STAR WARS
JEDI COUNCIL
ACTS OF WAR

Script
RANDY STRADLEY

Pencils
DAVIDÉ FABBRI

Inks
CHRISTIAN DALLA VECCHIA

Colors
DAVE McCAIG

Letters
STEVE DUTRO

Collection Cover Artist
DAVID MICHAEL BECK

TITAN BOOKS

STAR WARS®
JEDI COUNCIL

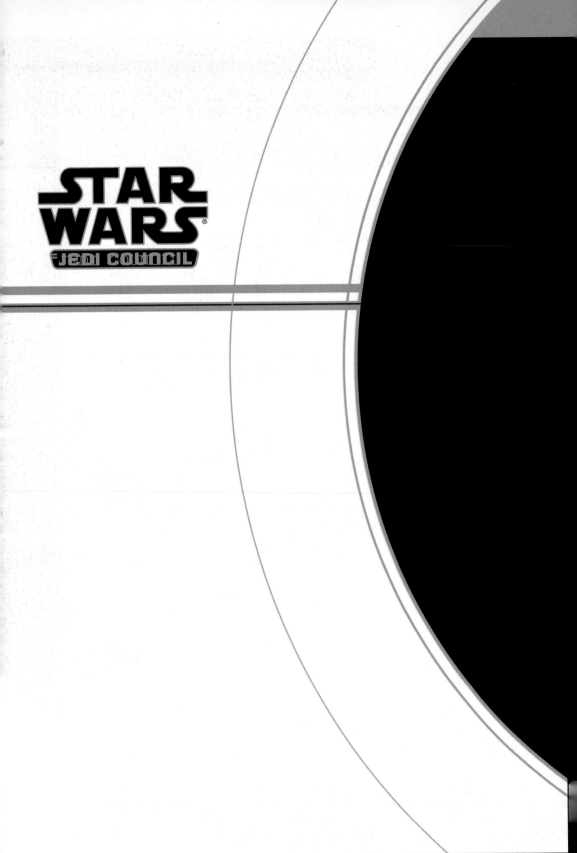

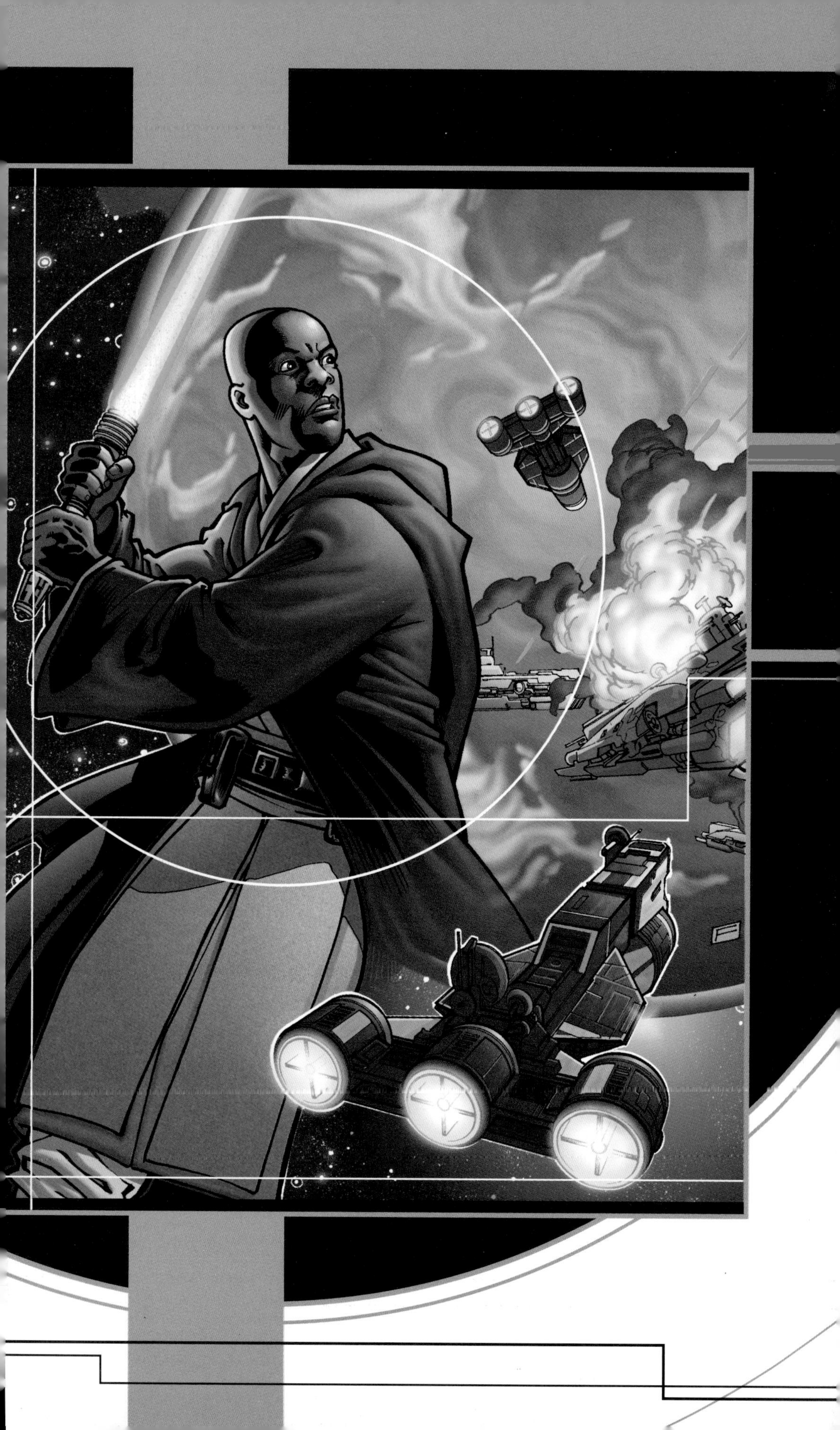

Publisher
MIKE RICHARDSON

Editor
DAVID LAND WITH PHILIP SIMON

Series Designer
JEREMY PERKINS

Collection Designer
LIA RIBACCHI

Art Director
MARK COX

Special thanks to **Lucy Autrey Wilson** and
Allan Kausch at Lucas Licensing

STAR WARS°:
JEDI COUNCIL — ACTS OF WAR

This book collects issues 1 through 4 of the Dark Horse
comic-book series *Star Wars*° : *Jedi Council Acts   of War.*

Published by
Titan Books
144 Southwark St
London SE1 0UP

First edition: July 2001
ISBN: 1 84023 286 2

1 2 3 4 5 6 7 8 9 10
PRINTED IN ITALY

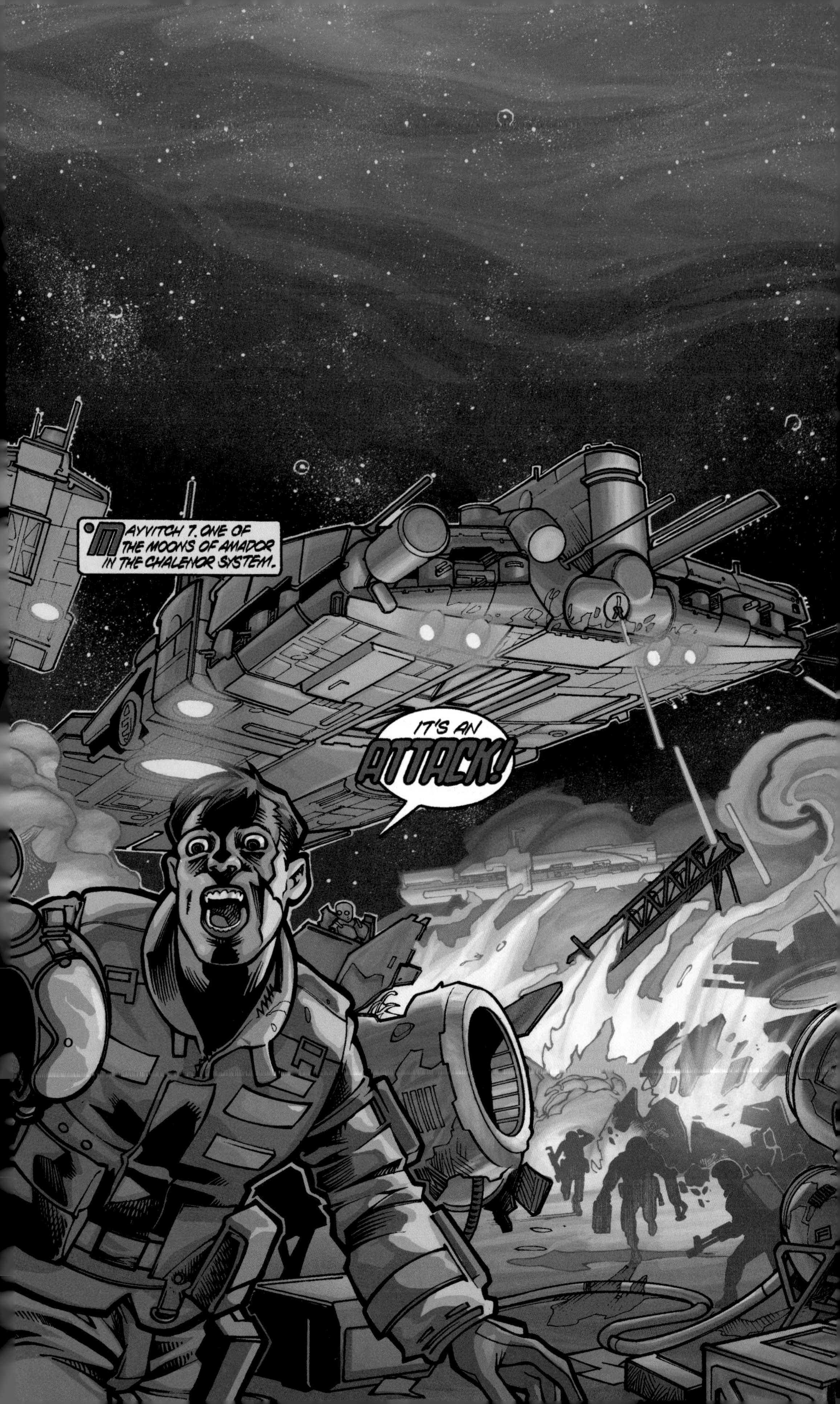
MAYVITCH 7. ONE OF THE MOONS OF AMADOR IN THE CHALENOR SYSTEM.
IT'S AN ATTACK!

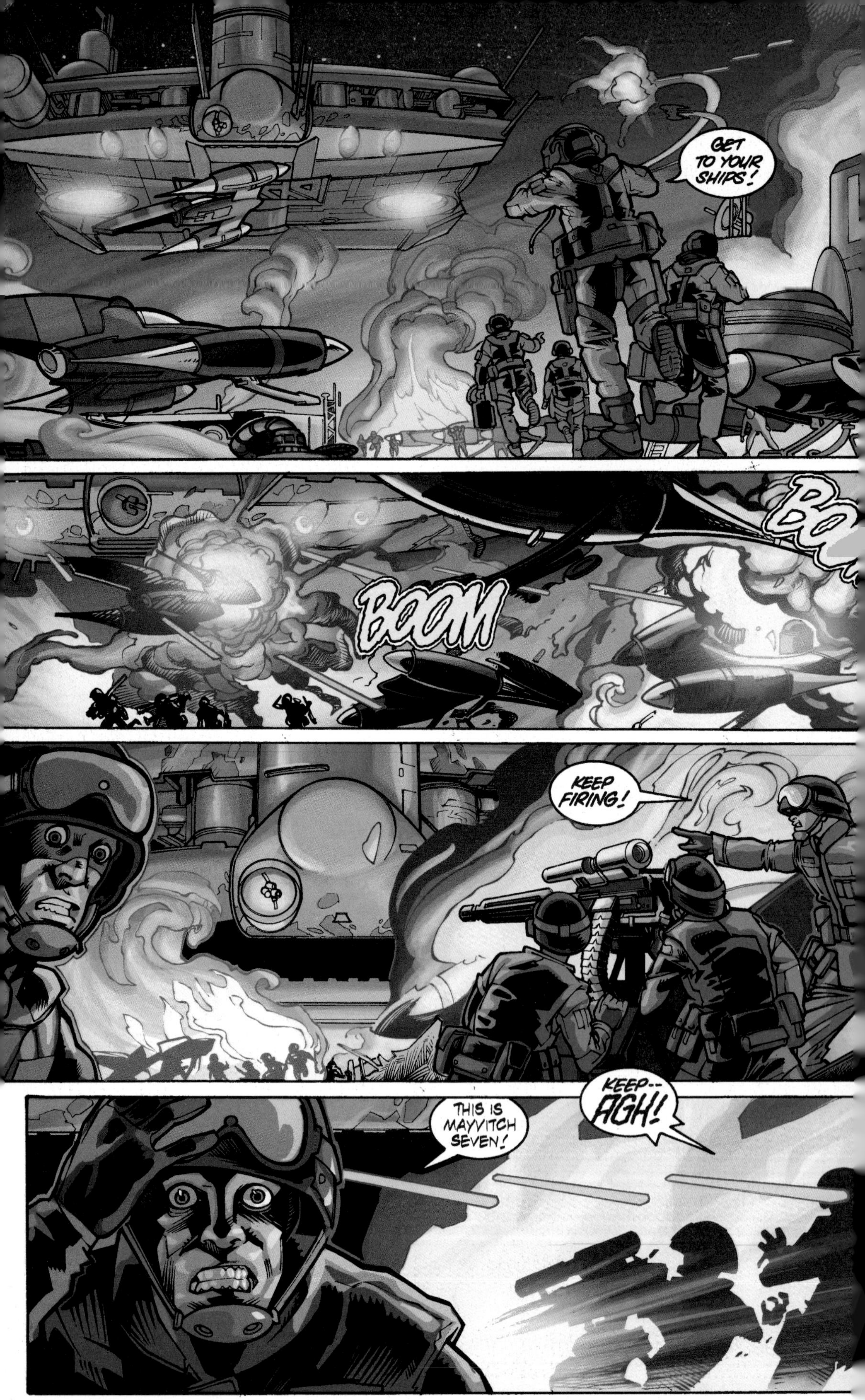
GET TO YOUR SHIPS!
BOOM
BO
KEEP FIRING!
THIS IS MAYVITCH SEVEN!
KEEP-- AGH!

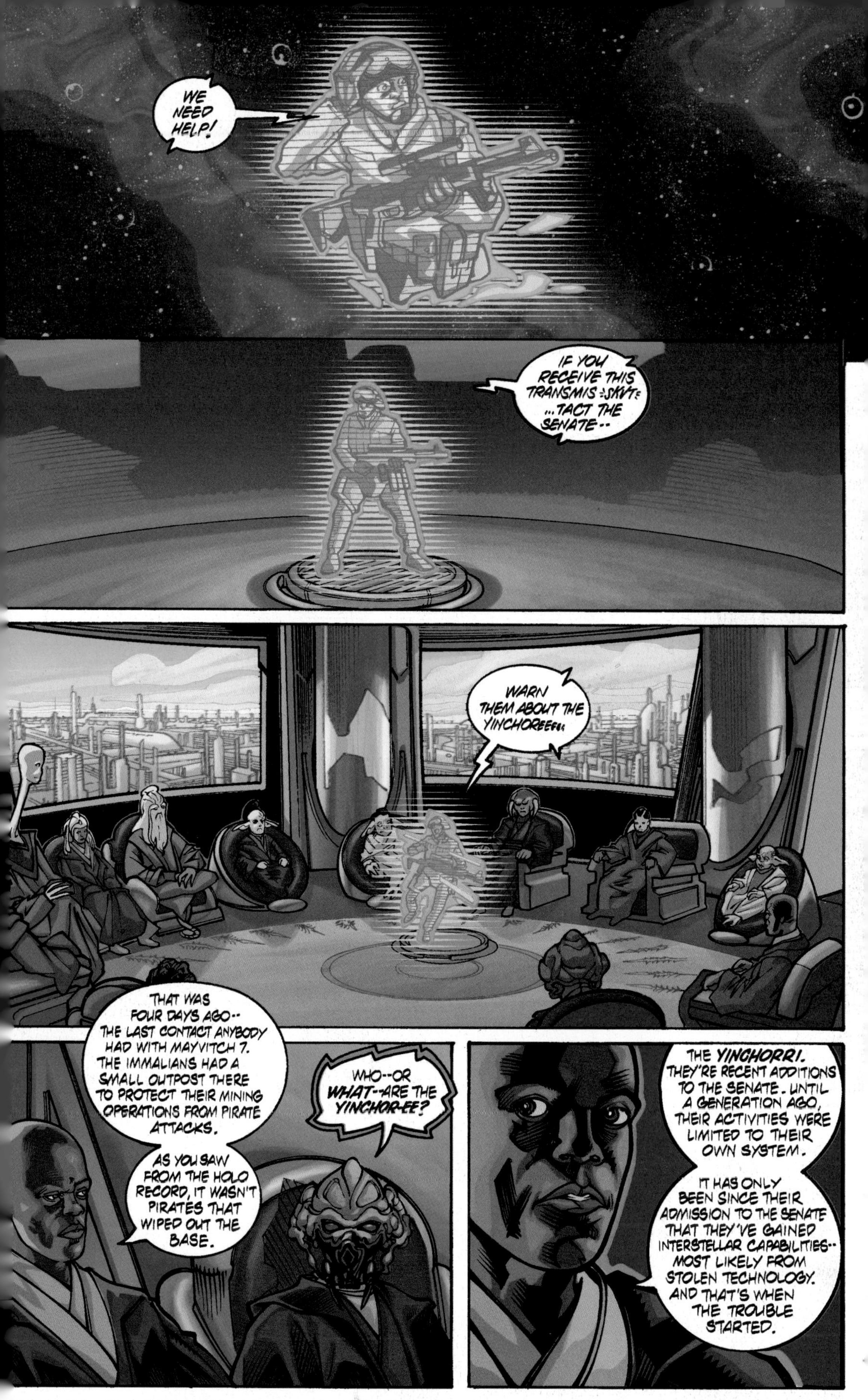
WE NEED HELP!
IF YOU RECEIVE THIS TRANSMIS :SKVT: ...TACT THE SENATE--
WARN THEM ABOUT THE YINCHOREEE...
THAT WAS FOUR DAYS AGO-- THE LAST CONTACT ANYBODY HAD WITH MAYVITCH 7. THE IMMALIANS HAD A SMALL OUTPOST THERE TO PROTECT THEIR MINING OPERATIONS FROM PIRATE ATTACKS.
AS YOU SAW FROM THE HOLO RECORD, IT WASN'T PIRATES THAT WIPED OUT THE BASE.
WHO--OR WHAT--ARE THE YINCHOR-EE?
THE YINCHORRI. THEY'RE RECENT ADDITIONS TO THE SENATE. UNTIL A GENERATION AGO, THEIR ACTIVITIES WERE LIMITED TO THEIR OWN SYSTEM.
IT HAS ONLY BEEN SINCE THEIR ADMISSION TO THE SENATE THAT THEY'VE GAINED INTERSTELLAR CAPABILITIES-- MOST LIKELY FROM STOLEN TECHNOLOGY. AND THAT'S WHEN THE TROUBLE STARTED.

THE YINCHORRI BELIEVE THAT IF THEY'RE STRONG ENOUGH TO TAKE SOMETHING AND HOLD ON TO IT, IT IS, BY RIGHTS, THEIRS.

"MIGHT MAKES RIGHT." A SHORT-SIGHTED PHILOSOPHY--

--AND ONE THAT IS OFTEN REGANTED UPON MEETING A MORE POWERFUL ADVERSARY. YOU TOOK APPROPRIATE ACTION, I TRUST?

SO I BELIEVED, OPPO RANCISIS.

AT CHANCELLO VALORUM'S REQU I DISPATCHE! TWO KNIGHTS ' YINCHORR-- NAESHAHN AN HER PADAWAN EBOR TAULK.

LAST NIGHT, THEIR MUTILATED BODIES WERE DELIVERED TO CHANCELLOR VALORUM'S CHAMBERS...

WITHIN YOUR RIGHTS, YOU WERE, MACE WINDU, TO SEND JEDI INTO DANGER WITHOUT CONSULTING THE REST OF THE COUNCIL.

BUT HAD YOU DONE SO, GREATER INSIGH INTO THE PROBLEM YOU MIGHT HAVE OBTAINED.

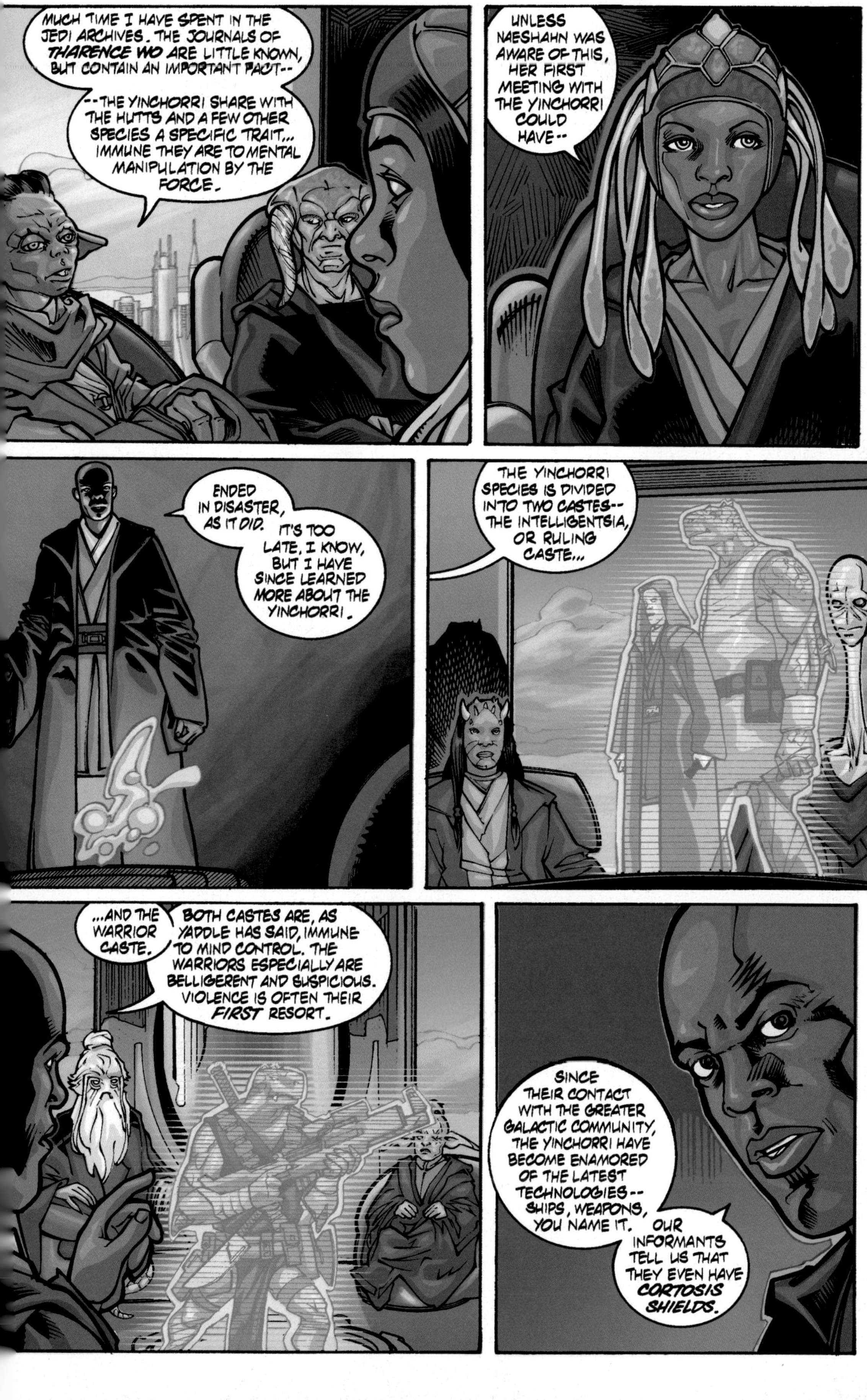
MUCH TIME I HAVE SPENT IN THE JEDI ARCHIVES. THE JOURNALS OF THARENCE WO ARE LITTLE KNOWN, BUT CONTAIN AN IMPORTANT FACT--
--THE YINCHORRI SHARE WITH THE HUTTS AND A FEW OTHER SPECIES A SPECIFIC TRAIT... IMMUNE THEY ARE TO MENTAL MANIPULATION BY THE FORCE.
UNLESS NAESHAHN WAS AWARE OF THIS, HER FIRST MEETING WITH THE YINCHORRI COULD HAVE--
ENDED IN DISASTER, AS IT DID.
IT'S TOO LATE, I KNOW, BUT I HAVE SINCE LEARNED MORE ABOUT THE YINCHORRI.
THE YINCHORRI SPECIES IS DIVIDED INTO TWO CASTES--THE INTELLIGENTSIA, OR RULING CASTE...
...AND THE WARRIOR CASTE.
BOTH CASTES ARE, AS YADDLE HAS SAID, IMMUNE TO MIND CONTROL. THE WARRIORS ESPECIALLY ARE BELLIGERENT AND SUSPICIOUS. VIOLENCE IS OFTEN THEIR FIRST RESORT.
SINCE THEIR CONTACT WITH THE GREATER GALACTIC COMMUNITY, THE YINCHORRI HAVE BECOME ENAMORED OF THE LATEST TECHNOLOGIES--SHIPS, WEAPONS, YOU NAME IT.
OUR INFORMANTS TELL US THAT THEY EVEN HAVE CORTOSIS SHIELDS.

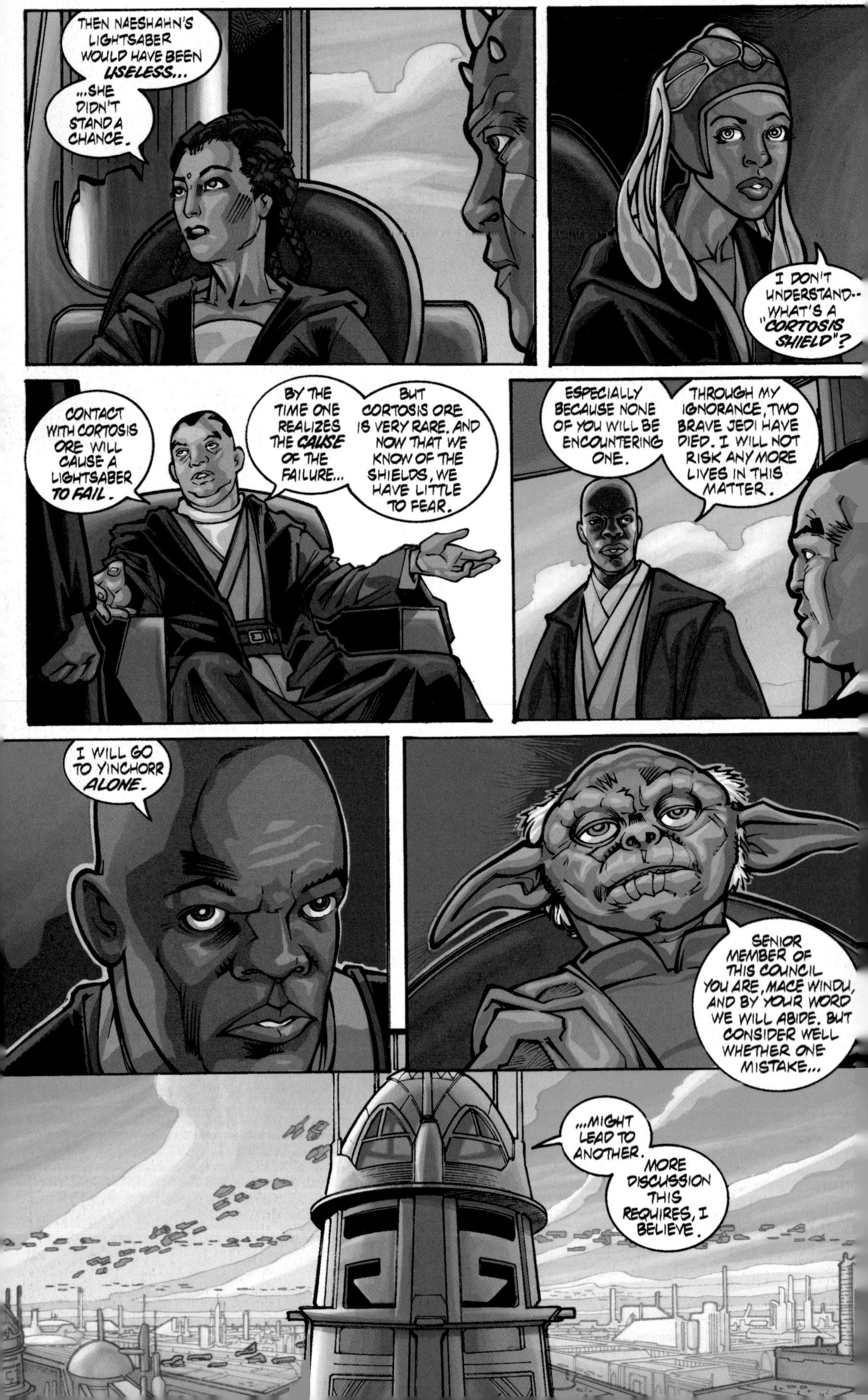

THEN NAESHAHN'S LIGHTSABER WOULD HAVE BEEN USELESS...
...SHE DIDN'T STAND A CHANCE.
I DON'T UNDERSTAND-- WHAT'S A "CORTOSIS SHIELD"?
CONTACT WITH CORTOSIS ORE WILL CAUSE A LIGHTSABER TO FAIL.
BY THE TIME ONE REALIZES THE CAUSE OF THE FAILURE...
BUT CORTOSIS ORE IS VERY RARE. AND NOW THAT WE KNOW OF THE SHIELDS, WE HAVE LITTLE TO FEAR.
ESPECIALLY BECAUSE NONE OF YOU WILL BE ENCOUNTERING ONE.
THROUGH MY IGNORANCE, TWO BRAVE JEDI HAVE DIED. I WILL NOT RISK ANY MORE LIVES IN THIS MATTER.
I WILL GO TO YINCHORR ALONE.
SENIOR MEMBER OF THIS COUNCIL YOU ARE, MACE WINDU, AND BY YOUR WORD WE WILL ABIDE. BUT CONSIDER WELL WHETHER ONE MISTAKE...
...MIGHT LEAD TO ANOTHER.
MORE DISCUSSION THIS REQUIRES, I BELIEVE.

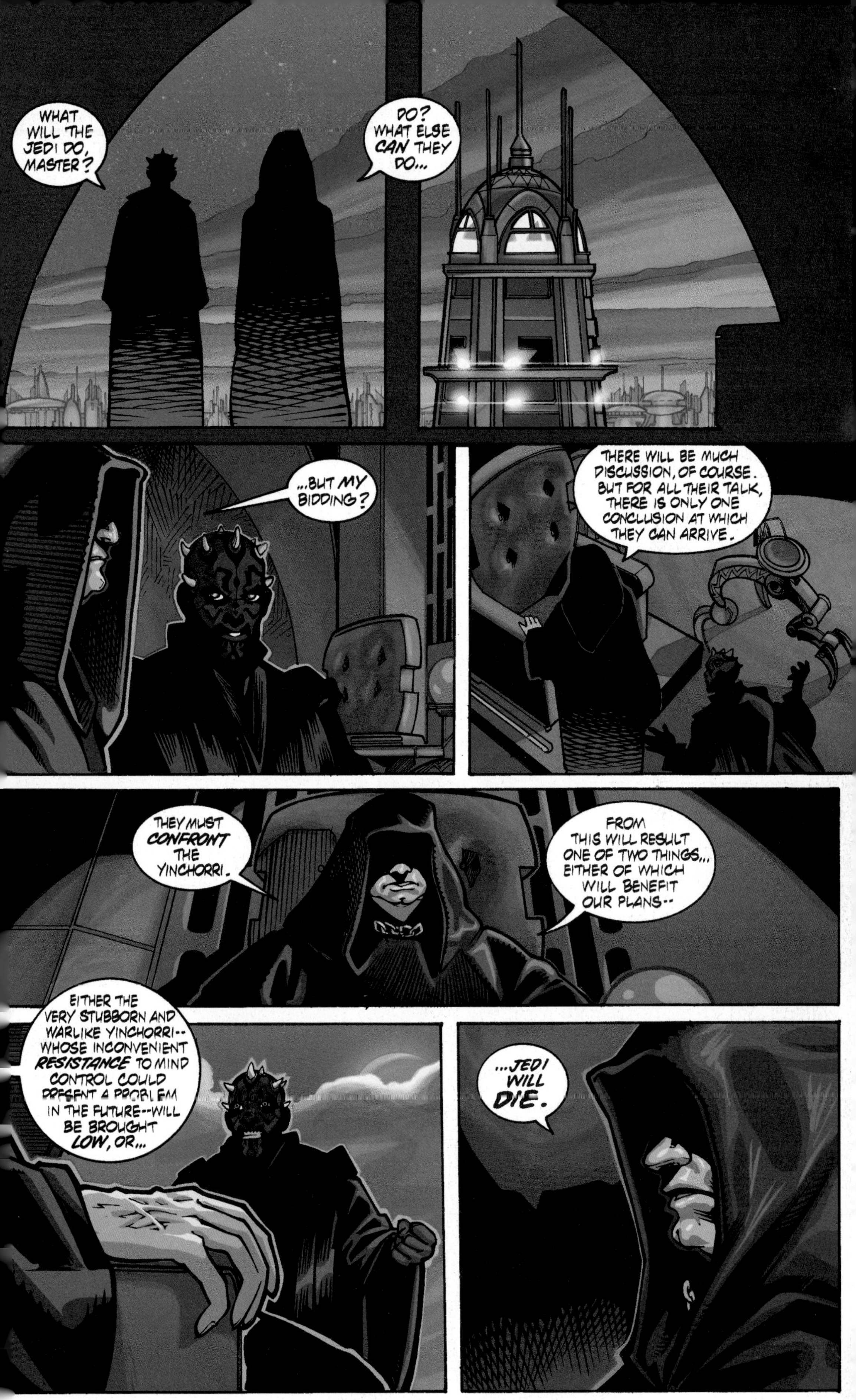
WHAT WILL THE JEDI DO, MASTER?
DO? WHAT ELSE CAN THEY DO...
...BUT MY BIDDING?
THERE WILL BE MUCH DISCUSSION, OF COURSE. BUT FOR ALL THEIR TALK, THERE IS ONLY ONE CONCLUSION AT WHICH THEY CAN ARRIVE.
THEY MUST CONFRONT THE YINCHORRI.
FROM THIS WILL RESULT ONE OF TWO THINGS... EITHER OF WHICH WILL BENEFIT OUR PLANS--
EITHER THE VERY STUBBORN AND WARLIKE YINCHORRI--WHOSE INCONVENIENT RESISTANCE TO MIND CONTROL COULD PRESENT A PROBLEM IN THE FUTURE--WILL BE BROUGHT LOW, OR...
...JEDI WILL DIE.

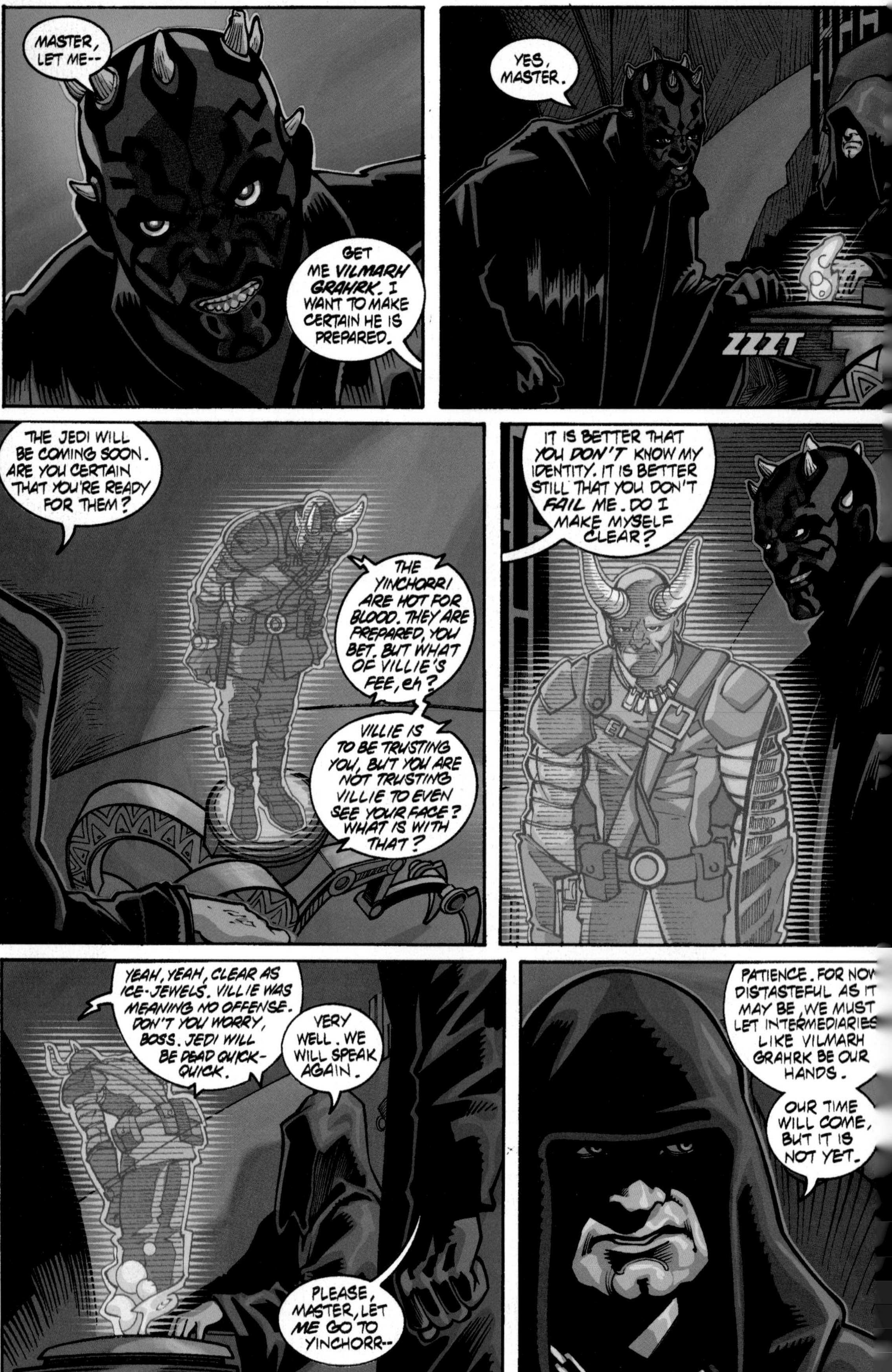
MASTER, LET ME--
GET ME VILMARH GRAHRK. I WANT TO MAKE CERTAIN HE IS PREPARED.
YES, MASTER.
ZZZT
THE JEDI WILL BE COMING SOON. ARE YOU CERTAIN THAT YOU'RE READY FOR THEM?
THE YINCHORRI ARE HOT FOR BLOOD. THEY ARE PREPARED, YOU BET. BUT WHAT OF VILLIE'S FEE, eh?
VILLIE IS TO BE TRUSTING YOU, BUT YOU ARE NOT TRUSTING VILLIE TO EVEN SEE YOUR FACE? WHAT IS WITH THAT?
IT IS BETTER THAT YOU DON'T KNOW MY IDENTITY. IT IS BETTER STILL THAT YOU DON'T FAIL ME. DO I MAKE MYSELF CLEAR?
YEAH, YEAH, CLEAR AS ICE-JEWELS. VILLIE WAS MEANING NO OFFENSE. DON'T YOU WORRY, BOSS. JEDI WILL BE DEAD QUICK-QUICK.
VERY WELL. WE WILL SPEAK AGAIN.
PLEASE, MASTER, LET ME GO TO YINCHORR--
PATIENCE. FOR NOW DISTASTEFUL AS IT MAY BE, WE MUST LET INTERMEDIARIES LIKE VILMARH GRAHRK BE OUR HANDS.
OUR TIME WILL COME, BUT IT IS NOT YET.

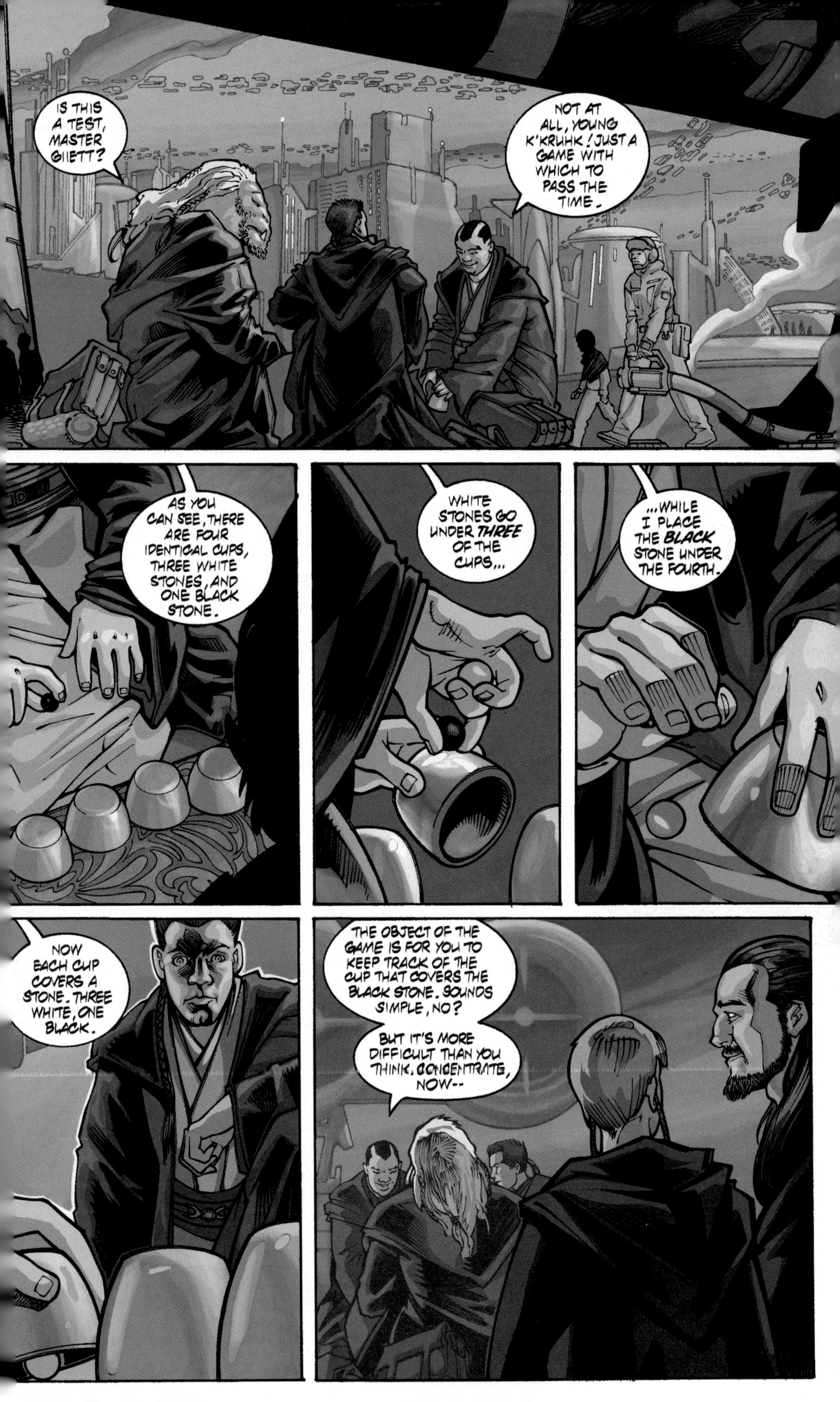
IS THIS A TEST, MASTER GIIETT?
NOT AT ALL, YOUNG K'KRUHK! JUST A GAME WITH WHICH TO PASS THE TIME.
AS YOU CAN SEE, THERE ARE FOUR IDENTICAL CUPS, THREE WHITE STONES, AND ONE BLACK STONE.
WHITE STONES GO UNDER *THREE* OF THE CUPS...
...WHILE I PLACE THE *BLACK* STONE UNDER THE FOURTH.
NOW EACH CUP COVERS A STONE. THREE WHITE, ONE BLACK.
THE OBJECT OF THE GAME IS FOR YOU TO KEEP TRACK OF THE CUP THAT COVERS THE BLACK STONE. SOUNDS SIMPLE, NO?
BUT IT'S MORE DIFFICULT THAN YOU THINK. CONCENTRATE, NOW--

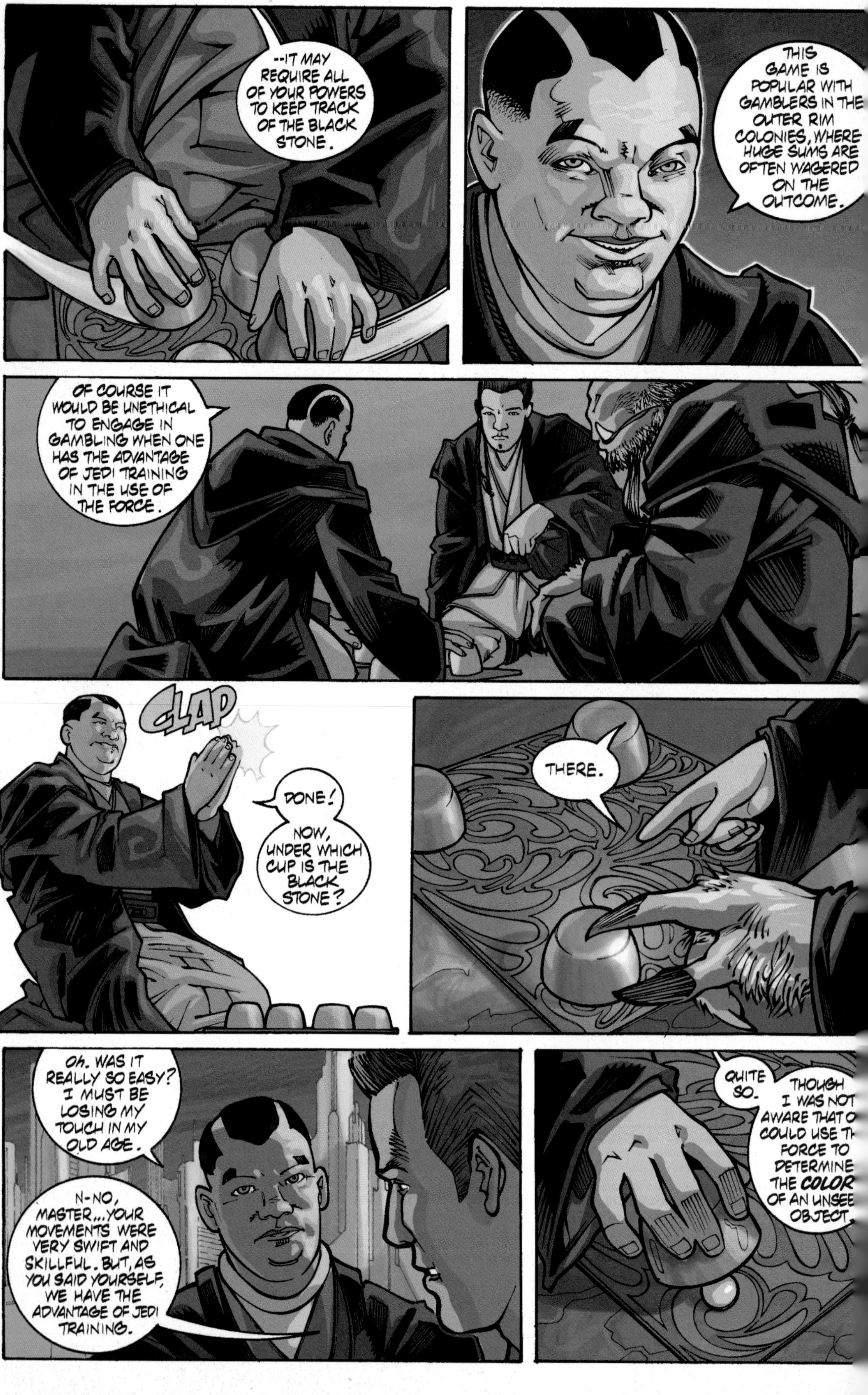
--IT MAY REQUIRE ALL OF YOUR POWERS TO KEEP TRACK OF THE BLACK STONE.
THIS GAME IS POPULAR WITH GAMBLERS IN THE OUTER RIM COLONIES, WHERE HUGE SUMS ARE OFTEN WAGERED ON THE OUTCOME.
OF COURSE IT WOULD BE UNETHICAL TO ENGAGE IN GAMBLING WHEN ONE HAS THE ADVANTAGE OF JEDI TRAINING IN THE USE OF THE FORCE.
CLAP
DONE!
NOW, UNDER WHICH CUP IS THE BLACK STONE?
THERE.
Oh. WAS IT REALLY SO EASY? I MUST BE LOSING MY TOUCH IN MY OLD AGE.
N-NO, MASTER... YOUR MOVEMENTS WERE VERY SWIFT AND SKILLFUL. BUT, AS YOU SAID YOURSELF, WE HAVE THE ADVANTAGE OF JEDI TRAINING.
QUITE SO.
THOUGH I WAS NOT AWARE THAT O COULD USE TH FORCE TO DETERMINE THE COLOR OF AN UNSEE OBJECT.

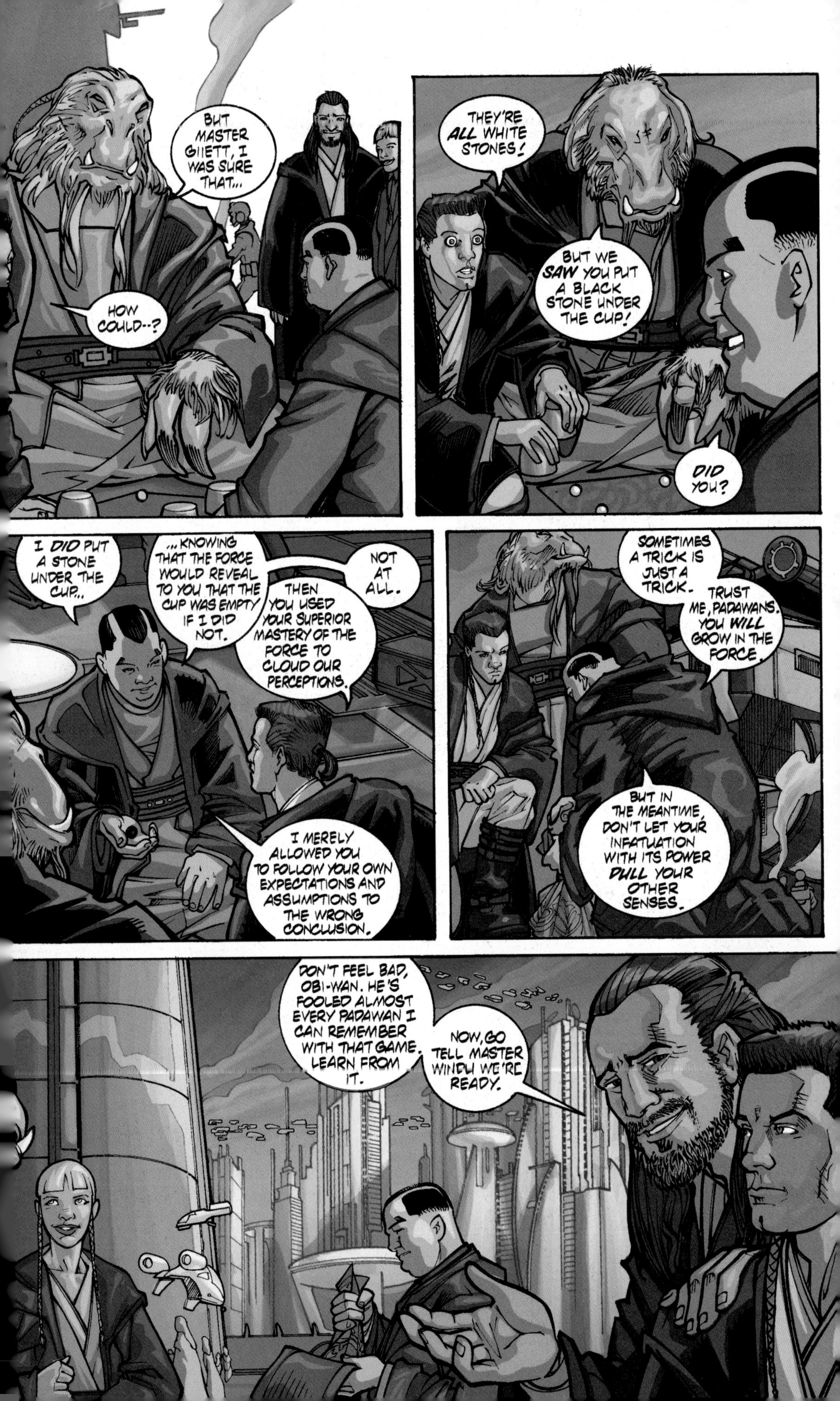
BUT MASTER GIIETT, I WAS SURE THAT...
HOW COULD--?
THEY'RE ALL WHITE STONES!
BUT WE SAW YOU PUT A BLACK STONE UNDER THE CUP!
DID YOU?
I DID PUT A STONE UNDER THE CUP...
...KNOWING THAT THE FORCE WOULD REVEAL TO YOU THAT THE CUP WAS EMPTY IF I DID NOT.
THEN YOU USED YOUR SUPERIOR MASTERY OF THE FORCE TO CLOUD OUR PERCEPTIONS.
NOT AT ALL.
I MERELY ALLOWED YOU TO FOLLOW YOUR OWN EXPECTATIONS AND ASSUMPTIONS TO THE WRONG CONCLUSION.
SOMETIMES A TRICK IS JUST A TRICK.
TRUST ME, PADAWANS. YOU WILL GROW IN THE FORCE.
BUT IN THE MEANTIME, DON'T LET YOUR INFATUATION WITH ITS POWER DULL YOUR OTHER SENSES.
DON'T FEEL BAD, OBI-WAN. HE'S FOOLED ALMOST EVERY PADAWAN I CAN REMEMBER WITH THAT GAME. LEARN FROM IT.
NOW, GO TELL MASTER WINDU WE'RE READY.

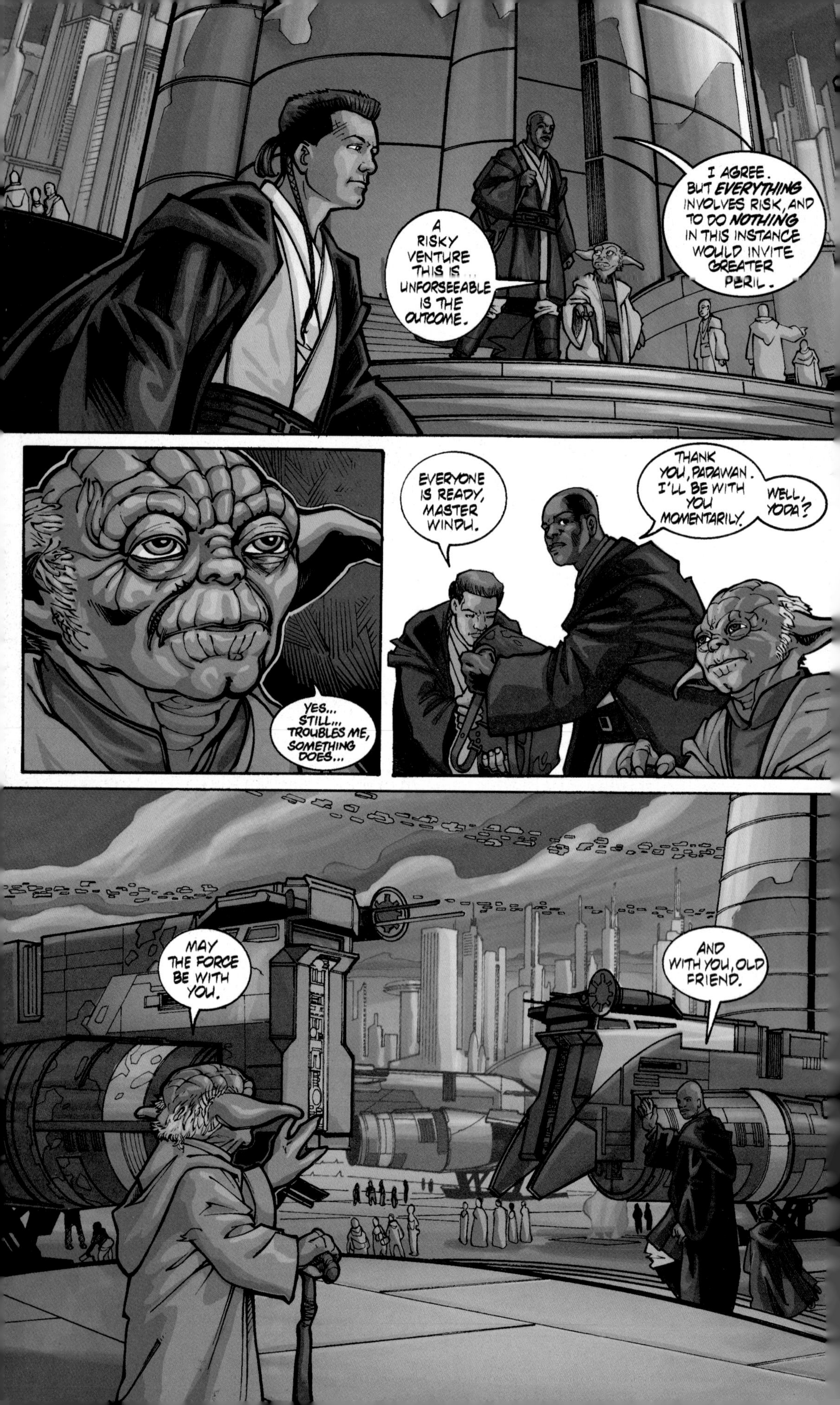
A RISKY VENTURE THIS IS... UNFORSEEABLE IS THE OUTCOME.
I AGREE. BUT EVERYTHING INVOLVES RISK, AND TO DO NOTHING IN THIS INSTANCE WOULD INVITE GREATER PERIL.
YES... STILL... TROUBLES ME, SOMETHING DOES...
EVERYONE IS READY, MASTER WINDU.
THANK YOU, PADAWAN. I'LL BE WITH YOU MOMENTARILY.
WELL, YODA?
MAY THE FORCE BE WITH YOU.
AND WITH YOU, OLD FRIEND.

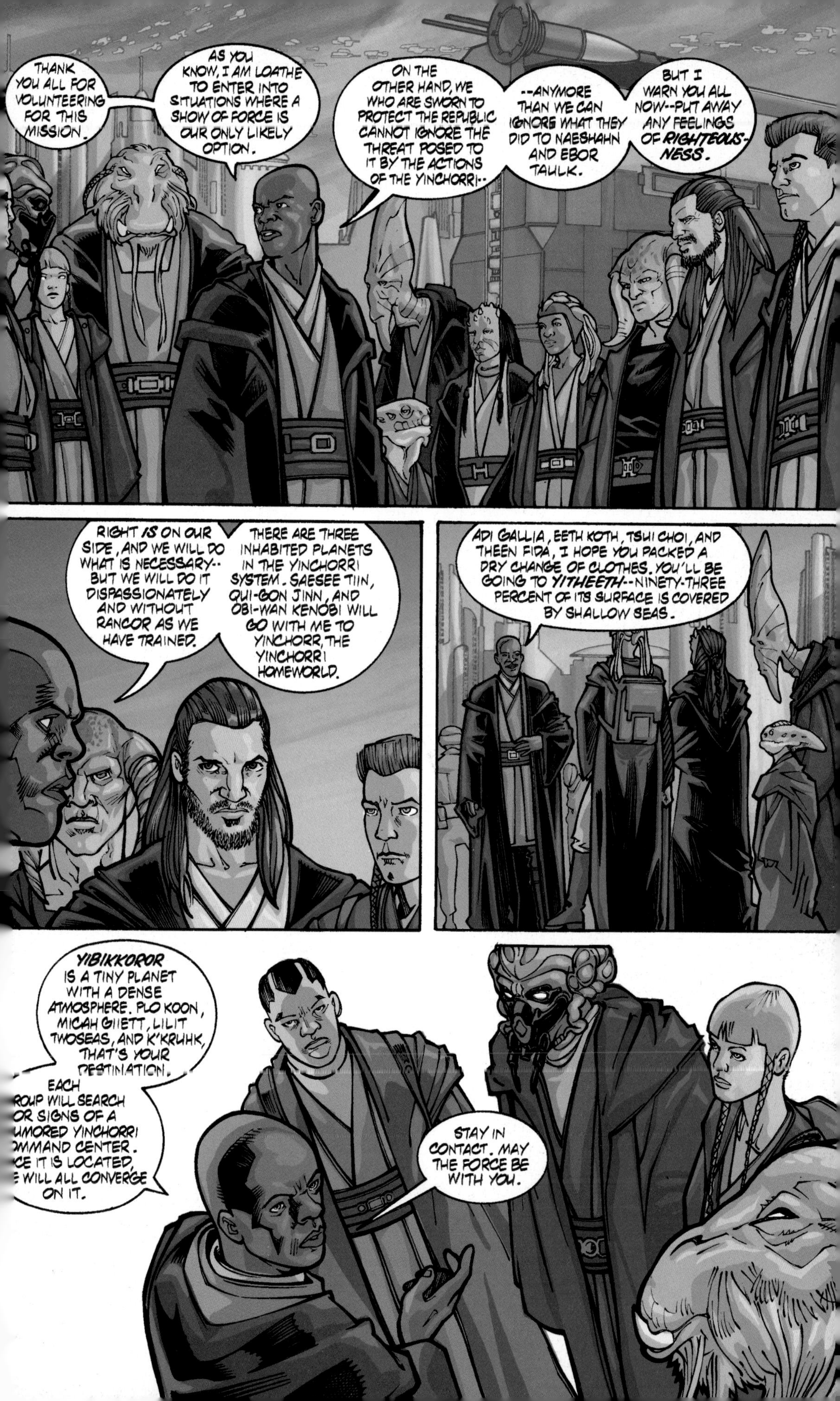
THANK YOU ALL FOR VOLUNTEERING FOR THIS MISSION.
AS YOU KNOW, I AM LOATHE TO ENTER INTO SITUATIONS WHERE A SHOW OF FORCE IS OUR ONLY LIKELY OPTION.
ON THE OTHER HAND, WE WHO ARE SWORN TO PROTECT THE REPUBLIC CANNOT IGNORE THE THREAT POSED TO IT BY THE ACTIONS OF THE YINCHORRI--
--ANYMORE THAN WE CAN IGNORE WHAT THEY DID TO NAESHAHN AND EBOR TAULK.
BUT I WARN YOU ALL NOW--PUT AWAY ANY FEELINGS OF *RIGHTEOUSNESS*.
RIGHT *IS* ON OUR SIDE, AND WE WILL DO WHAT IS NECESSARY-- BUT WE WILL DO IT DISPASSIONATELY AND WITHOUT RANCOR AS WE HAVE TRAINED.
THERE ARE THREE INHABITED PLANETS IN THE YINCHORRI SYSTEM. SAESEE TIIN, QUI-GON JINN, AND OBI-WAN KENOBI WILL *GO* WITH ME TO YINCHORR, THE YINCHORRI HOMEWORLD.
ADI GALLIA, EETH KOTH, TSUI CHOI, AND THEEN FIDA, I HOPE YOU PACKED A DRY CHANGE OF CLOTHES. YOU'LL BE GOING TO *YITHEETH*--NINETY-THREE PERCENT OF ITS SURFACE IS COVERED BY SHALLOW SEAS.
YIBIKKOROR IS A TINY PLANET WITH A DENSE ATMOSPHERE. PLO KOON, MICAH GIIETT, LILIT TWOSEAS, AND K'KRUHK, THAT'S YOUR DESTINATION.
EACH ROUP WILL SEARCH OR SIGNS OF A UMORED YINCHORRI OMMAND CENTER. CE IT IS LOCATED, E WILL ALL CONVERGE ON IT.
STAY IN CONTACT. MAY THE FORCE BE WITH YOU.

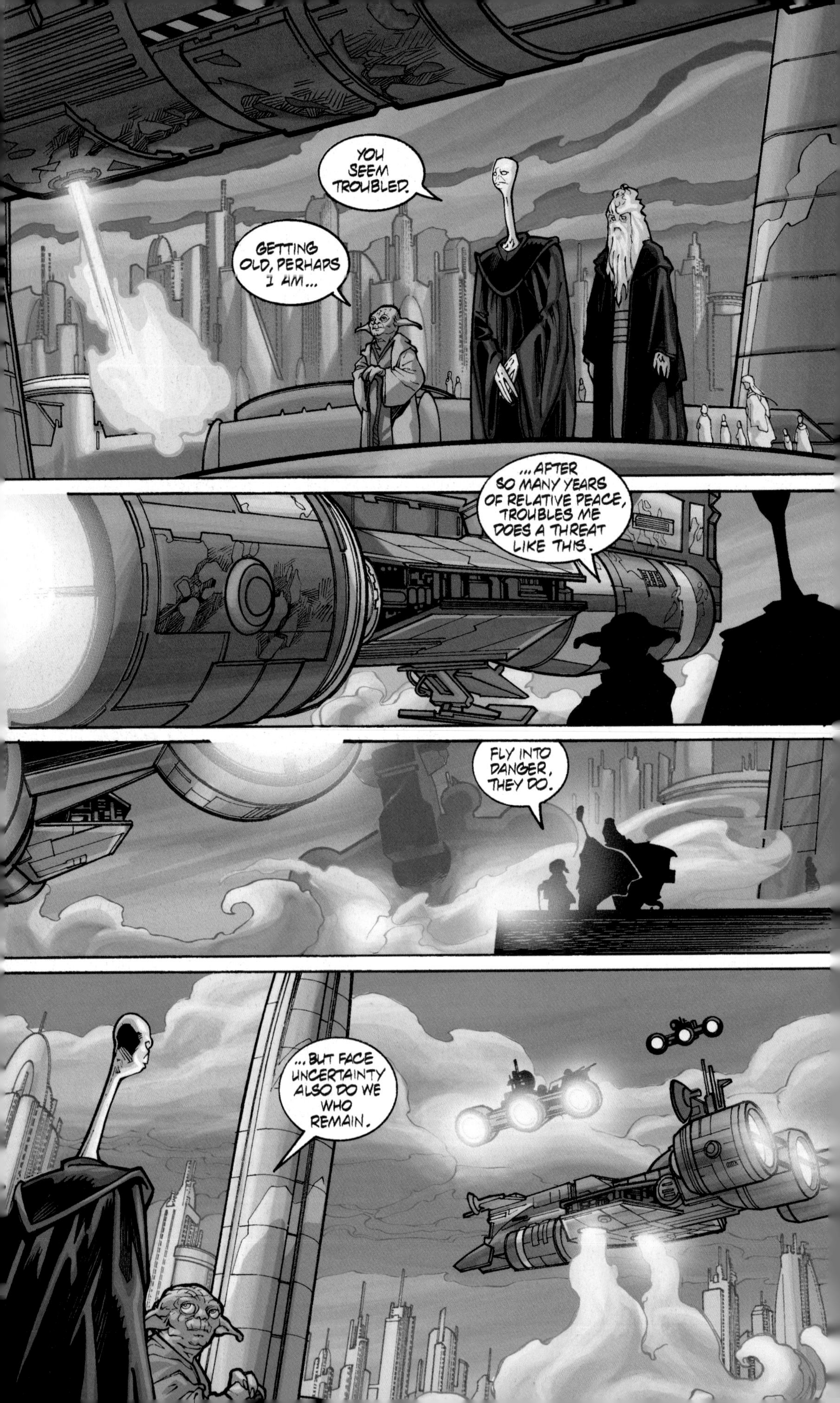
YOU SEEM TROUBLED.
GETTING OLD, PERHAPS I AM...
...AFTER SO MANY YEARS OF RELATIVE PEACE, TROUBLES ME DOES A THREAT LIKE THIS.
FLY INTO DANGER, THEY DO.
...BUT FACE UNCERTAINTY ALSO DO WE WHO REMAIN.

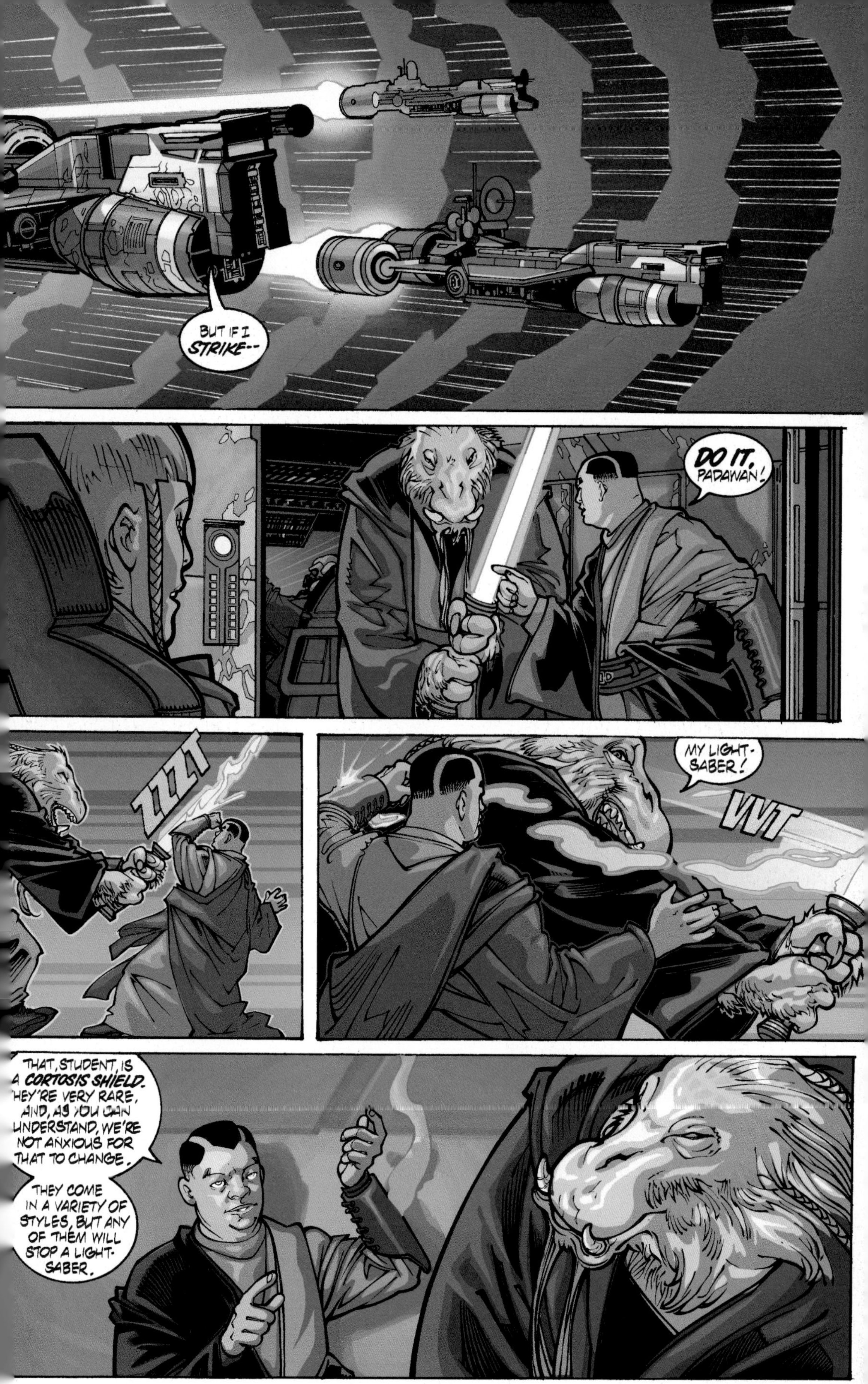

BUT IF I STRIKE--
DO IT, PADAWAN!
ZZZT
MY LIGHT-SABER!
VVT
THAT, STUDENT, IS A CORTOSIS SHIELD. THEY'RE VERY RARE, AND, AS YOU CAN UNDERSTAND, WE'RE NOT ANXIOUS FOR THAT TO CHANGE.
THEY COME IN A VARIETY OF STYLES, BUT ANY OF THEM WILL STOP A LIGHT-SABER.

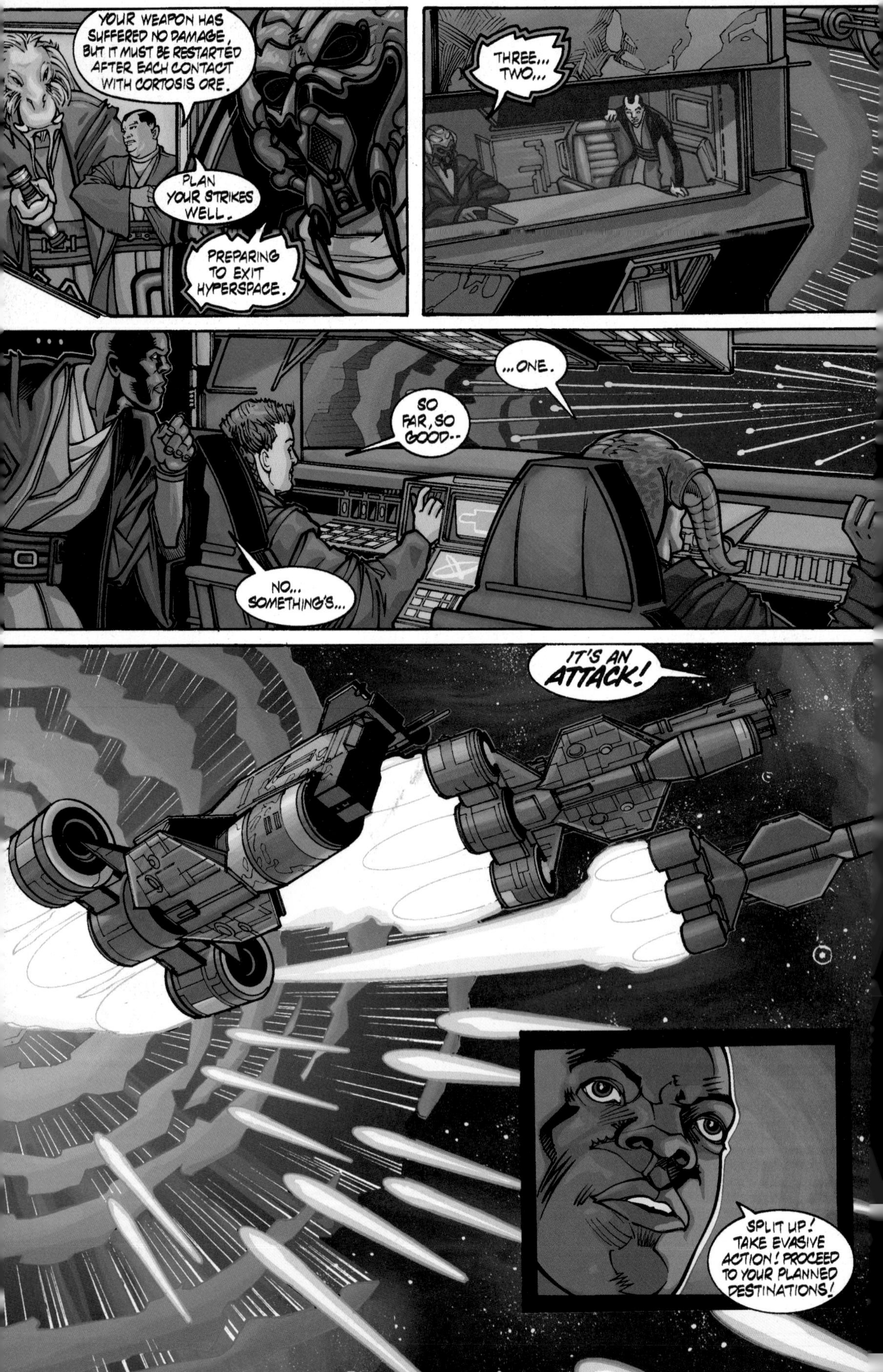
YOUR WEAPON HAS SUFFERED NO DAMAGE, BUT IT MUST BE RESTARTED AFTER EACH CONTACT WITH CORTOSIS ORE.
PLAN YOUR STRIKES WELL.
PREPARING TO EXIT HYPERSPACE.
THREE... TWO...
...ONE.
SO FAR, SO GOOD--
NO... SOMETHING'S...
IT'S AN ATTACK!
SPLIT UP! TAKE EVASIVE ACTION! PROCEED TO YOUR PLANNED DESTINATIONS!

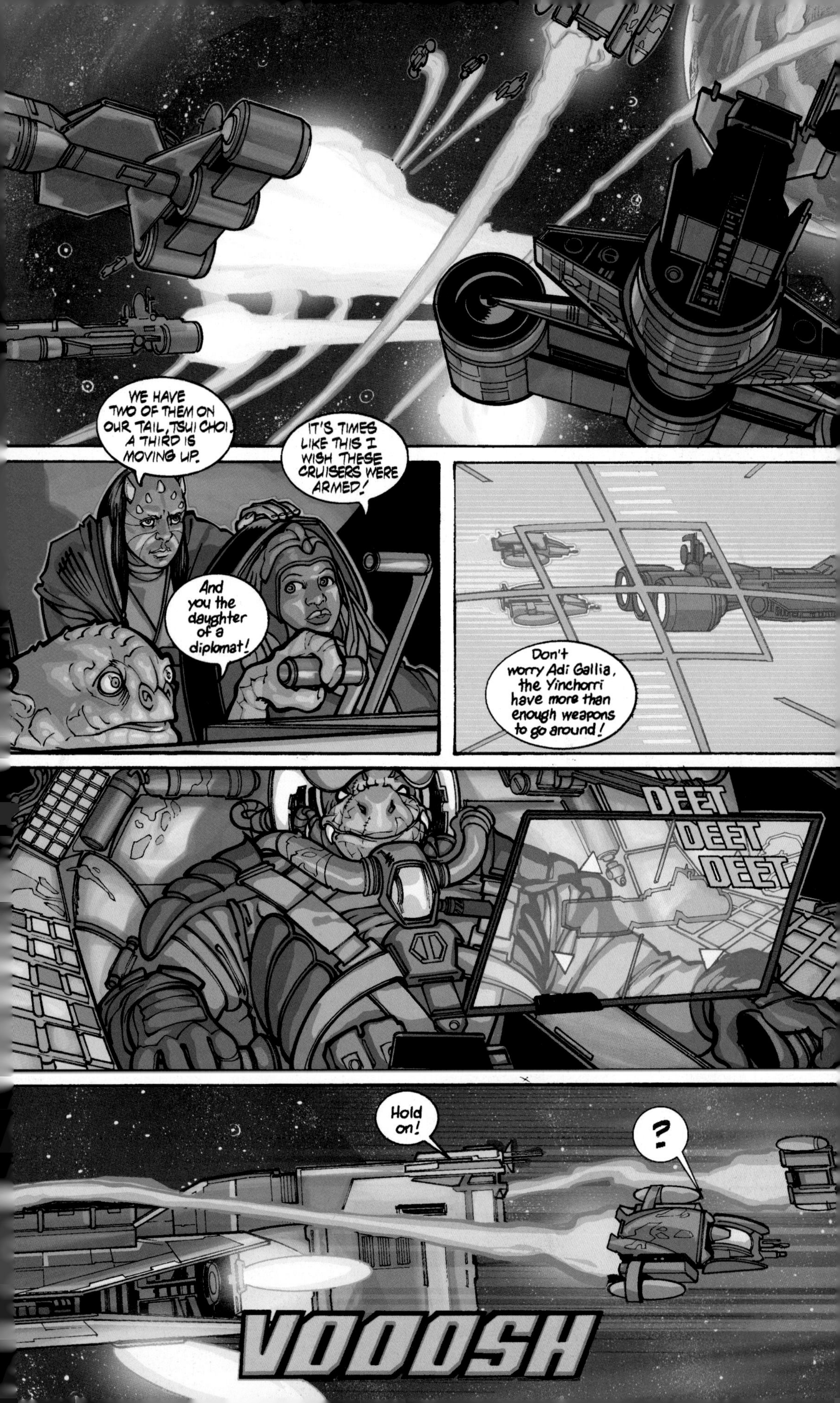
WE HAVE TWO OF THEM ON OUR TAIL, TSUI CHOI. A THIRD IS MOVING UP.
IT'S TIMES LIKE THIS I WISH THESE CRUISERS WERE ARMED!
And you the daughter of a diplomat!
Don't worry Adi Gallia, the Yinchorri have more than enough weapons to go around!
DEET
DEET
DEET
Hold on!
?
VOOOSH

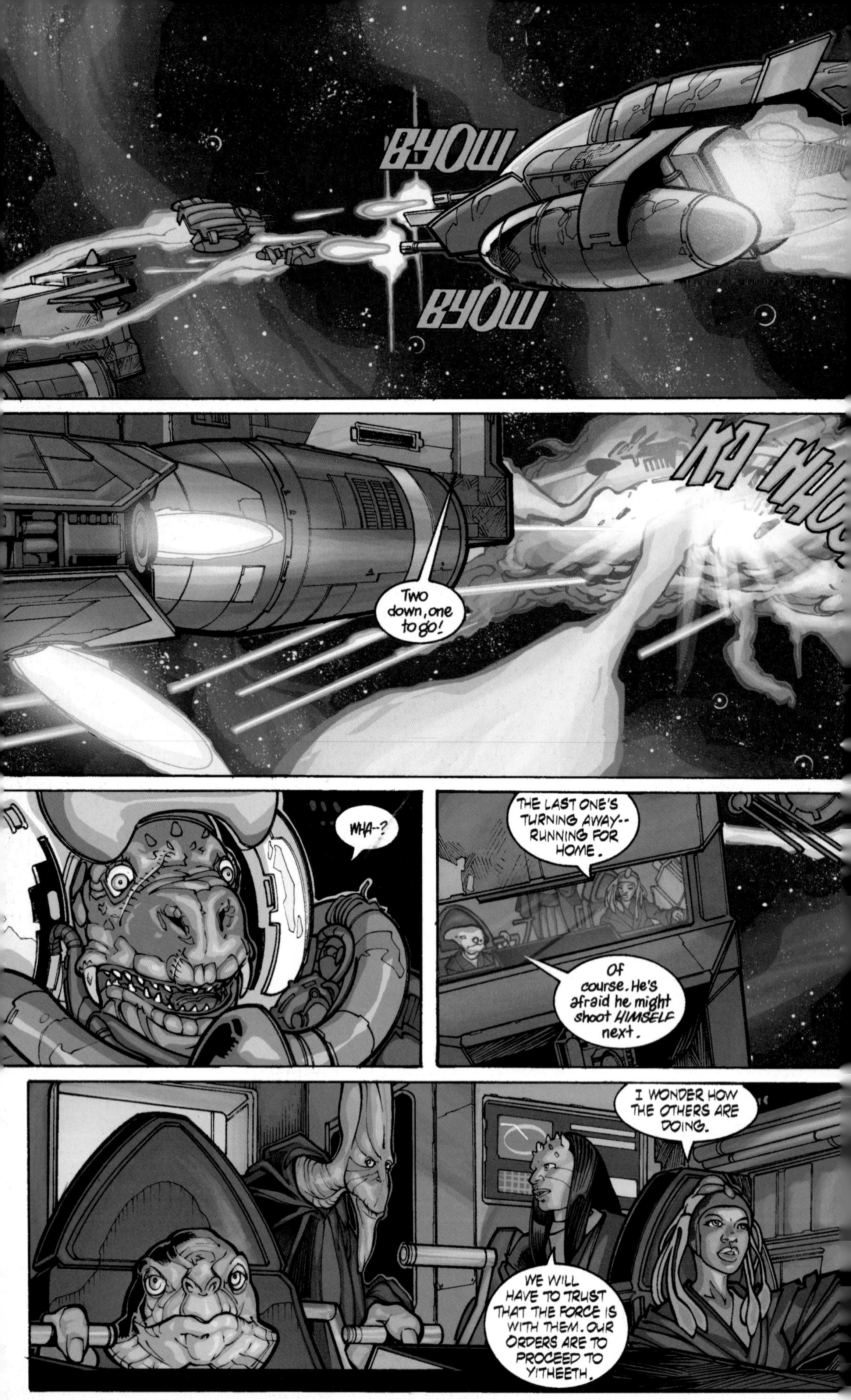
BYOW
BYOW
KA-WHOO
Two down, one to go!
WHA--?
THE LAST ONE'S TURNING AWAY-- RUNNING FOR HOME.
Of course. He's afraid he might shoot HIMSELF next.
I WONDER HOW THE OTHERS ARE DOING.
WE WILL HAVE TO TRUST THAT THE FORCE IS WITH THEM. OUR ORDERS ARE TO PROCEED TO YITHEETH.

THERE GO OUR SHIELDS!

BE CALM, OBI-WAN. ANY IDEAS, SAESEE?

ONE. BUT IT WILL REQUIRE SPLIT-SECOND TIMING.

UH, SAESEE, WE'RE HEADING RIGHT TOWARD THAT PLANET...

WE'LL BE IN ITS GRAVITY WELL.

I KNOW. QUI-GON, I'M TRANSFERRING COORDINATES TO YOU. LOCK THEM INTO THE NAVIGATION COMPUTER AND PREPARE TO JUMP TO HYPERSPACE.

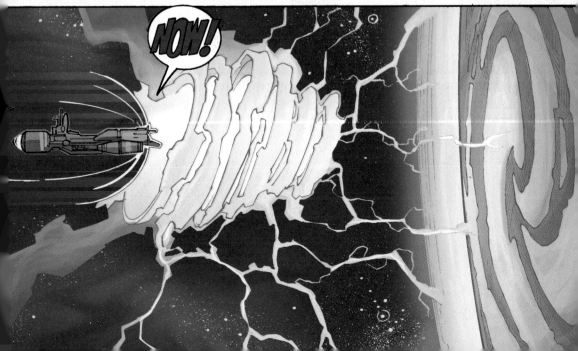

NOW!

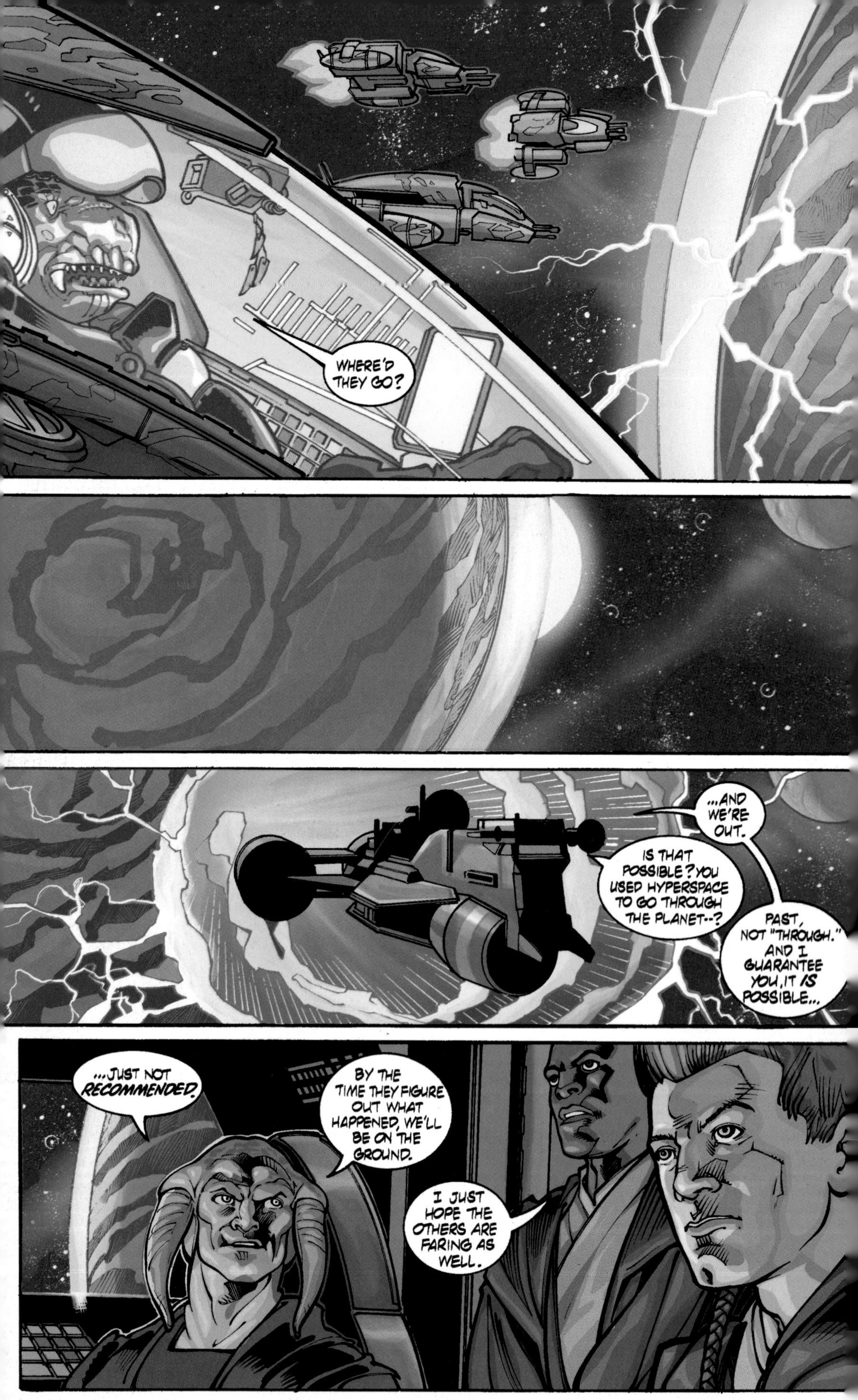
WHERE'D THEY GO?
...AND WE'RE OUT.
IS THAT POSSIBLE? YOU USED HYPERSPACE TO GO THROUGH THE PLANET--?
PAST, NOT "THROUGH." AND I GUARANTEE YOU, IT IS POSSIBLE...
...JUST NOT RECOMMENDED.
BY THE TIME THEY FIGURE OUT WHAT HAPPENED, WE'LL BE ON THE GROUND.
I JUST HOPE THE OTHERS ARE FARING AS WELL.

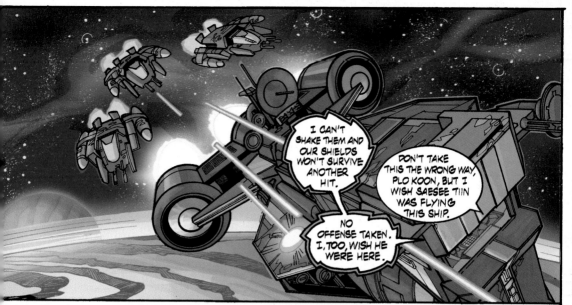

I CAN'T SHAKE THEM AND OUR SHIELDS WON'T SURVIVE ANOTHER HIT.

DON'T TAKE THIS THE WRONG WAY, PLO KOON, BUT I WISH SAESEE TIIN WAS FLYING THIS SHIP.

NO OFFENSE TAKEN. I, TOO, WISH HE WERE HERE.

OR EVEN OPPO RANCISIS-- I'M SURE HE'D HAVE A PLAN TO DEAL WITH THOSE FIGHTERS...

MASTER GIIETT, I KNOW A WAY! YOUR TRICK WITH THE CUPS AND STONES!

WHAT ARE YOU TALKING ABOUT?

MIS-DIRECTION, SIR. IF WE COULD MAKE THE YINCHORRI THINK WE HAD LEFT THE SHIP--

YES... YES!

K'KRUHK, COME WITH ME.

PLO KOON, I DON'T HAVE TIME TO EXPLAIN, BUT *LET* THE YINCHORRI HIT US!

SPIDOOW

YES, JUST LIKE THAT!

I DIDN'T *PLAN* THAT.

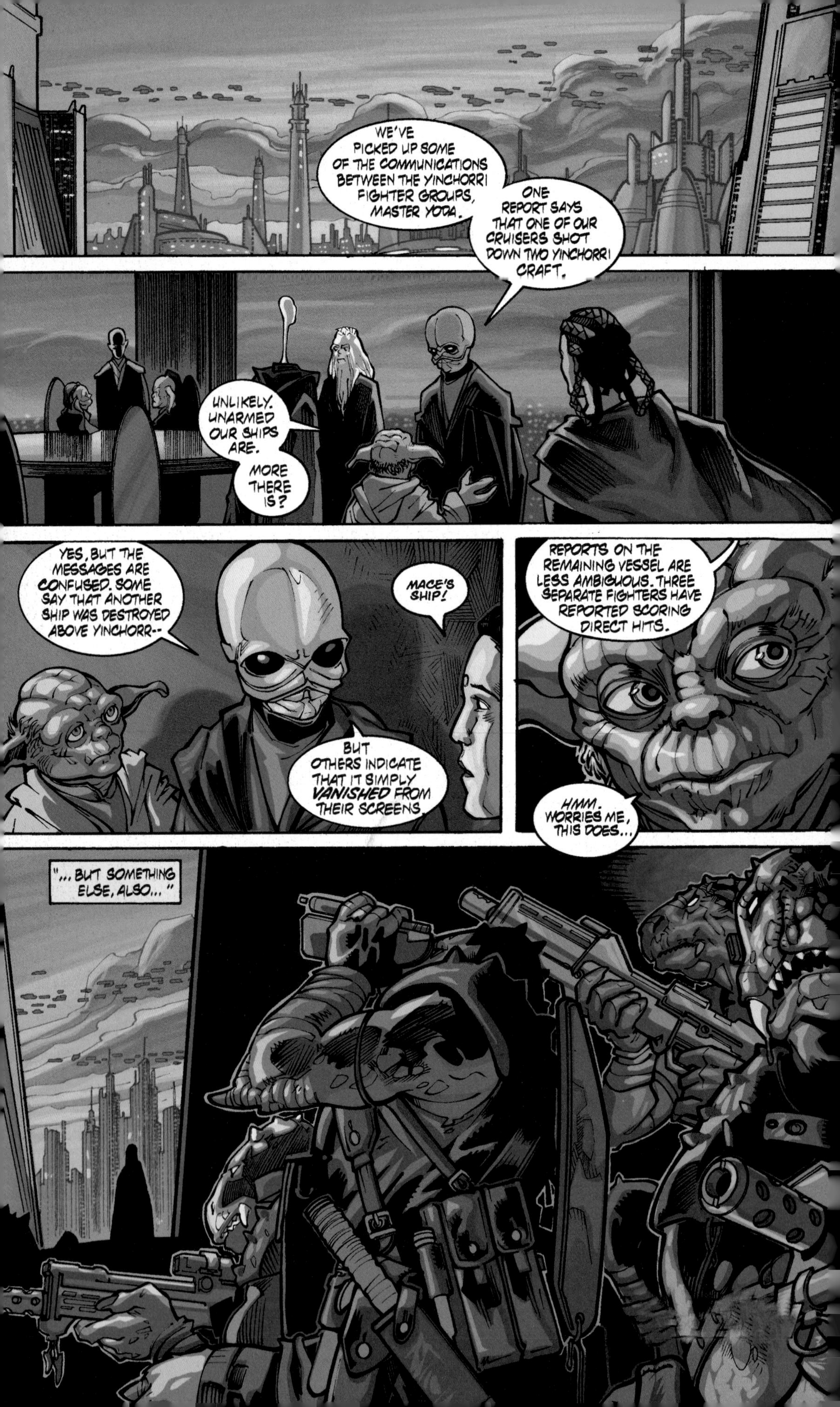
WE'VE PICKED UP SOME OF THE COMMUNICATIONS BETWEEN THE YINCHORRI FIGHTER GROUPS, MASTER YODA.
ONE REPORT SAYS THAT ONE OF OUR CRUISERS SHOT DOWN TWO YINCHORRI CRAFT.
UNLIKELY. UNARMED OUR SHIPS ARE.
MORE THERE IS?
YES, BUT THE MESSAGES ARE CONFUSED. SOME SAY THAT ANOTHER SHIP WAS DESTROYED ABOVE YINCHORR--
MACE'S SHIP!
BUT OTHERS INDICATE THAT IT SIMPLY VANISHED FROM THEIR SCREENS.
REPORTS ON THE REMAINING VESSEL ARE LESS AMBIGUOUS. THREE SEPARATE FIGHTERS HAVE REPORTED SCORING DIRECT HITS.
HMM. WORRIES ME, THIS DOES...
"... BUT SOMETHING ELSE, ALSO..."

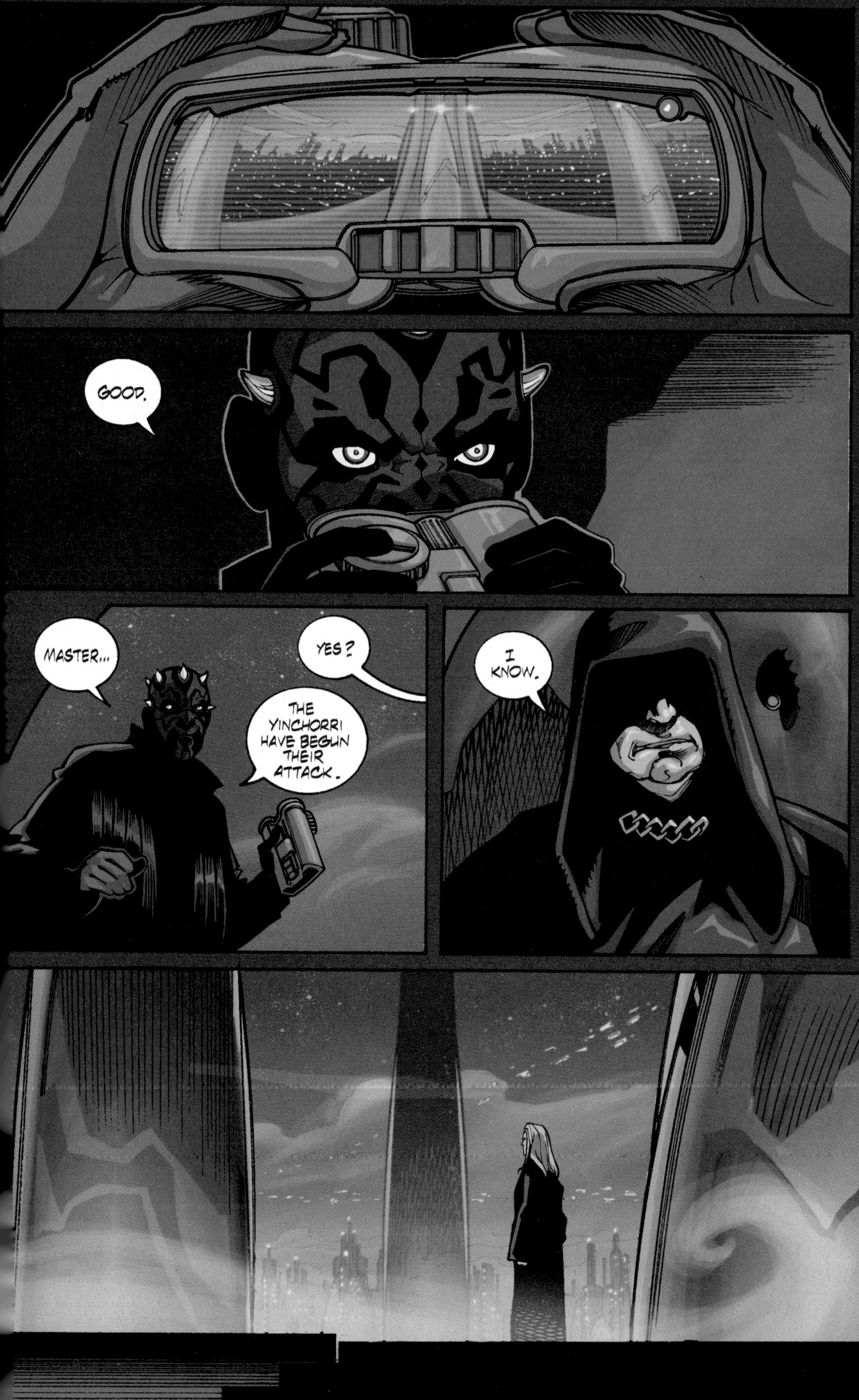
GOOD.
MASTER...
YES?
THE YINCHORRI HAVE BEGUN THEIR ATTACK.
I KNOW.

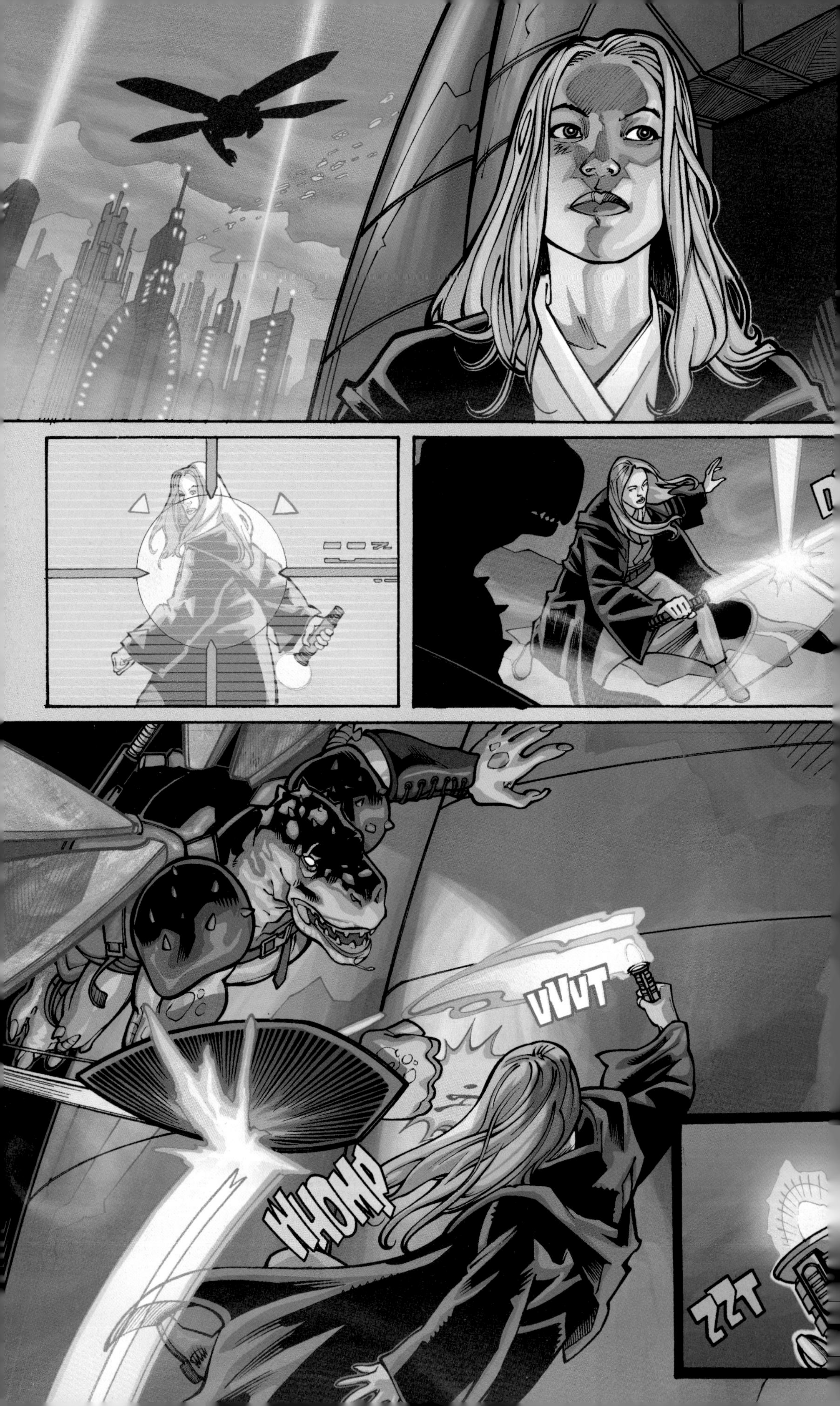
VVVT
WHOMP
ZZT

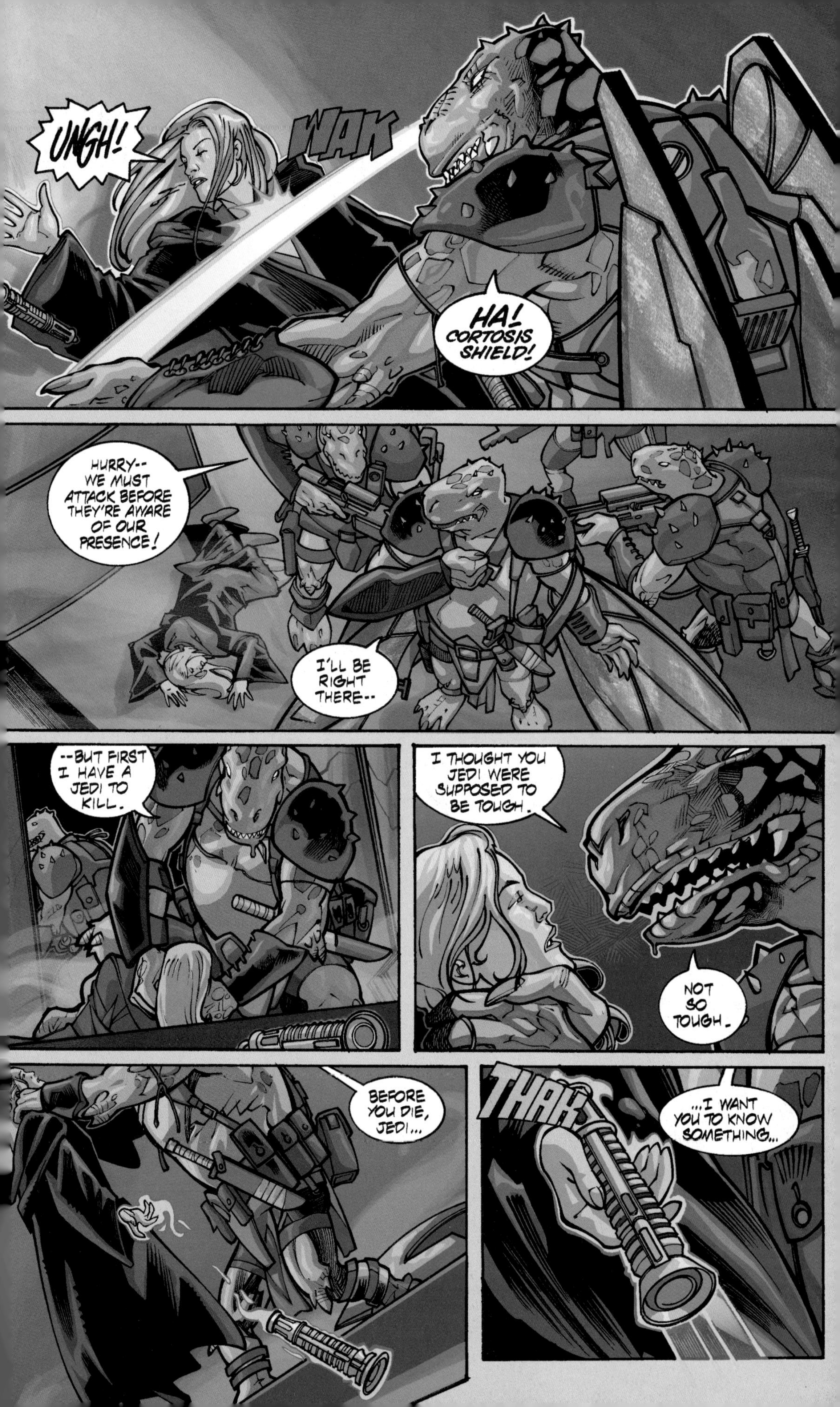
UNGH!
WAK
HA! CORTOSIS SHIELD!
HURRY-- WE MUST ATTACK BEFORE THEY'RE AWARE OF OUR PRESENCE!
I'LL BE RIGHT THERE--
--BUT FIRST I HAVE A JEDI TO KILL.
I THOUGHT YOU JEDI WERE SUPPOSED TO BE TOUGH.
NOT SO TOUGH.
BEFORE YOU DIE, JEDI...
THAK
...I WANT YOU TO KNOW SOMETHING...

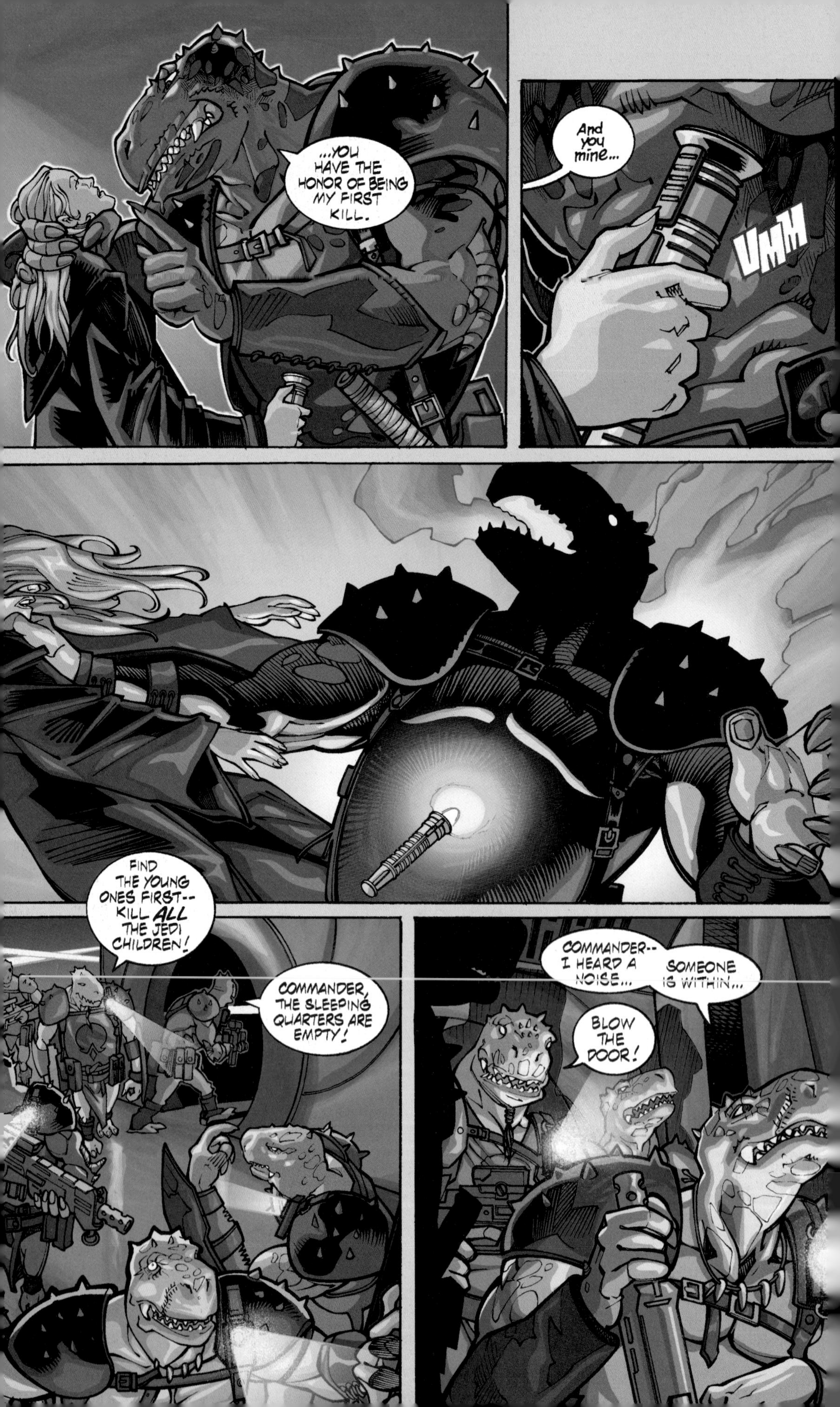
...YOU HAVE THE HONOR OF BEING MY FIRST KILL.
And you mine...
VMM
FIND THE YOUNG ONES FIRST-- KILL ALL THE JEDI CHILDREN!
COMMANDER, THE SLEEPING QUARTERS ARE EMPTY!
COMMANDER-- I HEARD A NOISE...
SOMEONE IS WITHIN...
BLOW THE DOOR!

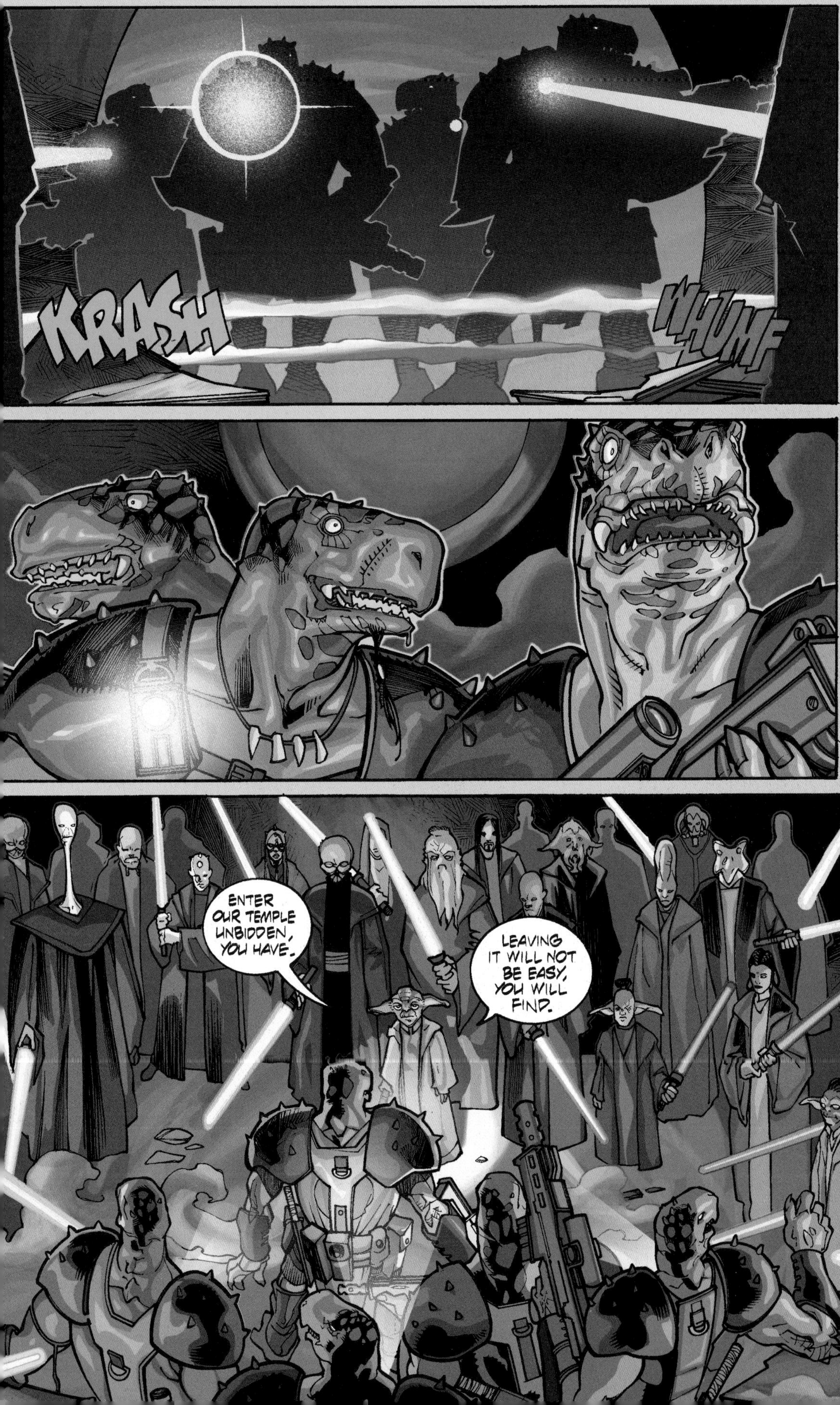
KRASH
WHUMF
ENTER OUR TEMPLE UNBIDDEN, YOU HAVE.
LEAVING IT WILL NOT BE EASY, YOU WILL FIND.

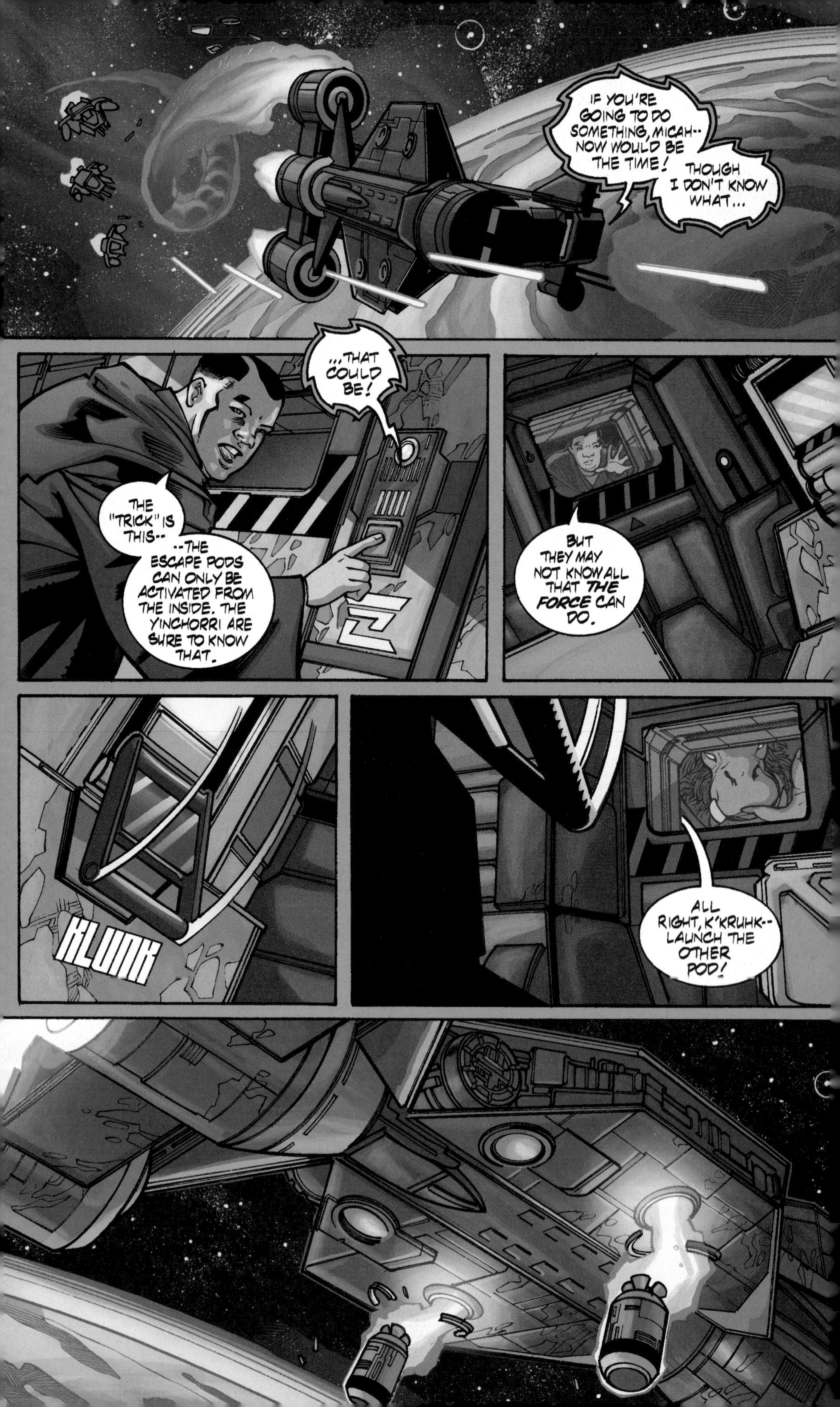
IF YOU'RE GOING TO DO SOMETHING, MICAH-- NOW WOULD BE THE TIME!
THOUGH I DON'T KNOW WHAT...
...THAT COULD BE!
THE "TRICK" IS THIS--
--THE ESCAPE PODS CAN ONLY BE ACTIVATED FROM THE INSIDE. THE YINCHORRI ARE SURE TO KNOW THAT.
BUT THEY MAY NOT KNOW ALL THAT THE FORCE CAN DO.
KLUNK
ALL RIGHT, K'KRUHK-- LAUNCH THE OTHER POD!

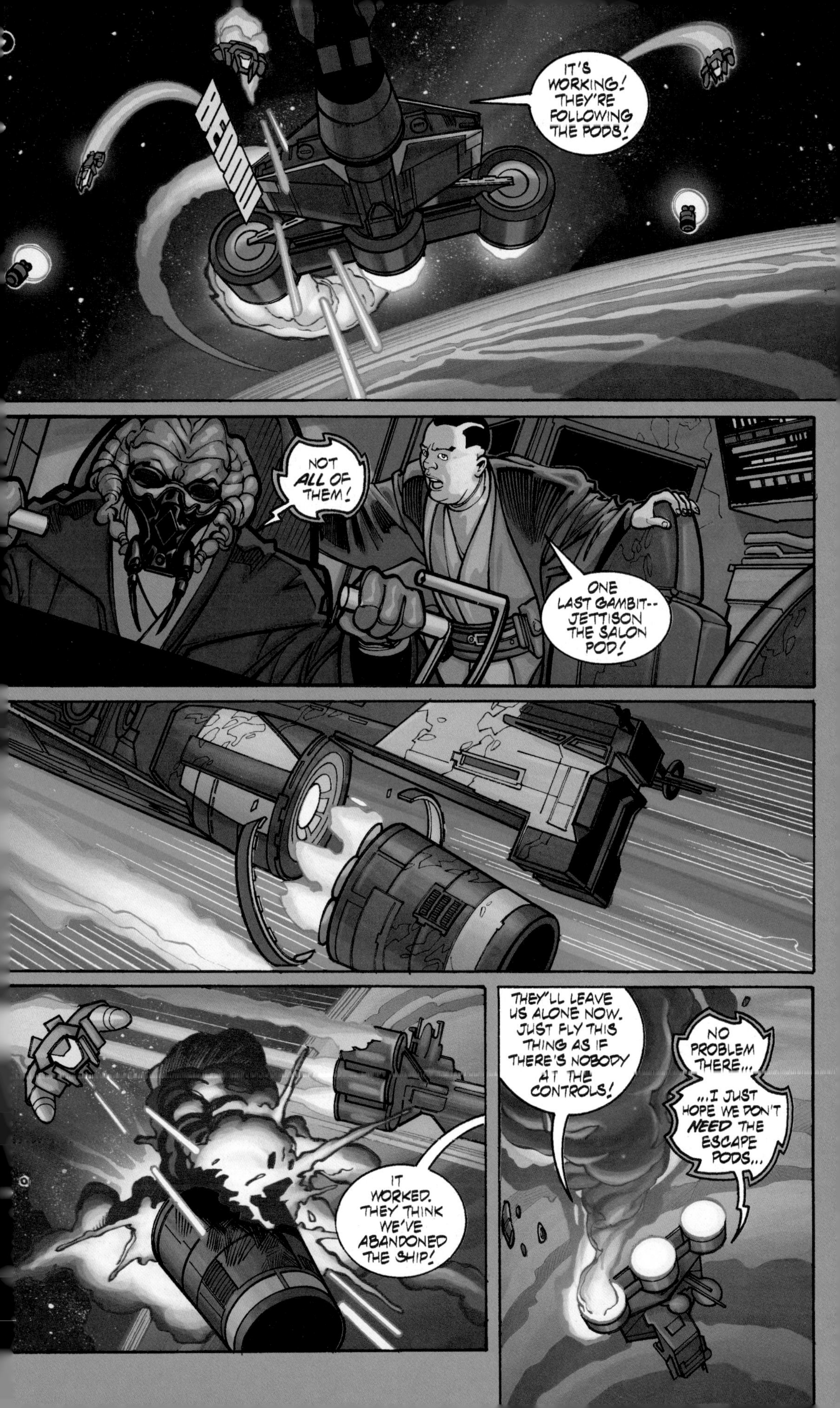
IT'S WORKING! THEY'RE FOLLOWING THE PODS!
NOT ALL OF THEM!
ONE LAST GAMBIT-- JETTISON THE SALON POD!
IT WORKED. THEY THINK WE'VE ABANDONED THE SHIP!
THEY'LL LEAVE US ALONE NOW. JUST FLY THIS THING AS IF THERE'S NOBODY AT THE CONTROLS!
NO PROBLEM THERE...
...I JUST HOPE WE DON'T NEED THE ESCAPE PODS...

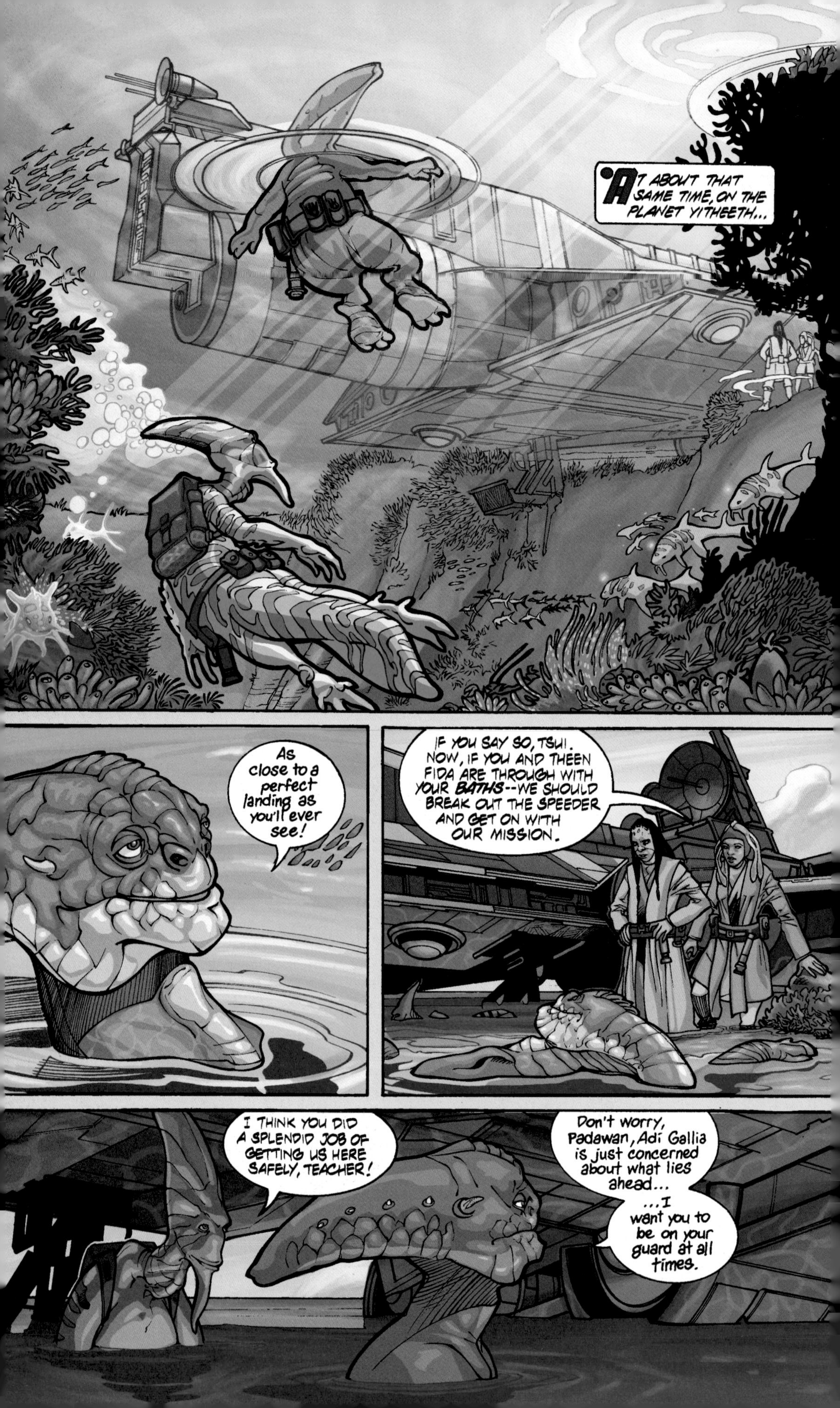
AT ABOUT THAT SAME TIME, ON THE PLANET YITHEETH...
As close to a perfect landing as you'll ever see!
IF YOU SAY SO, TSUI. NOW, IF YOU AND THEEN FIDA ARE THROUGH WITH YOUR BATHS--WE SHOULD BREAK OUT THE SPEEDER AND GET ON WITH OUR MISSION.
I THINK YOU DID A SPLENDID JOB OF GETTING US HERE SAFELY, TEACHER!
Don't worry, Padawan, Adi Gallia is just concerned about what lies ahead...
...I want you to be on your guard at all times.

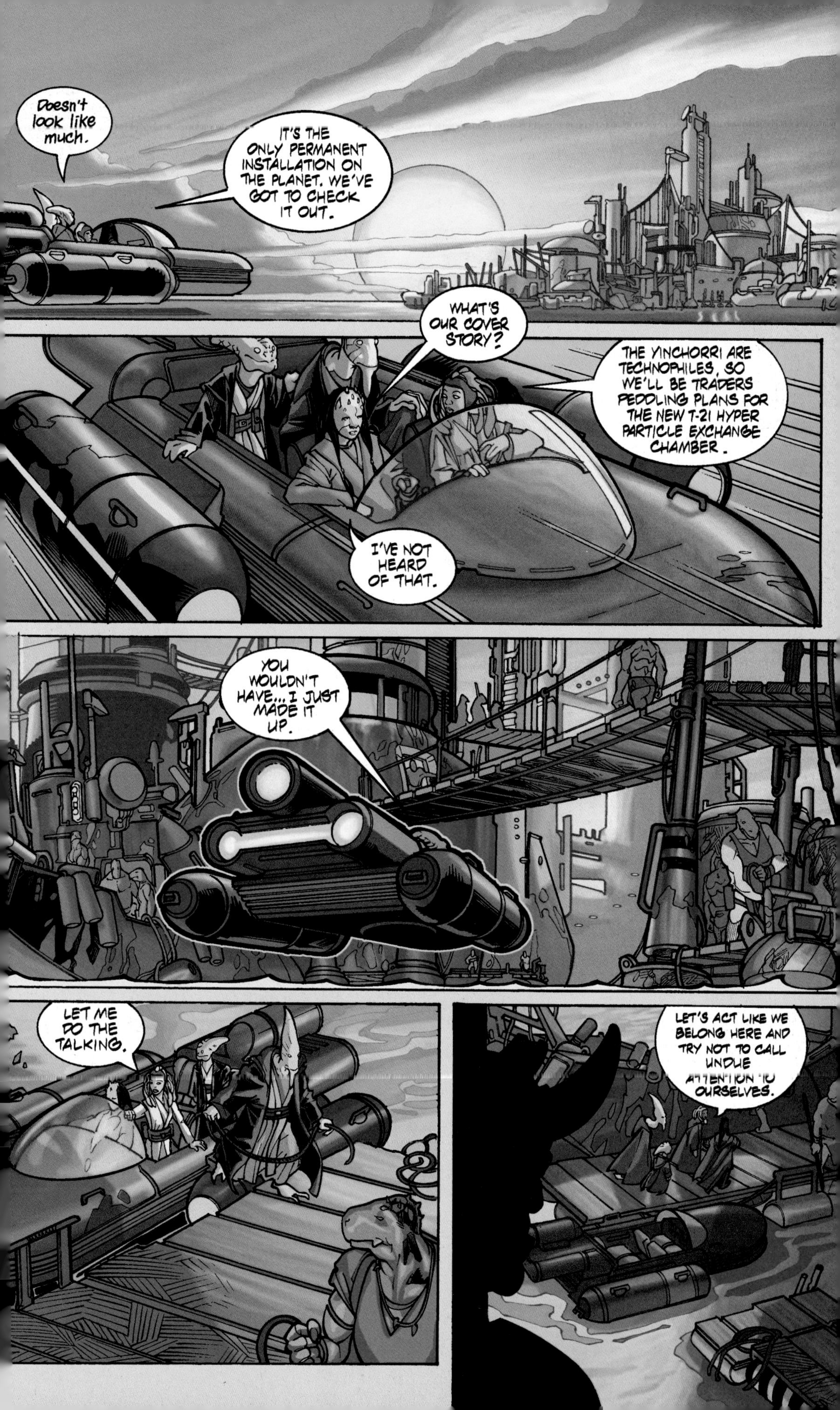
Doesn't look like much.
IT'S THE ONLY PERMANENT INSTALLATION ON THE PLANET. WE'VE GOT TO CHECK IT OUT.
WHAT'S OUR COVER STORY?
THE YINCHORRI ARE TECHNOPHILES, SO WE'LL BE TRADERS PEDDLING PLANS FOR THE NEW T-21 HYPER PARTICLE EXCHANGE CHAMBER.
I'VE NOT HEARD OF THAT.
YOU WOULDN'T HAVE... I JUST MADE IT UP.
LET ME DO THE TALKING.
LET'S ACT LIKE WE BELONG HERE AND TRY NOT TO CALL UNDUE ATTENTION TO OURSELVES.

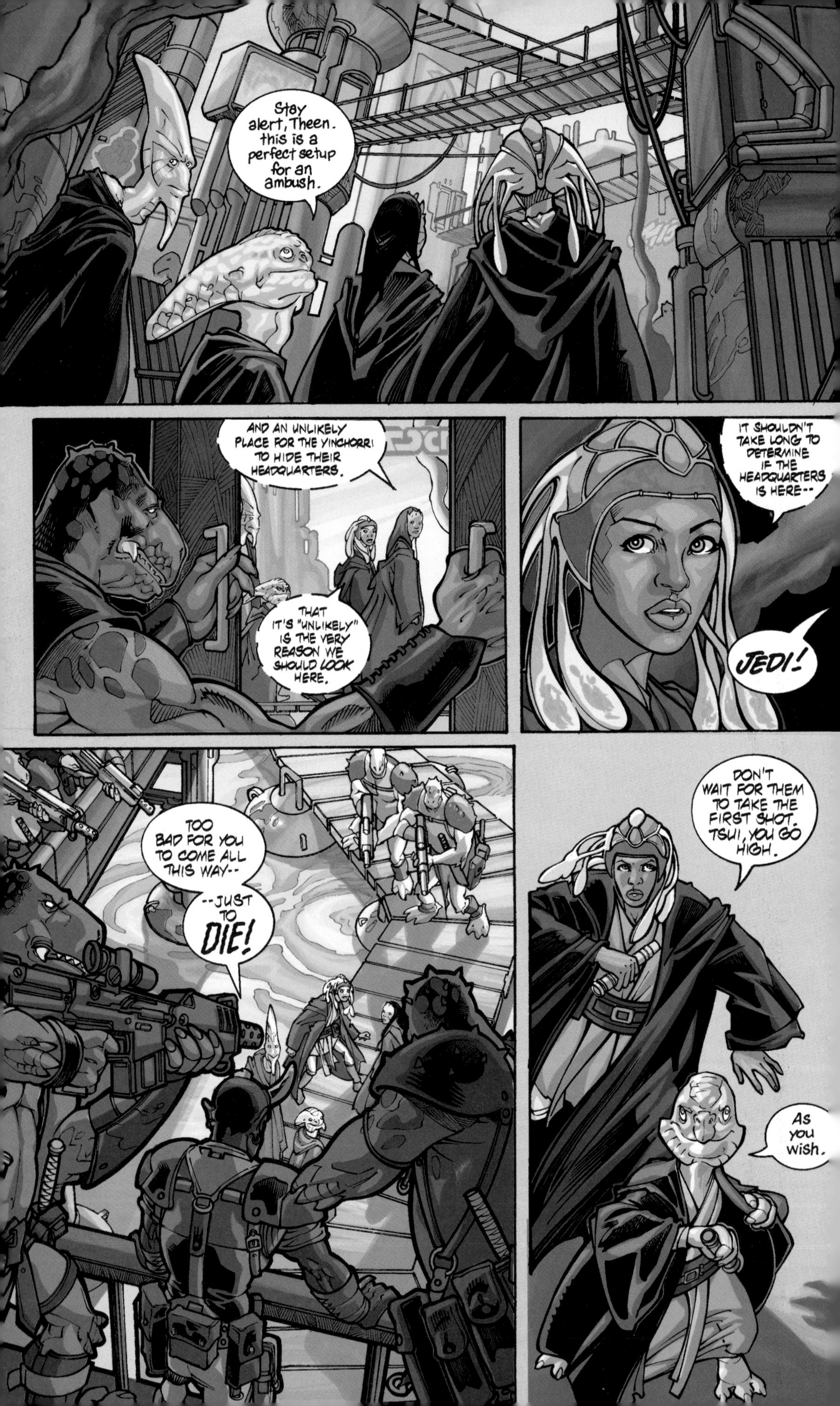

Stay alert, Theen. this is a perfect setup for an ambush.
AND AN UNLIKELY PLACE FOR THE YINCHORRI TO HIDE THEIR HEADQUARTERS.
THAT IT'S "UNLIKELY" IS THE VERY REASON WE SHOULD LOOK HERE.
IT SHOULDN'T TAKE LONG TO DETERMINE IF THE HEADQUARTERS IS HERE--
JEDI!
TOO BAD FOR YOU TO COME ALL THIS WAY--
--JUST TO DIE!
DON'T WAIT FOR THEM TO TAKE THE FIRST SHOT. TSUI, YOU GO HIGH.
As you wish.

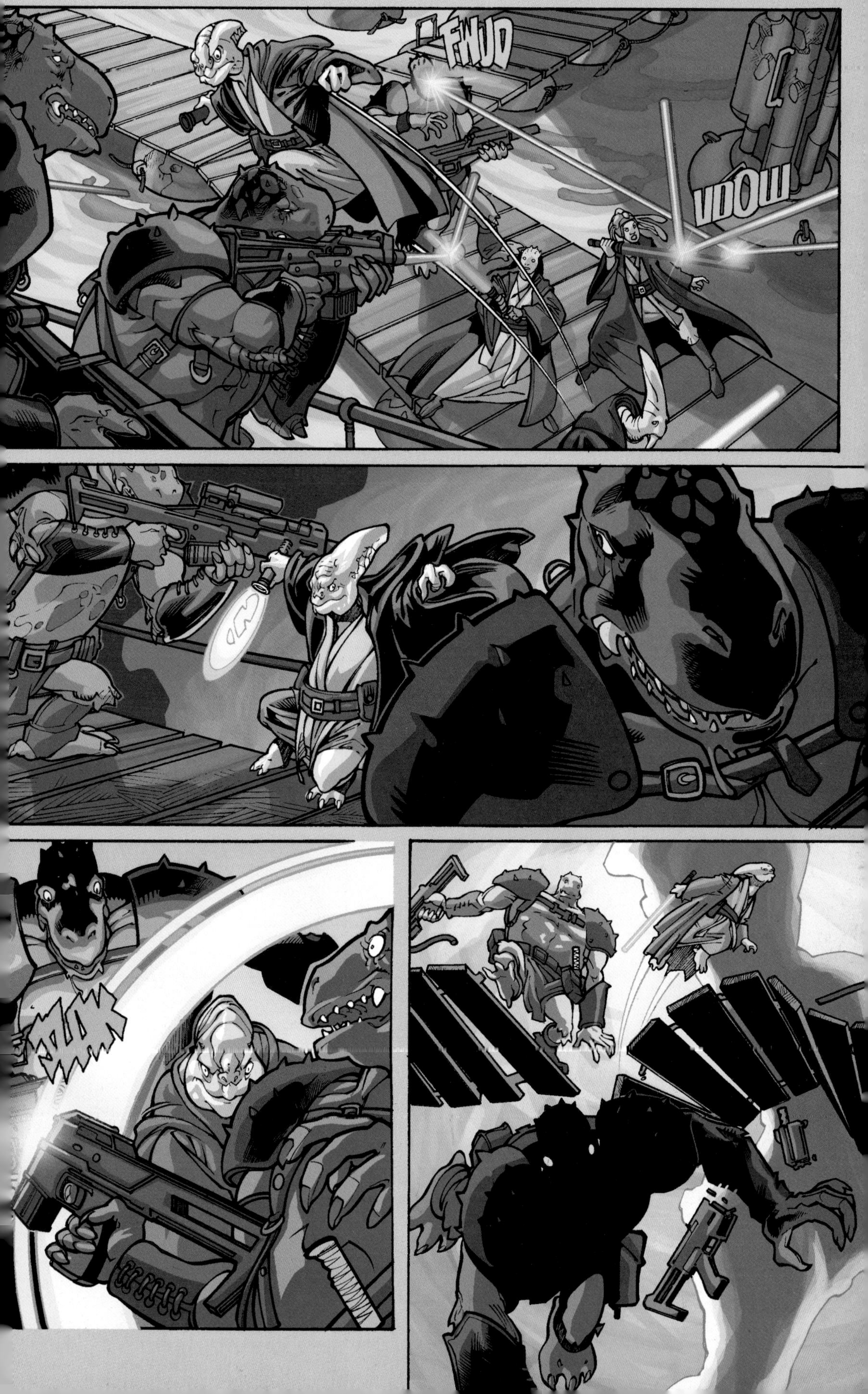
FNUD
VDOW
ZZAK

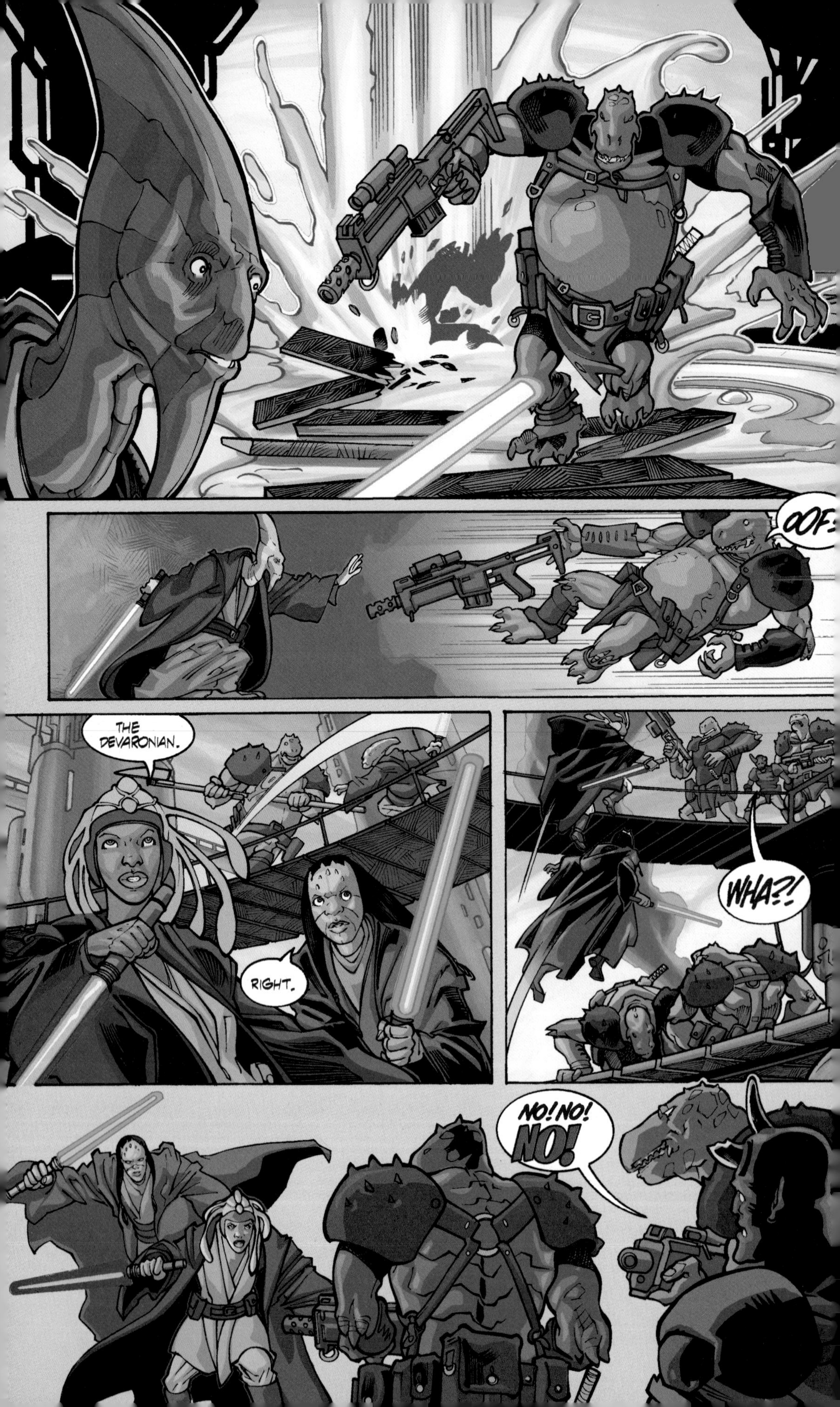
OOF!
THE DEVARONIAN.
RIGHT.
WHA?!
NO! NO! NO!

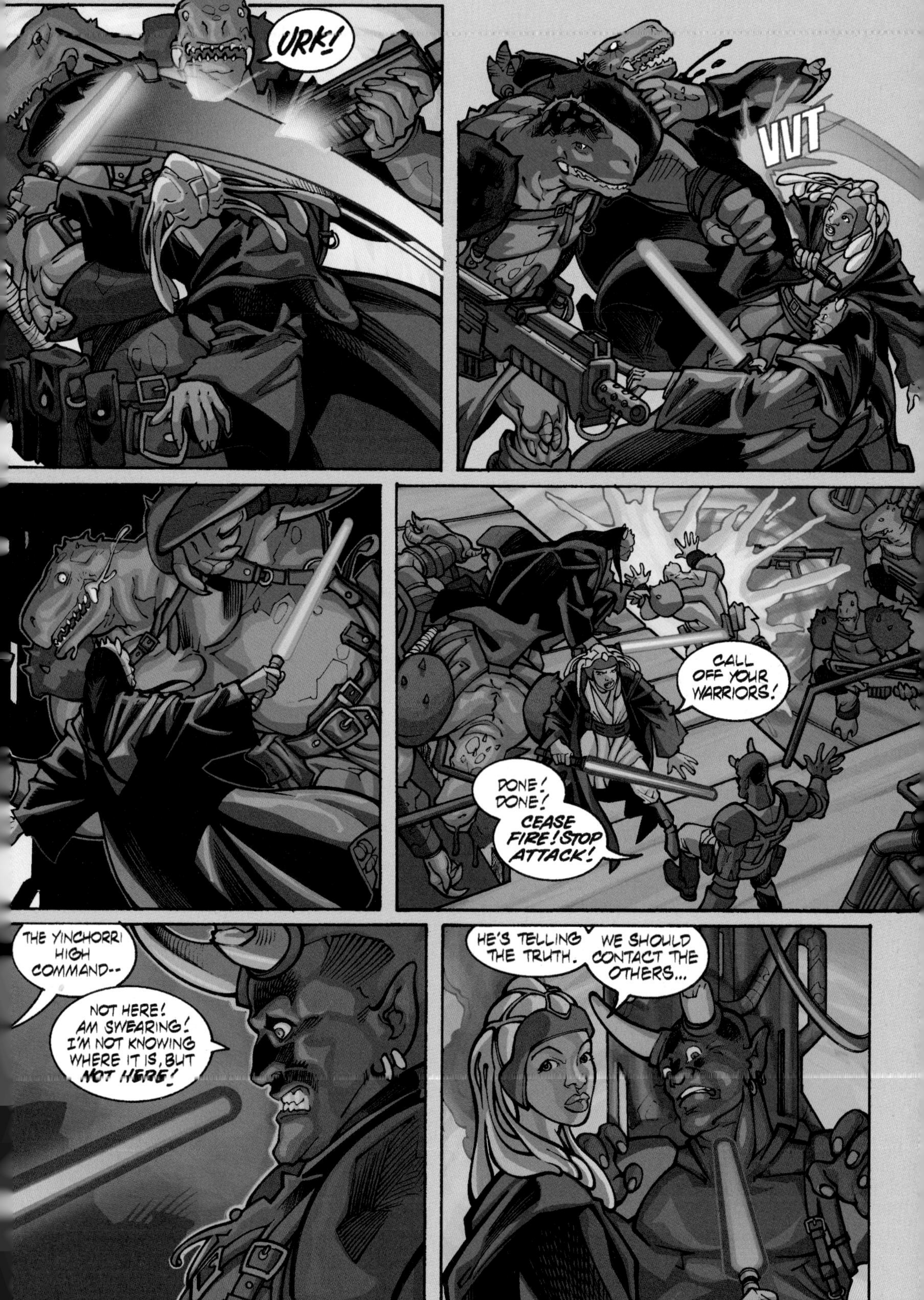
URK!
VVT
CALL OFF YOUR WARRIORS!
DONE! DONE! CEASE FIRE! STOP ATTACK!
THE YINCHORRI HIGH COMMAND--
NOT HERE! AM SWEARING! I'M NOT KNOWING WHERE IT IS, BUT NOT HERE!
HE'S TELLING THE TRUTH.
WE SHOULD CONTACT THE OTHERS...

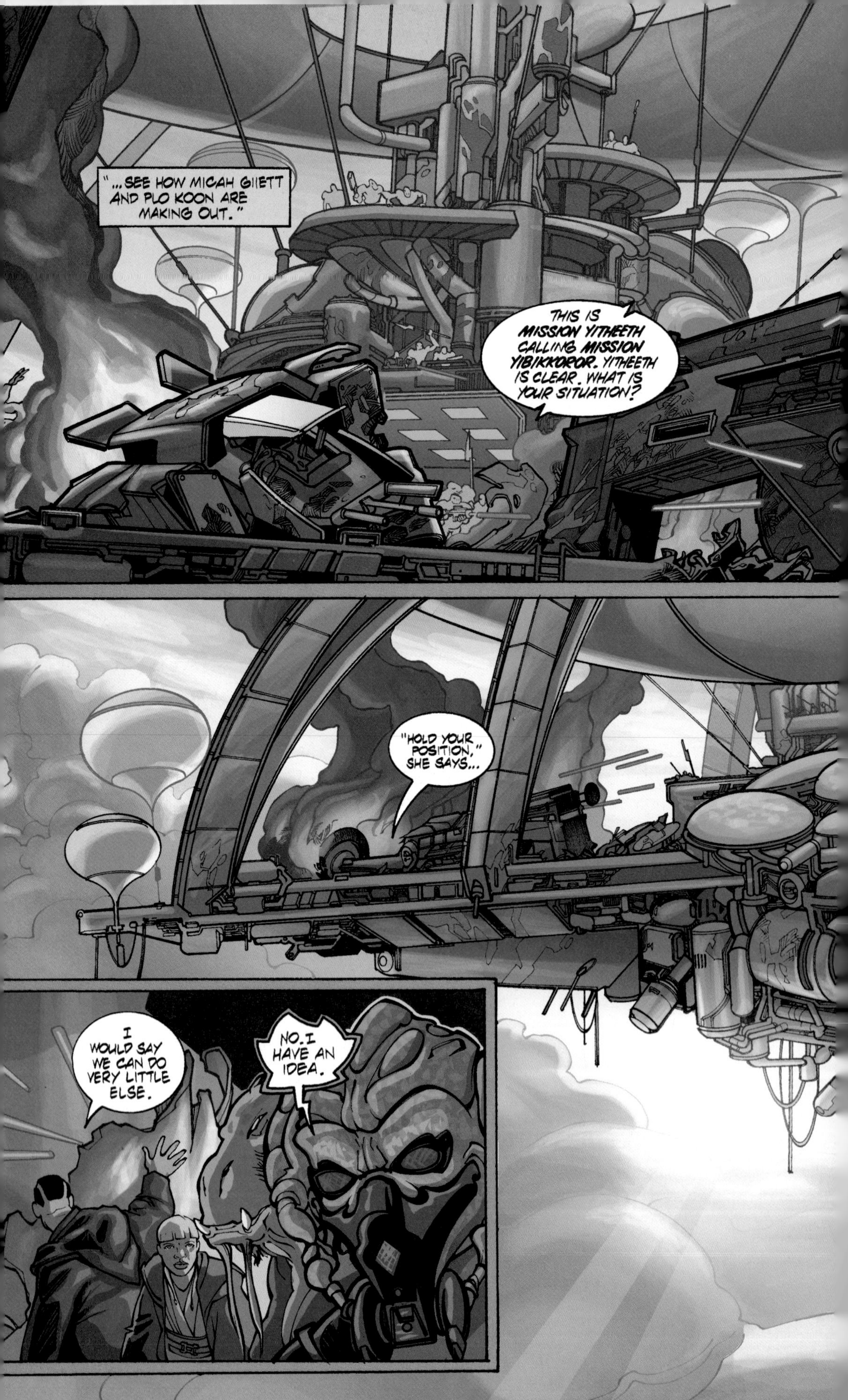
"...SEE HOW MICAH GIIETT AND PLO KOON ARE MAKING OUT."
THIS IS MISSION YITHEETH CALLING MISSION YIBIKKOROR. YITHEETH IS CLEAR. WHAT IS YOUR SITUATION?
"HOLD YOUR POSITION," SHE SAYS...
I WOULD SAY WE CAN DO VERY LITTLE ELSE.
NO. I HAVE AN IDEA.

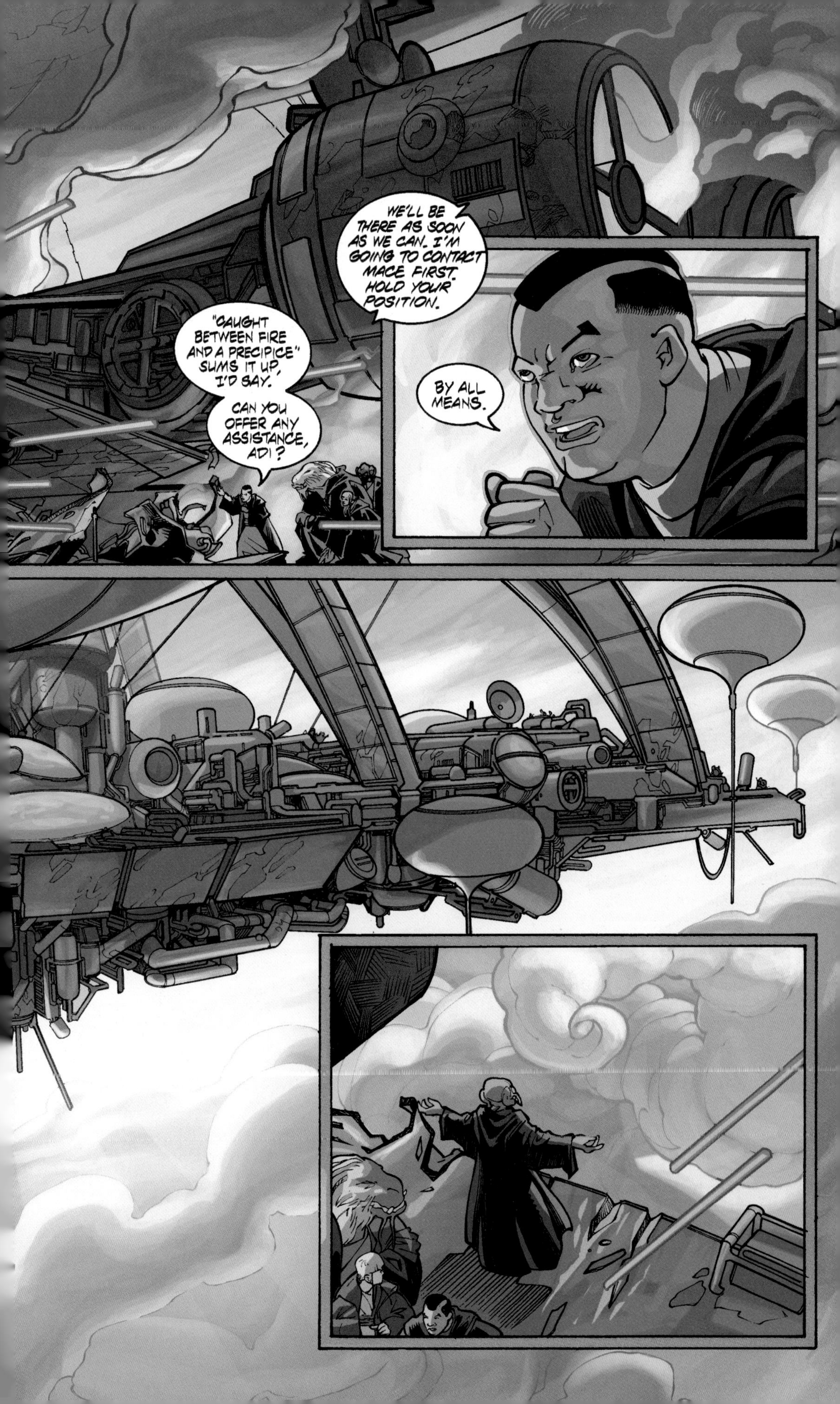

"CAUGHT BETWEEN FIRE AND A PRECIPICE" SUMS IT UP, I'D SAY.
CAN YOU OFFER ANY ASSISTANCE, ADI?
WE'LL BE THERE AS SOON AS WE CAN. I'M GOING TO CONTACT MACE FIRST. HOLD YOUR POSITION.
BY ALL MEANS.

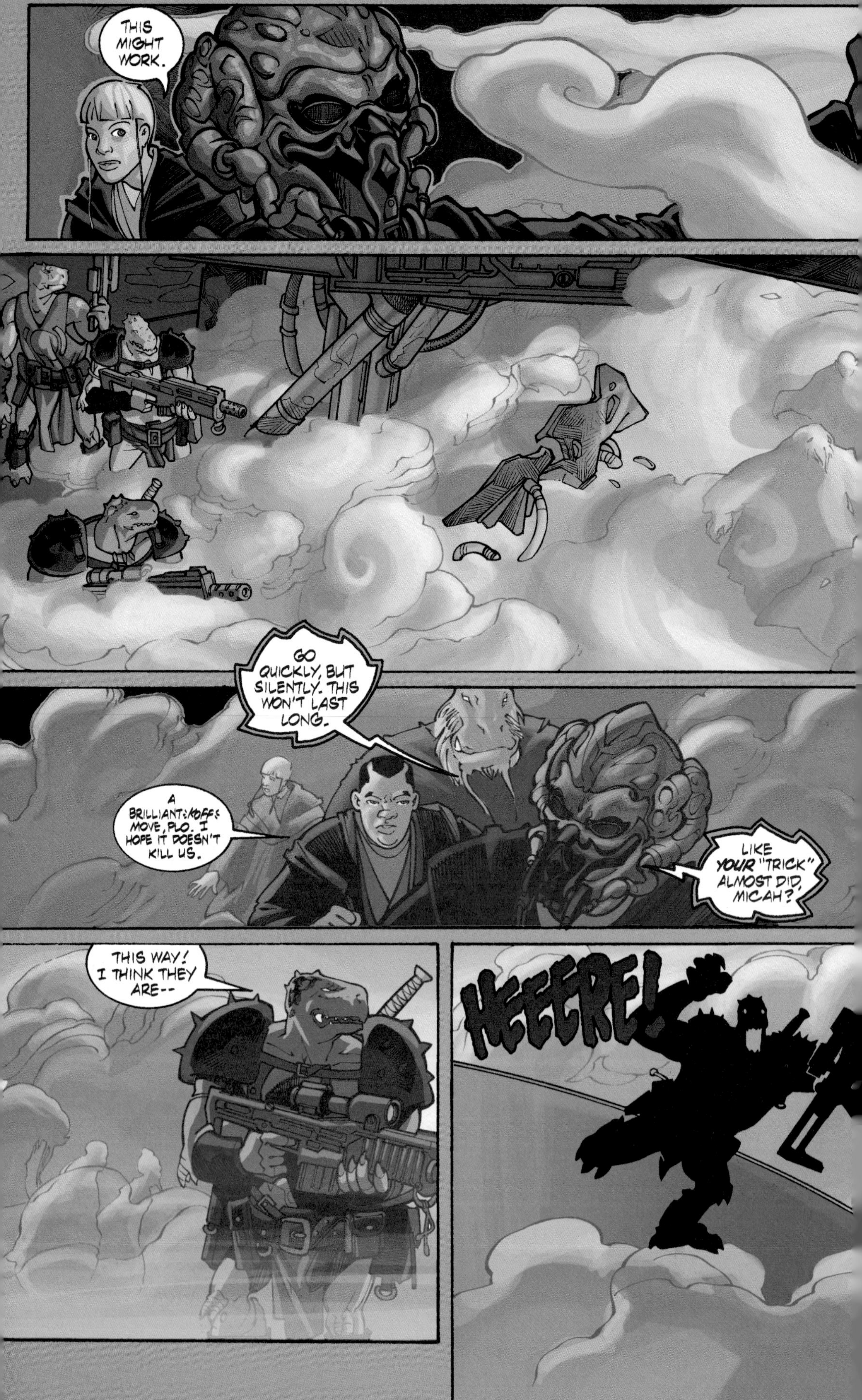
THIS MIGHT WORK.
GO QUICKLY, BUT SILENTLY. THIS WON'T LAST LONG.
A BRILLIANT :KOFF: MOVE, PLO. I HOPE IT DOESN'T KILL US.
LIKE ***YOUR*** "TRICK" ALMOST DID, MICAH?
THIS WAY! I THINK THEY ARE--
HEEERE!

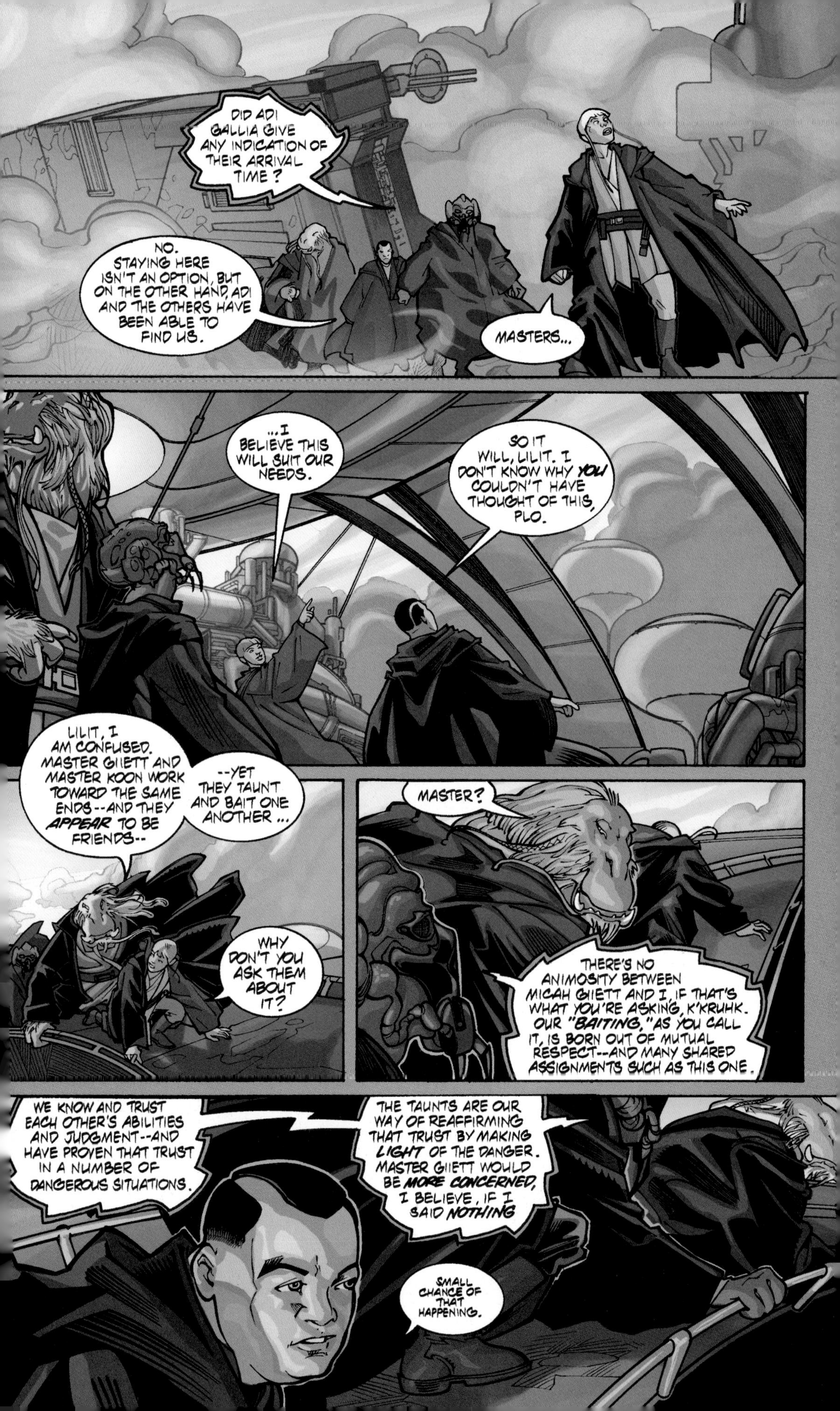
DID ADI GALLIA GIVE ANY INDICATION OF THEIR ARRIVAL TIME ?
NO. STAYING HERE ISN'T AN OPTION, BUT ON THE OTHER HAND, ADI AND THE OTHERS HAVE BEEN ABLE TO FIND US.
MASTERS...
...I BELIEVE THIS WILL SUIT OUR NEEDS.
SO IT WILL, LILIT. I DON'T KNOW WHY YOU COULDN'T HAVE THOUGHT OF THIS, PLO.
LILIT, I AM CONFUSED. MASTER GIIETT AND MASTER KOON WORK TOWARD THE SAME ENDS--AND THEY APPEAR TO BE FRIENDS--
--YET THEY TAUNT AND BAIT ONE ANOTHER ...
WHY DON'T YOU ASK THEM ABOUT IT?
MASTER?
THERE'S NO ANIMOSITY BETWEEN MICAH GIIETT AND I, IF THAT'S WHAT YOU'RE ASKING, K'KRUHK. OUR "BAITING," AS YOU CALL IT, IS BORN OUT OF MUTUAL RESPECT--AND MANY SHARED ASSIGNMENTS SUCH AS THIS ONE.
WE KNOW AND TRUST EACH OTHER'S ABILITIES AND JUDGMENT--AND HAVE PROVEN THAT TRUST IN A NUMBER OF DANGEROUS SITUATIONS.
THE TAUNTS ARE OUR WAY OF REAFFIRMING THAT TRUST BY MAKING LIGHT OF THE DANGER. MASTER GIIETT WOULD BE MORE CONCERNED, I BELIEVE, IF I SAID NOTHING
SMALL CHANCE OF THAT HAPPENING.

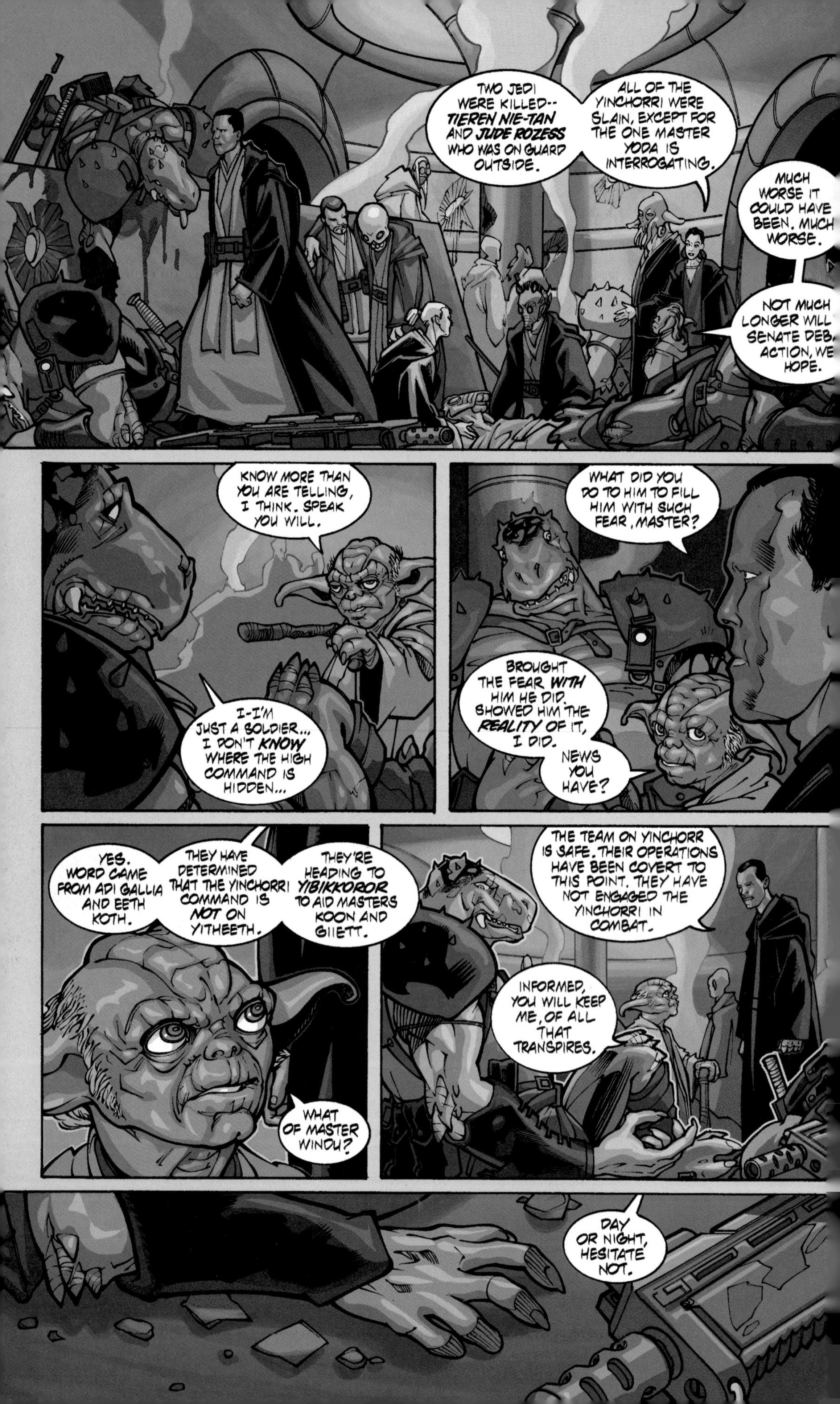
TWO JEDI WERE KILLED-- TIEREN NIE-TAN AND JUDE ROZESS WHO WAS ON GUARD OUTSIDE.
ALL OF THE YINCHORRI WERE SLAIN, EXCEPT FOR THE ONE MASTER YODA IS INTERROGATING.
MUCH WORSE IT COULD HAVE BEEN. MUCH WORSE.
NOT MUCH LONGER WILL SENATE DEB ACTION, WE HOPE.
KNOW MORE THAN YOU ARE TELLING, I THINK. SPEAK YOU WILL.
I-I'M JUST A SOLDIER... I DON'T KNOW WHERE THE HIGH COMMAND IS HIDDEN...
WHAT DID YOU DO TO HIM TO FILL HIM WITH SUCH FEAR, MASTER?
BROUGHT THE FEAR WITH HIM HE DID. SHOWED HIM THE REALITY OF IT, I DID.
NEWS YOU HAVE?
YES. WORD CAME FROM ADI GALLIA AND EETH KOTH.
THEY HAVE DETERMINED THAT THE YINCHORRI COMMAND IS NOT ON YITHEETH.
THEY'RE HEADING TO YIBIKKOROR TO AID MASTERS KOON AND GIIETT.
WHAT OF MASTER WINDU?
THE TEAM ON YINCHORR IS SAFE. THEIR OPERATIONS HAVE BEEN COVERT TO THIS POINT. THEY HAVE NOT ENGAGED THE YINCHORRI IN COMBAT.
INFORMED, YOU WILL KEEP ME, OF ALL THAT TRANSPIRES.
DAY OR NIGHT, HESITATE NOT.

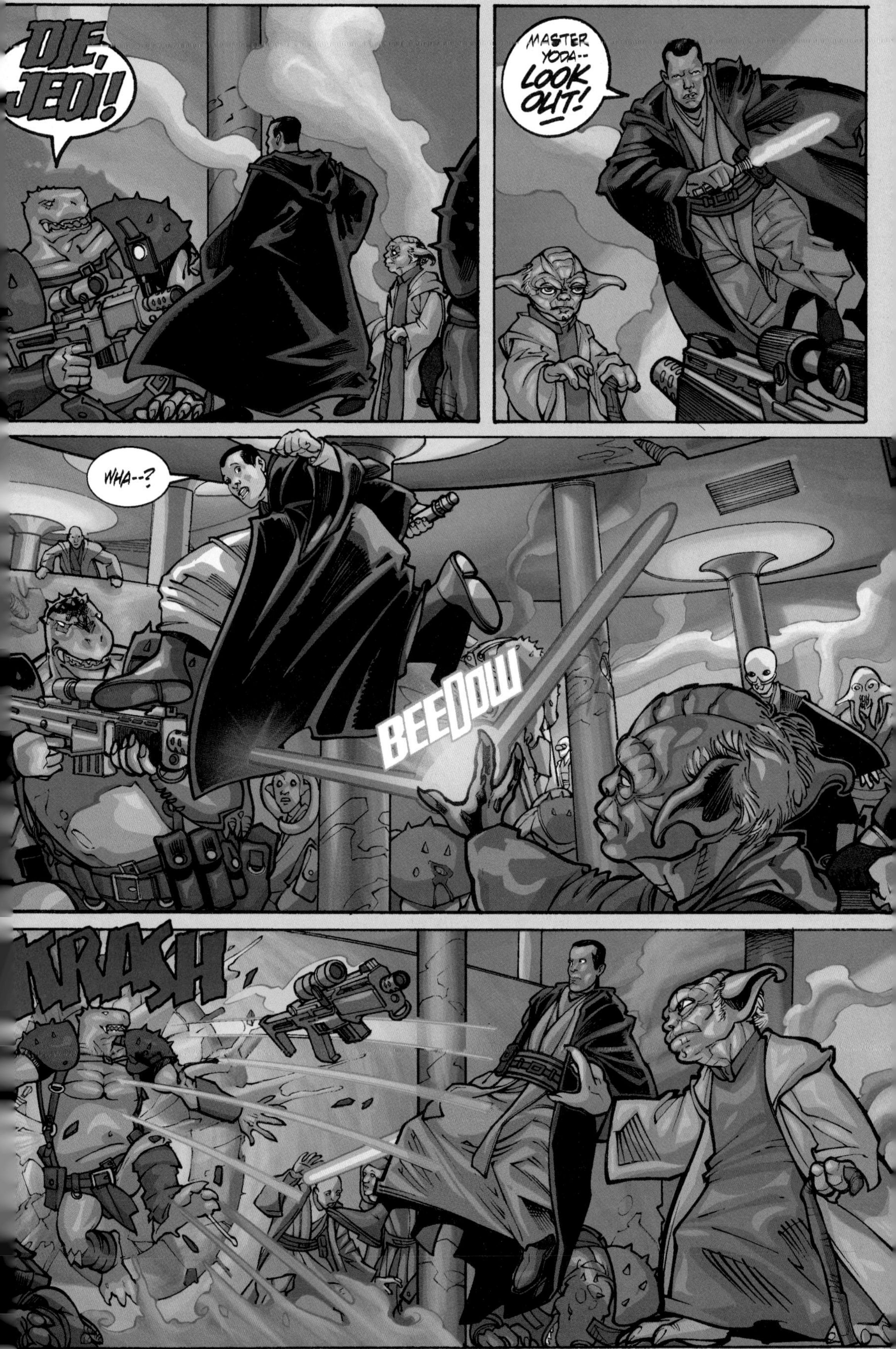
DIE, JEDI!
MASTER YODA-- LOOK OUT!
WHA--?
BEEDOW
KRASH

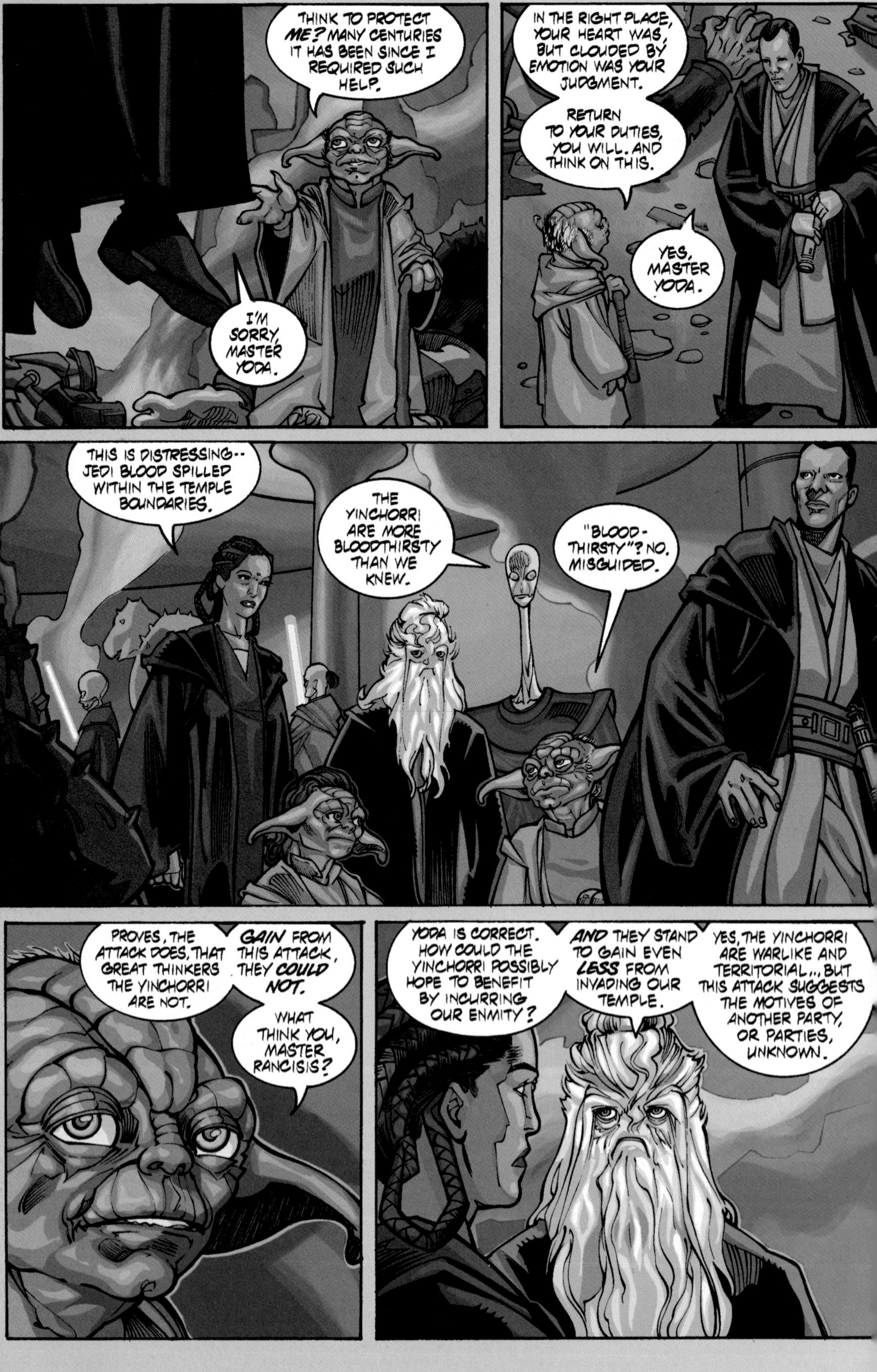
THINK TO PROTECT *ME?* MANY CENTURIES IT HAS BEEN SINCE I REQUIRED SUCH HELP.
I'M SORRY, MASTER YODA.
IN THE RIGHT PLACE, YOUR HEART WAS, BUT CLOUDED BY EMOTION WAS YOUR JUDGMENT.
RETURN TO YOUR DUTIES, YOU WILL. AND THINK ON THIS.
YES, MASTER YODA.
THIS IS DISTRESSING-- JEDI BLOOD SPILLED WITHIN THE TEMPLE BOUNDARIES.
THE YINCHORRI ARE MORE BLOODTHIRSTY THAN WE KNEW.
"BLOOD-THIRSTY"? NO. MISGUIDED.
PROVES, THE ATTACK DOES, THAT GREAT THINKERS THE YINCHORRI ARE NOT.
GAIN FROM THIS ATTACK, THEY *COULD NOT.*
WHAT THINK YOU, MASTER RANCISIS?
YODA IS CORRECT. HOW COULD THE YINCHORRI POSSIBLY HOPE TO BENEFIT BY INCURRING OUR ENMITY?
AND THEY STAND TO GAIN EVEN *LESS* FROM INVADING OUR TEMPLE.
YES, THE YINCHORRI ARE WARLIKE AND TERRITORIAL... BUT THIS ATTACK SUGGESTS THE MOTIVES OF ANOTHER PARTY, OR PARTIES, UNKNOWN.

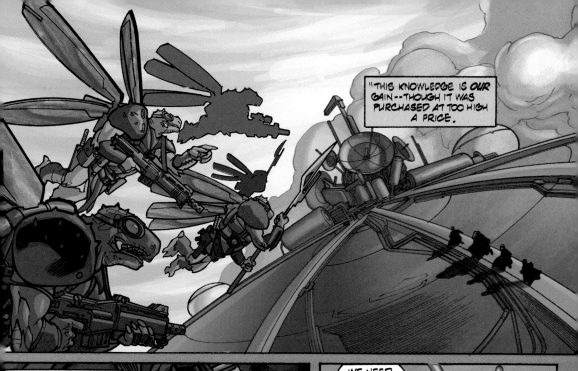

"THIS KNOWLEDGE IS *OUR* GAIN--THOUGH IT WAS PURCHASED AT TOO HIGH A PRICE."

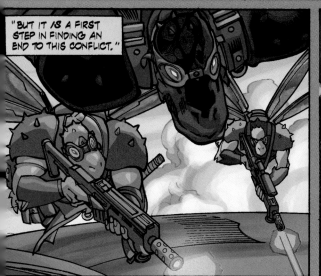

"BUT IT *IS* A FIRST STEP IN FINDING AN END TO THIS CONFLICT."

WE NEED TO FIND COVER!

THERE ISN'T ENOUGH TIME FOR ME TO TRY MY "TRICK" AGAIN...

NO NEED, PLO. *FOLLOW* ME.

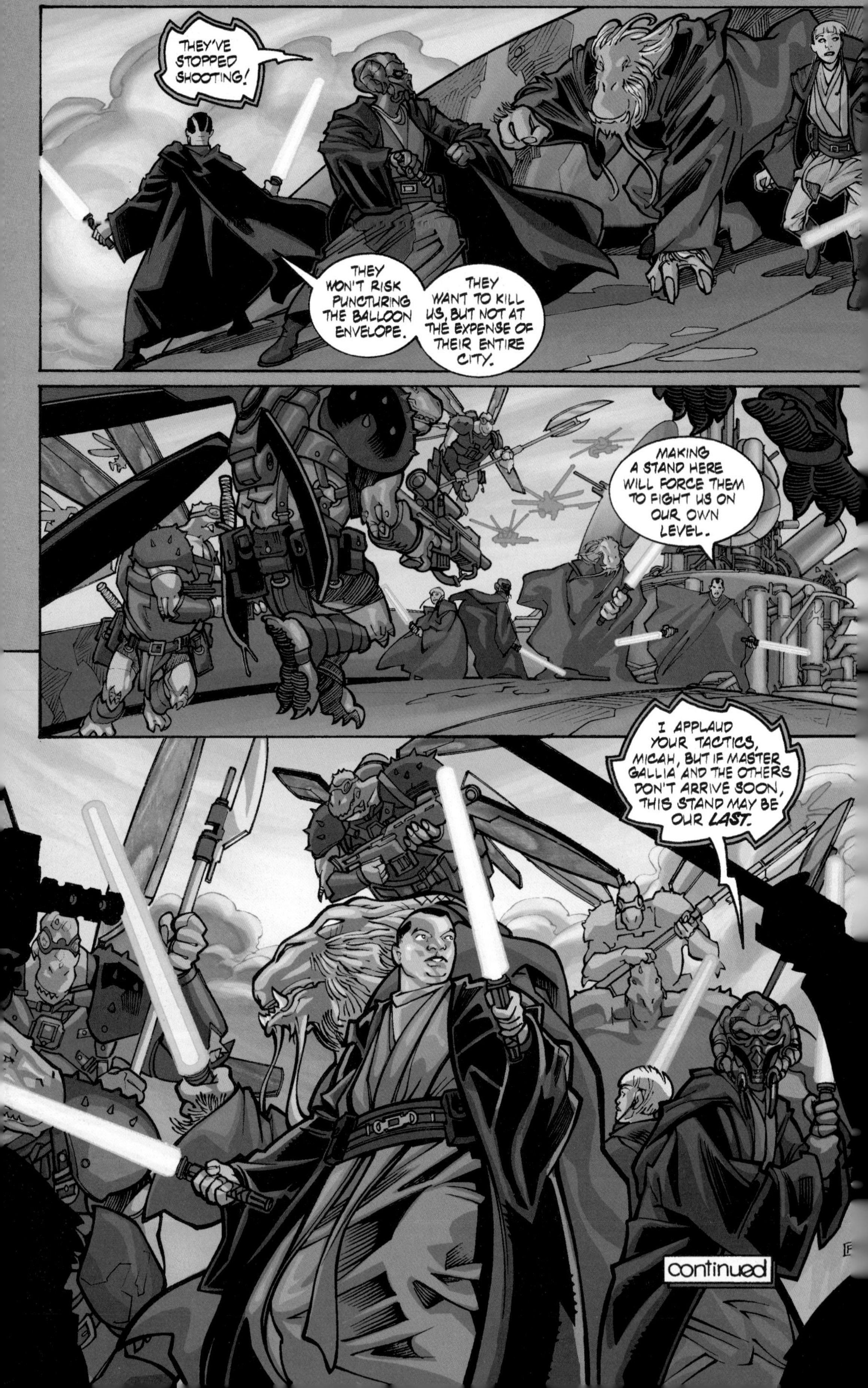
THEY'VE STOPPED SHOOTING!
THEY WON'T RISK PUNCTURING THE BALLOON ENVELOPE.
THEY WANT TO KILL US, BUT NOT AT THE EXPENSE OF THEIR ENTIRE CITY.
MAKING A STAND HERE WILL FORCE THEM TO FIGHT US ON OUR OWN LEVEL.
I APPLAUD YOUR TACTICS, MICAH, BUT IF MASTER GALLIA AND THE OTHERS DON'T ARRIVE SOON, THIS STAND MAY BE OUR LAST.
continued

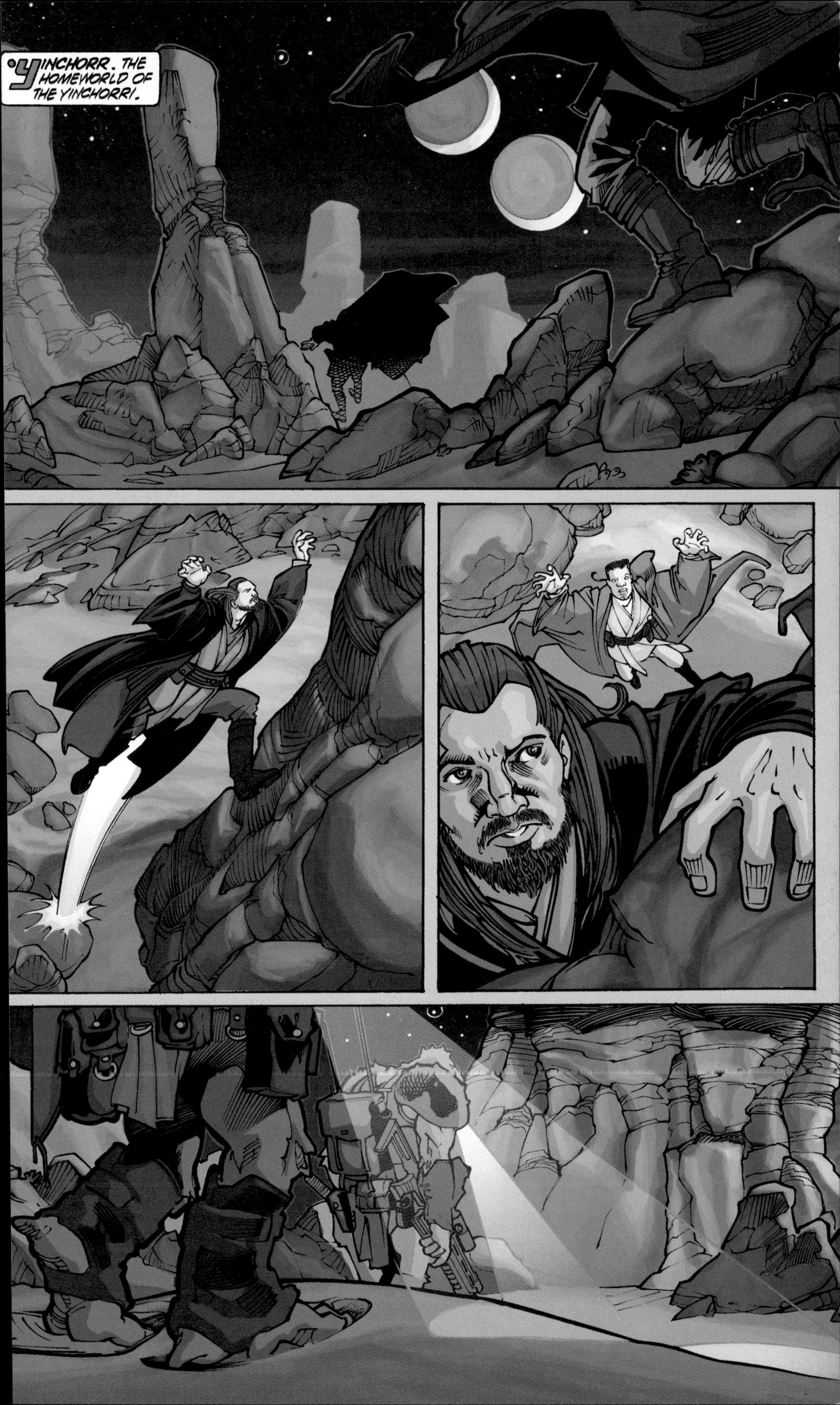
YINCHORR. THE HOMEWORLD OF THE YINCHORRI.

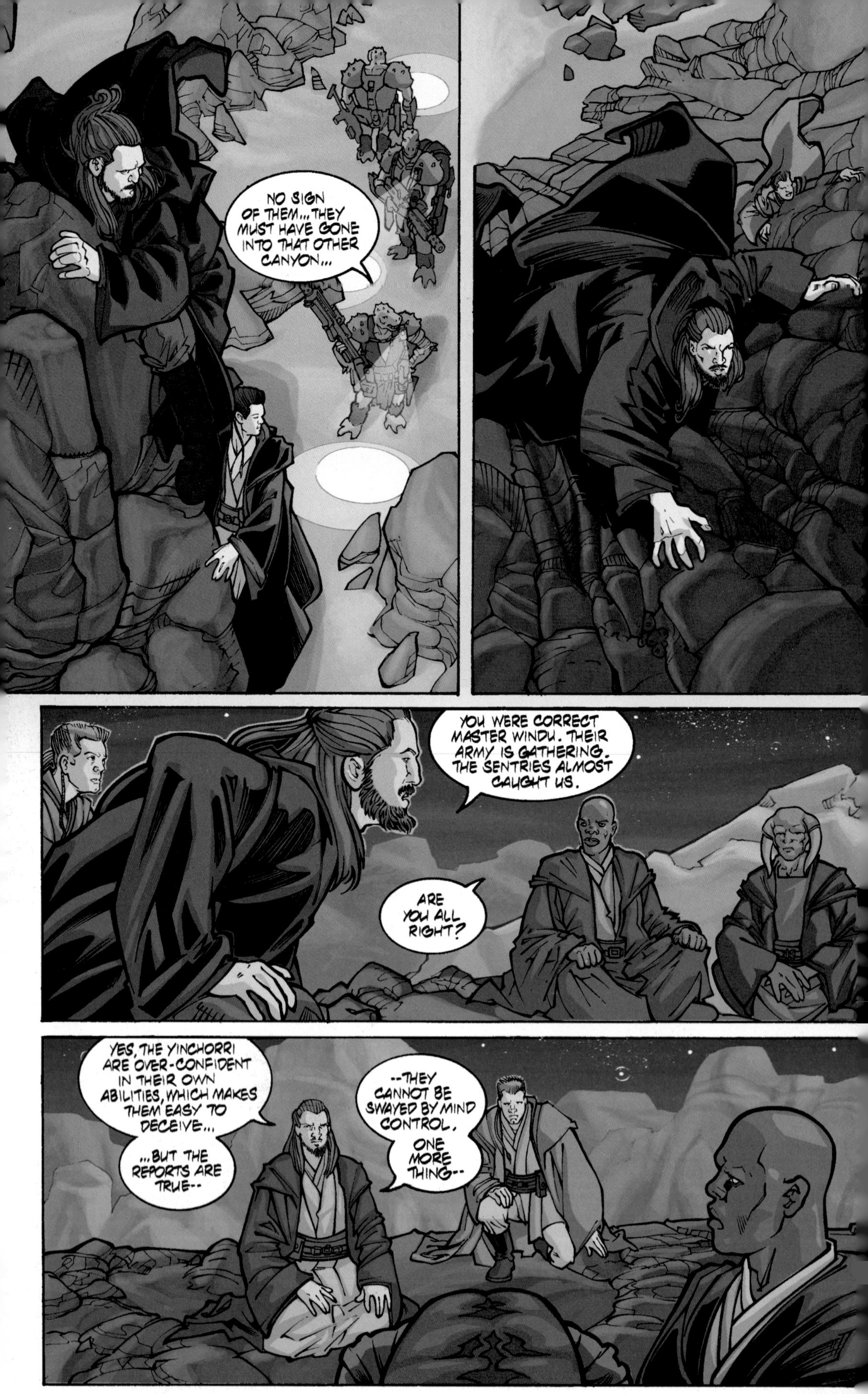
NO SIGN OF THEM... THEY MUST HAVE GONE INTO THAT OTHER CANYON...
YOU WERE CORRECT MASTER WINDU. THEIR ARMY IS GATHERING. THE SENTRIES ALMOST CAUGHT US.
ARE YOU ALL RIGHT?
YES, THE YINCHORRI ARE OVER-CONFIDENT IN THEIR OWN ABILITIES, WHICH MAKES THEM EASY TO DECEIVE...
...BUT THE REPORTS ARE TRUE--
--THEY CANNOT BE SWAYED BY MIND CONTROL.
ONE MORE THING--

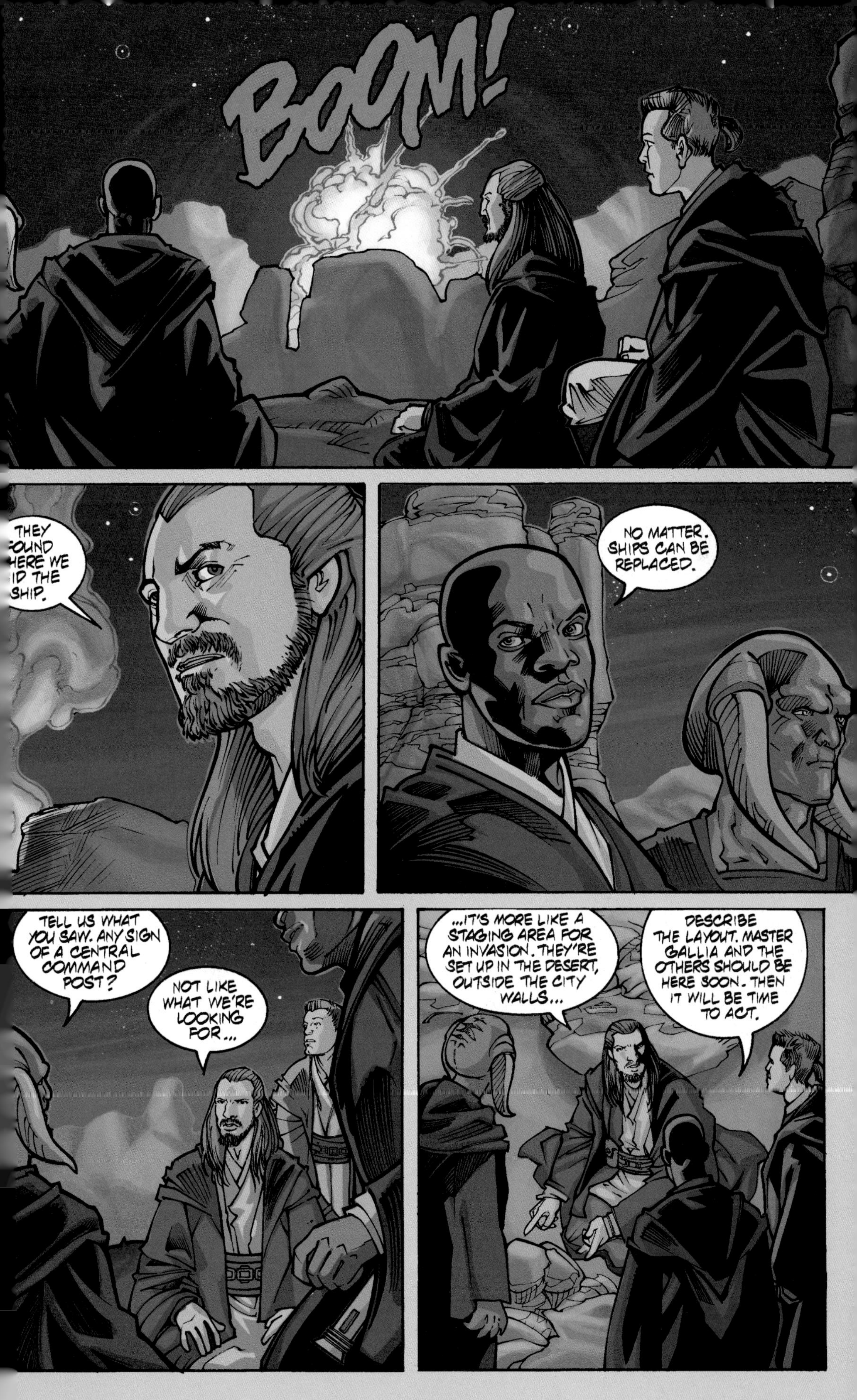
BOOM!
THEY FOUND HERE WE ID THE SHIP.
NO MATTER. SHIPS CAN BE REPLACED.
TELL US WHAT YOU SAW. ANY SIGN OF A CENTRAL COMMAND POST?
NOT LIKE WHAT WE'RE LOOKING FOR...
...IT'S MORE LIKE A STAGING AREA FOR AN INVASION. THEY'RE SET UP IN THE DESERT, OUTSIDE THE CITY WALLS...
DESCRIBE THE LAYOUT. MASTER GALLIA AND THE OTHERS SHOULD BE HERE SOON. THEN IT WILL BE TIME TO ACT.

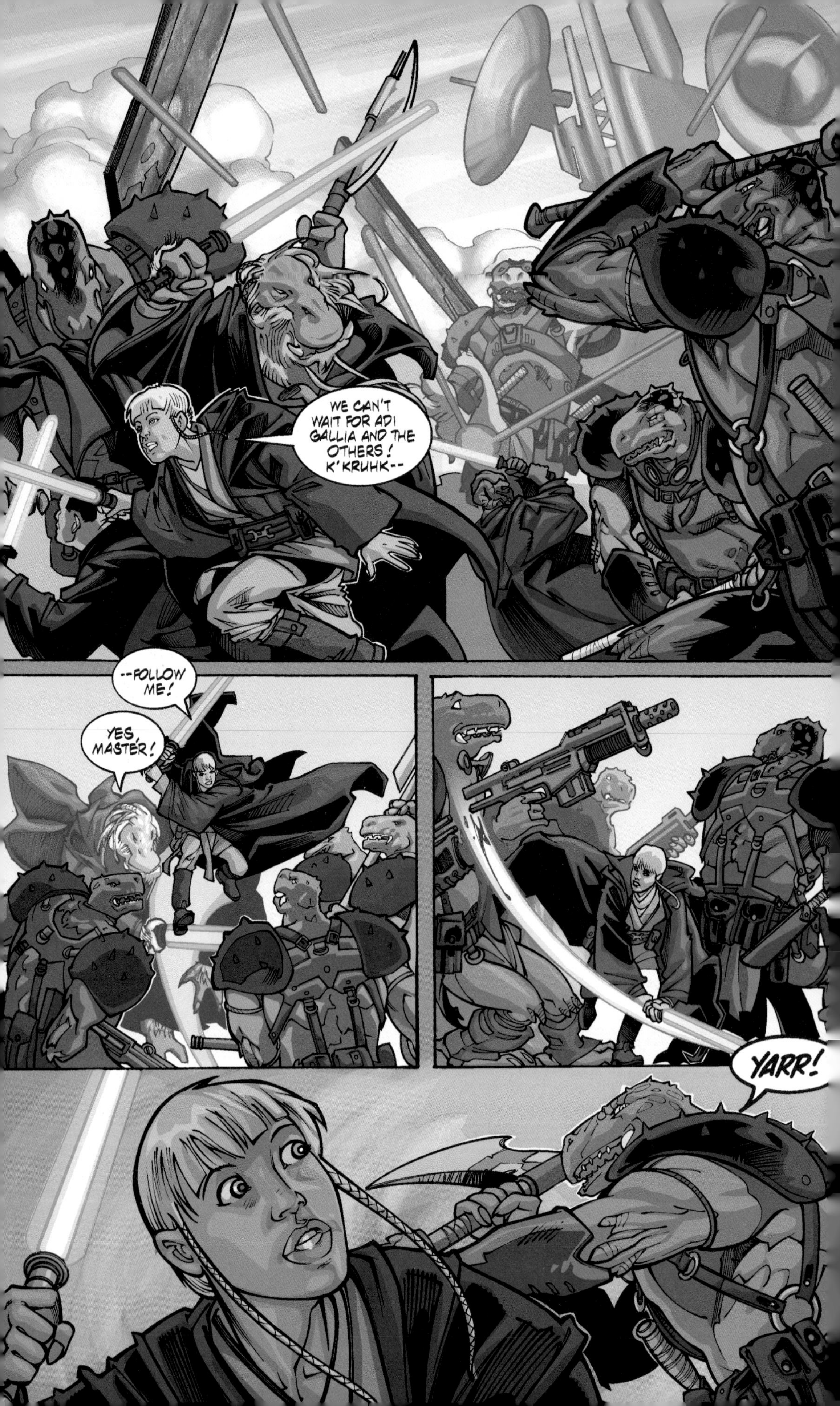
WE CAN'T WAIT FOR ADI GALLIA AND THE OTHERS! K'KRUHK--
--FOLLOW ME!
YES, MASTER!
YARR!

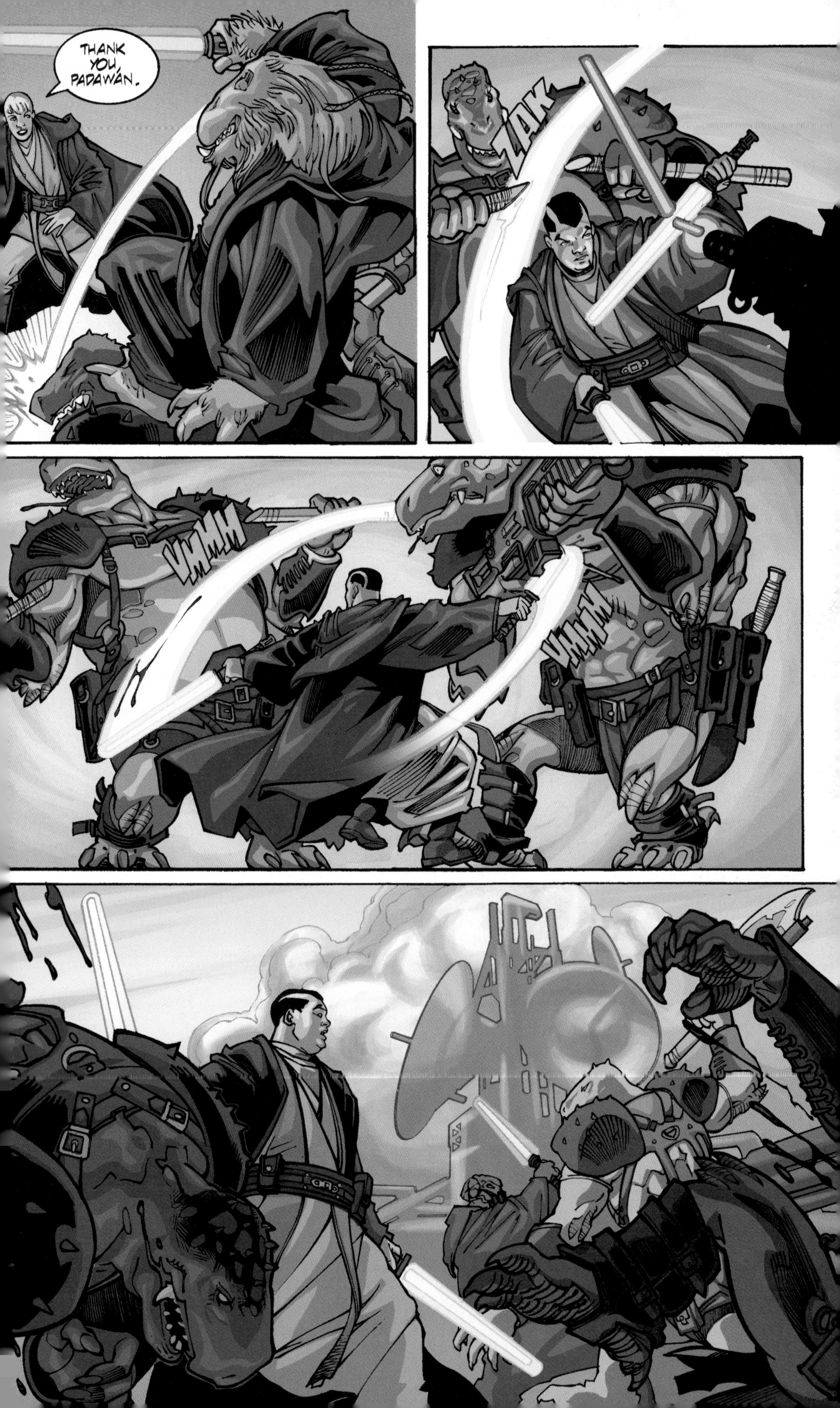
THANK YOU, PADAWAN.
ZAK
VMMM
VMMM

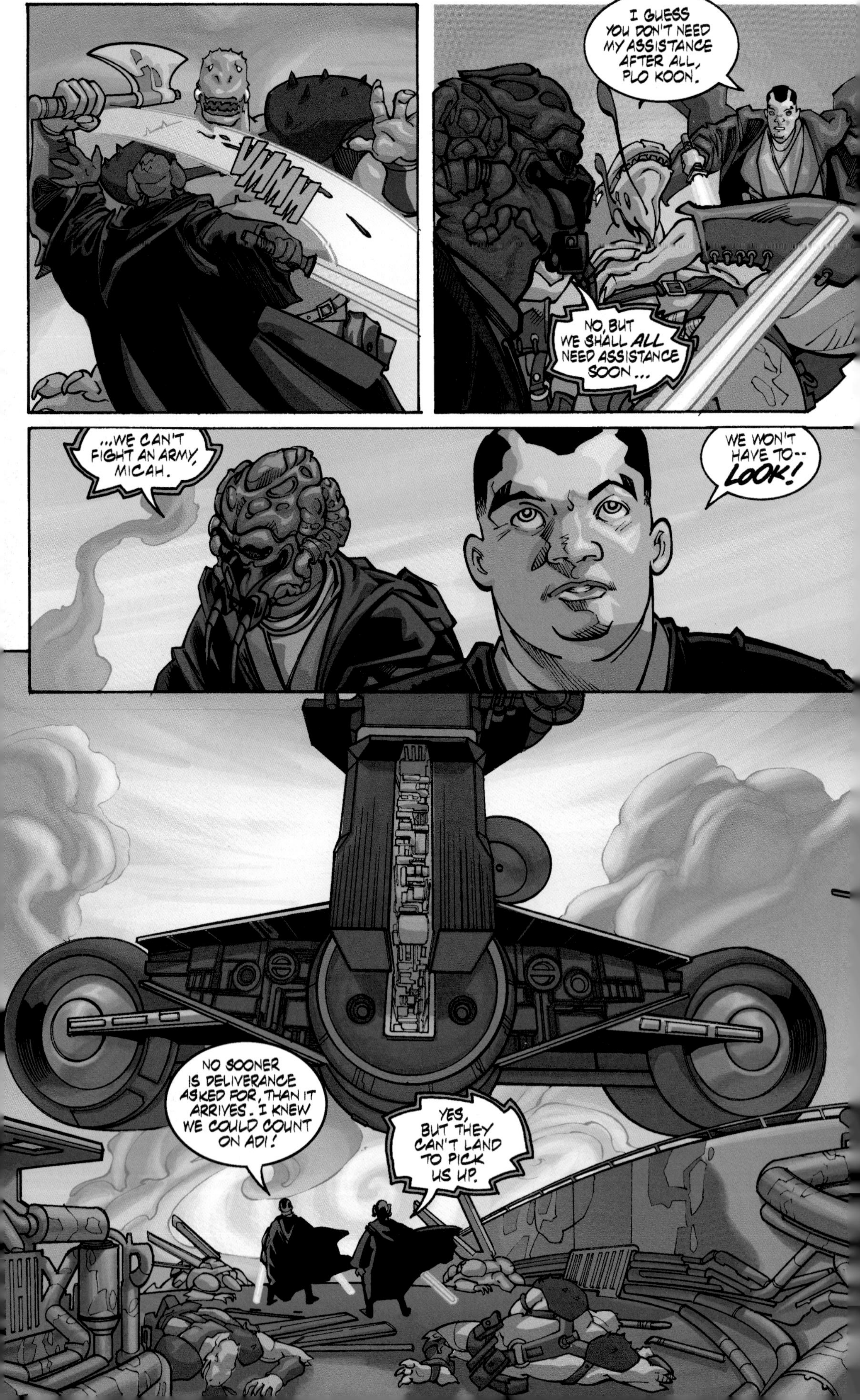
VMMM
I GUESS YOU DON'T NEED MY ASSISTANCE AFTER ALL, PLO KOON.
NO, BUT WE SHALL ALL NEED ASSISTANCE SOON...
...WE CAN'T FIGHT AN ARMY, MICAH.
WE WON'T HAVE TO-- LOOK!
NO SOONER IS DELIVERANCE ASKED FOR, THAN IT ARRIVES. I KNEW WE COULD COUNT ON ADI!
YES, BUT THEY CAN'T LAND TO PICK US UP.

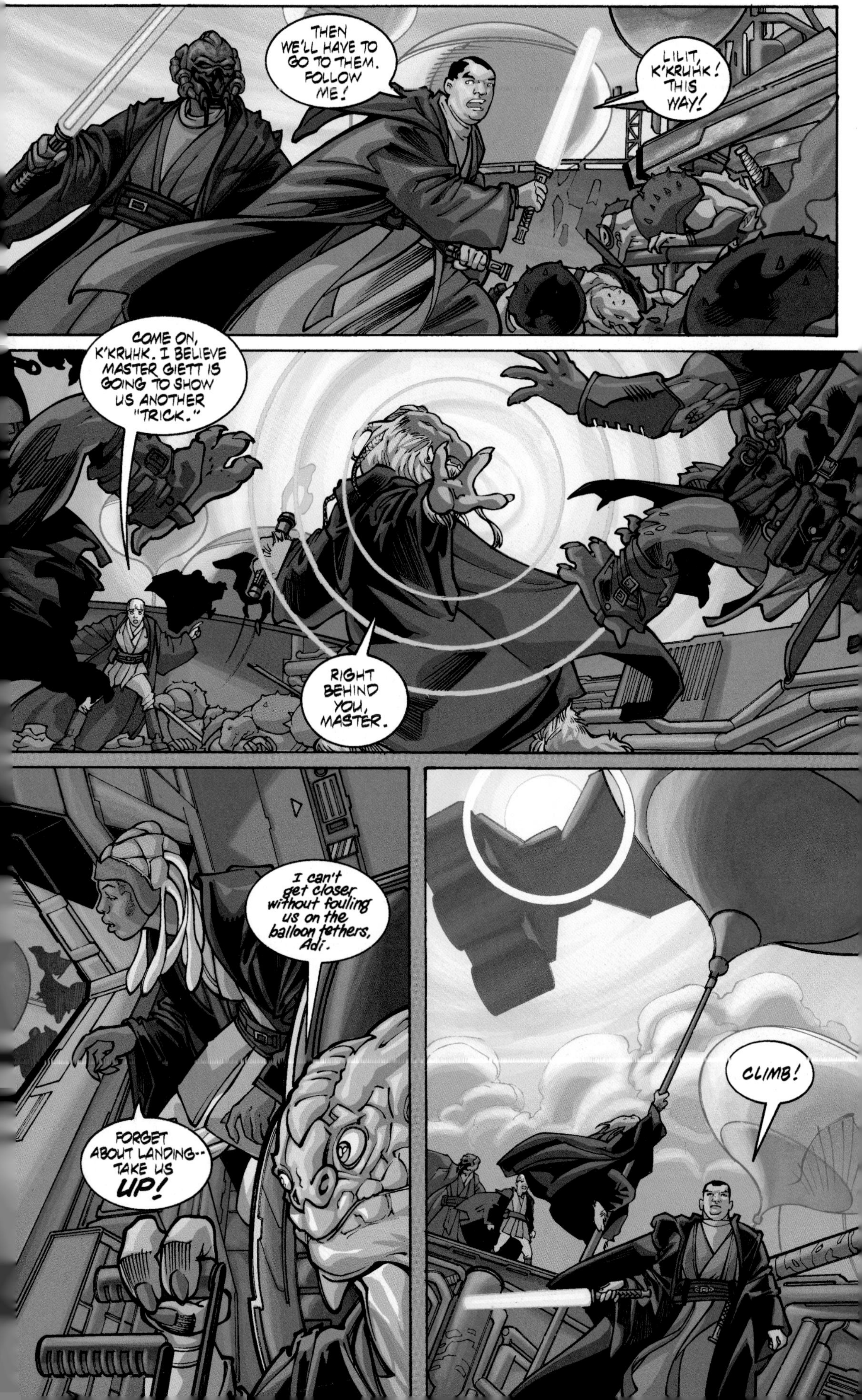
THEN WE'LL HAVE TO GO TO THEM. FOLLOW ME!
LILIT, K'KRUHK! THIS WAY!
COME ON, K'KRUHK. I BELIEVE MASTER GIETT IS GOING TO SHOW US ANOTHER "TRICK."
RIGHT BEHIND YOU, MASTER.
I can't get closer without fouling us on the balloon tethers, Adi.
FORGET ABOUT LANDING-- TAKE US UP!
CLIMB!

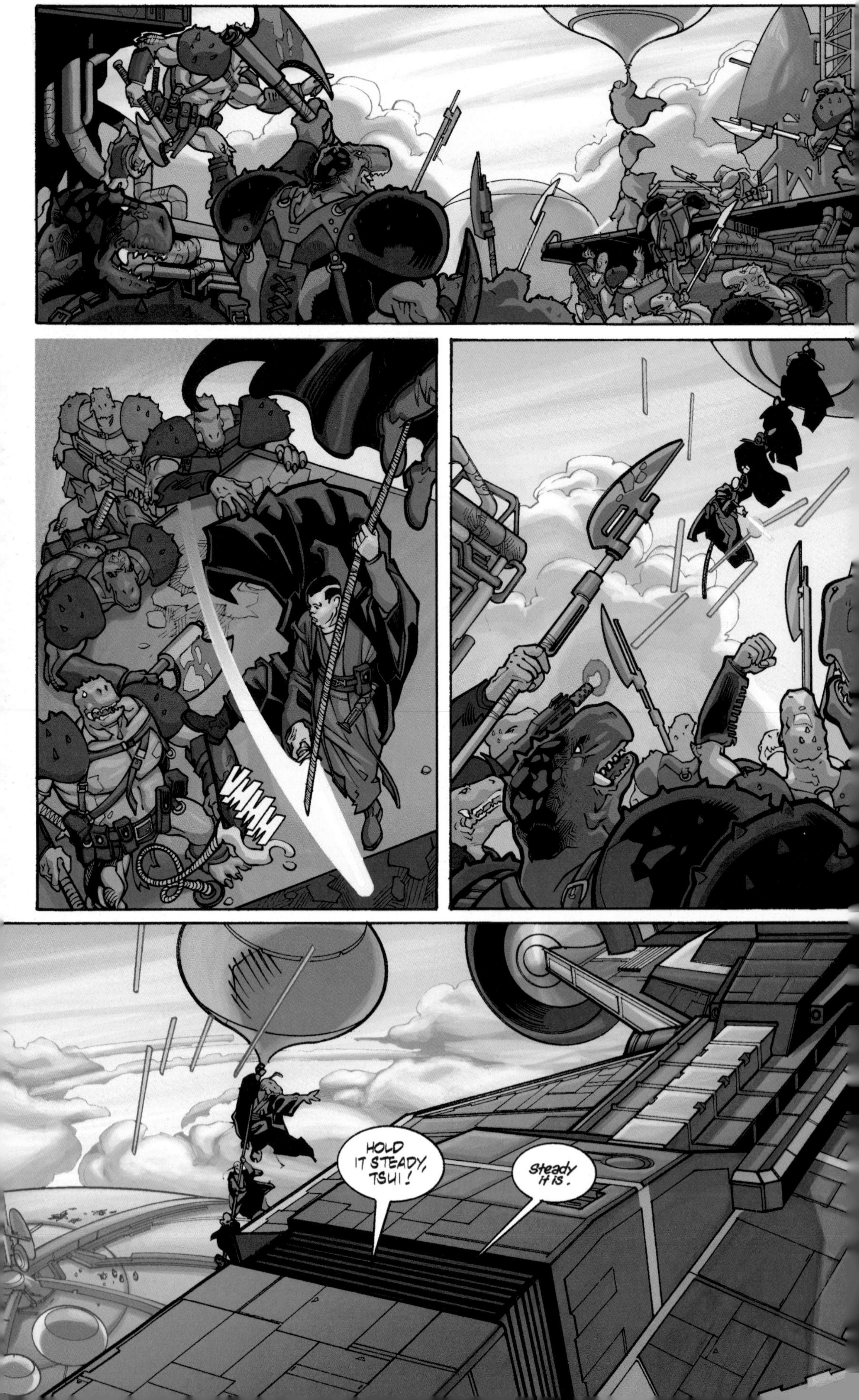
VMMM
HOLD IT STEADY, TSUI!
Steady it is.

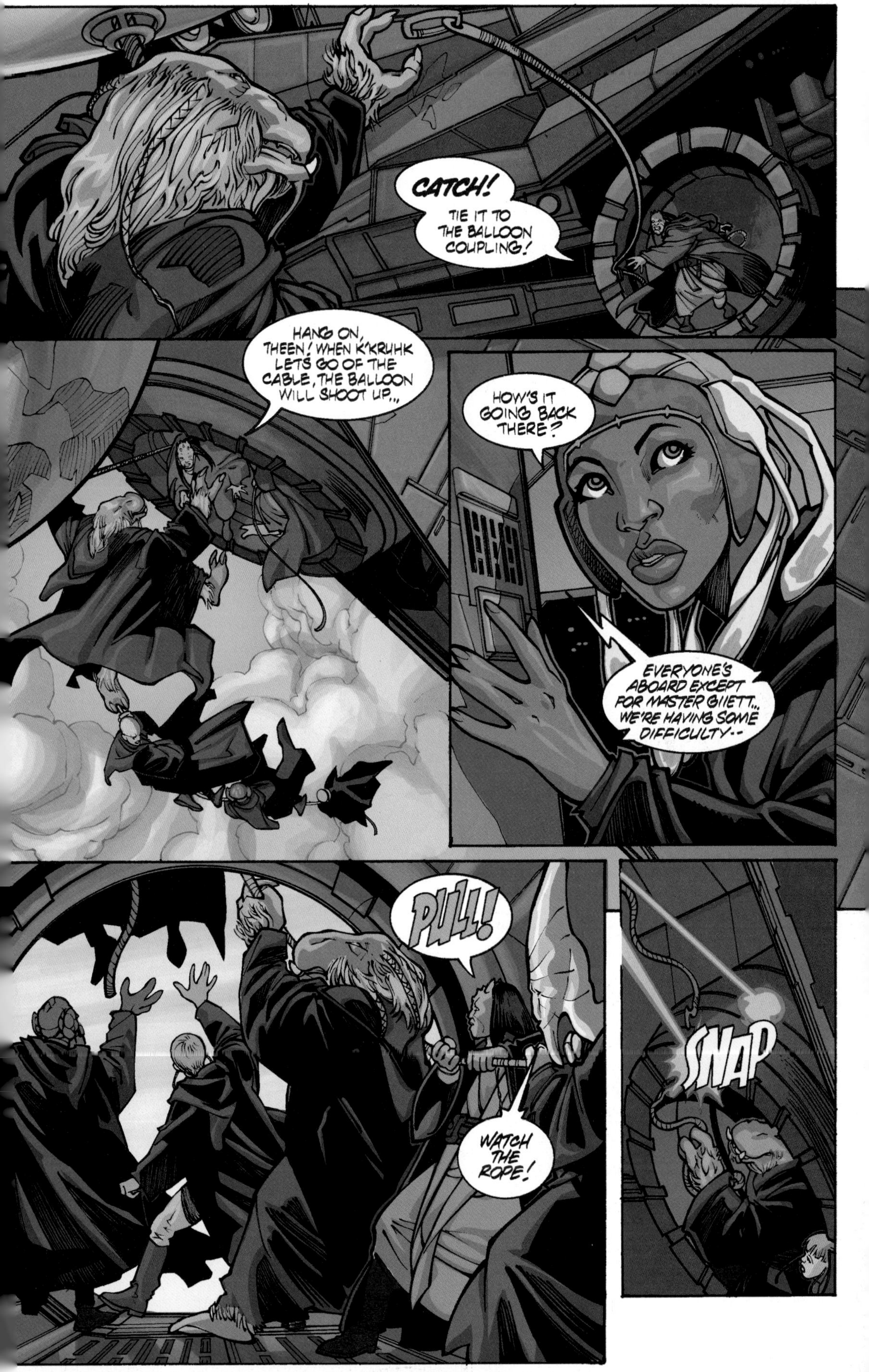
CATCH!
TIE IT TO THE BALLOON COUPLING!
HANG ON, THEEN! WHEN K'KRUHK LETS GO OF THE CABLE, THE BALLOON WILL SHOOT UP...
HOW'S IT GOING BACK THERE?
EVERYONE'S ABOARD EXCEPT FOR MASTER GIIETT... WE'RE HAVING SOME DIFFICULTY--
PULL!
WATCH THE ROPE!
SNAP

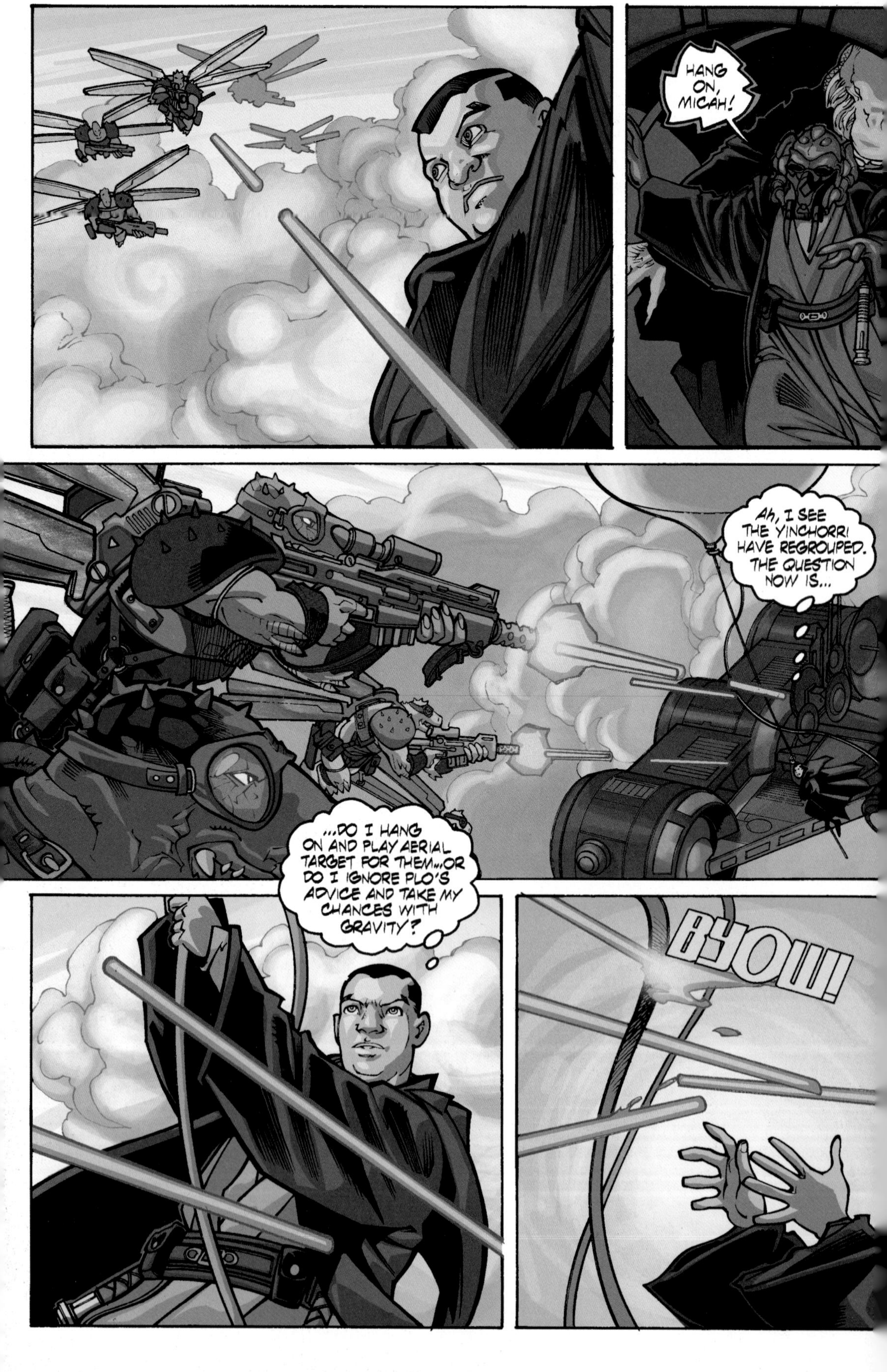
HANG ON, MICAH!
Ah, I SEE THE YINCHORRI HAVE REGROUPED. THE QUESTION NOW IS...
...DO I HANG ON AND PLAY AERIAL TARGET FOR THEM...OR DO I IGNORE PLO'S ADVICE AND TAKE MY CHANCES WITH GRAVITY?
BYOW!

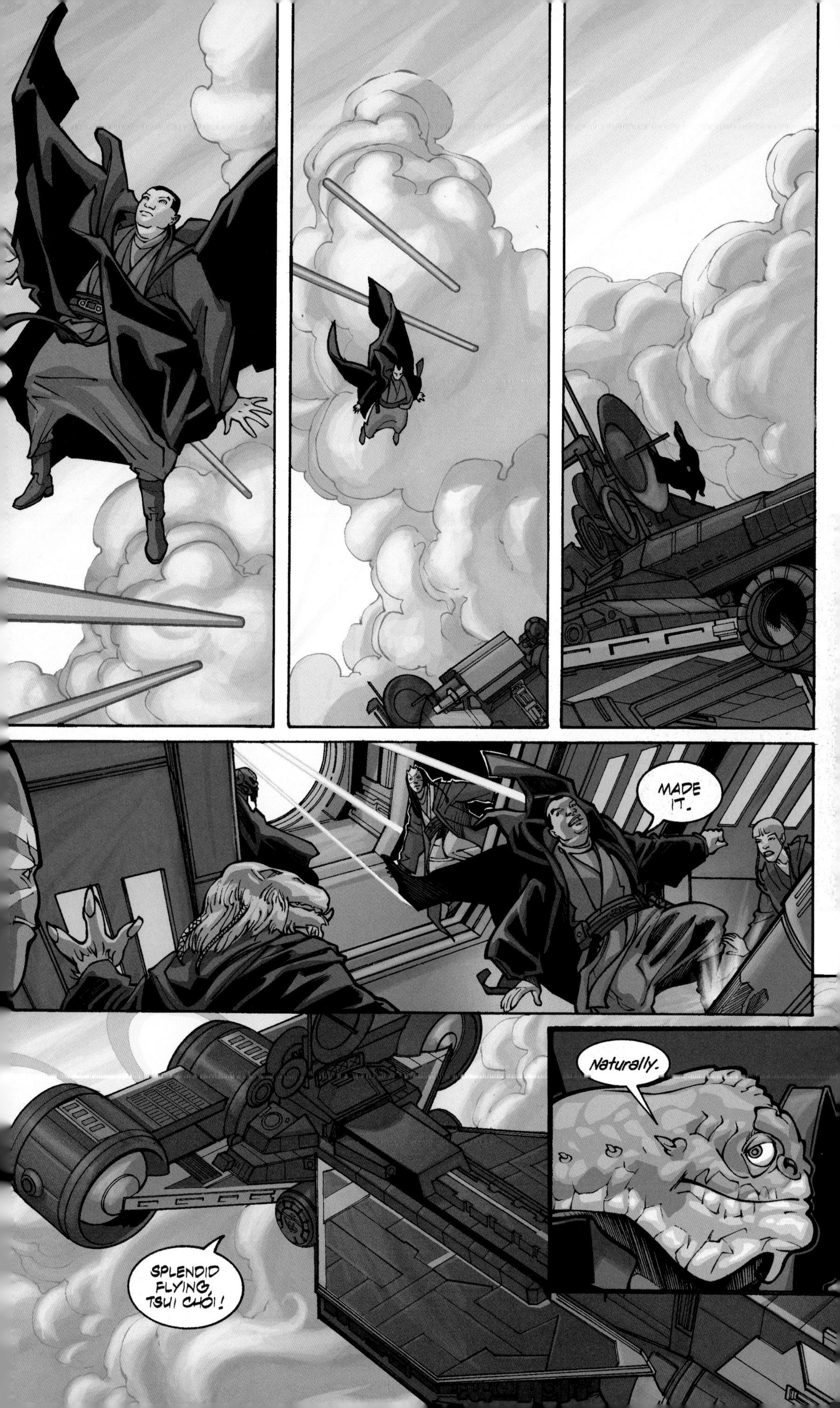
MADE IT.
SPLENDID FLYING, TSUI CHÓI!
Naturally.

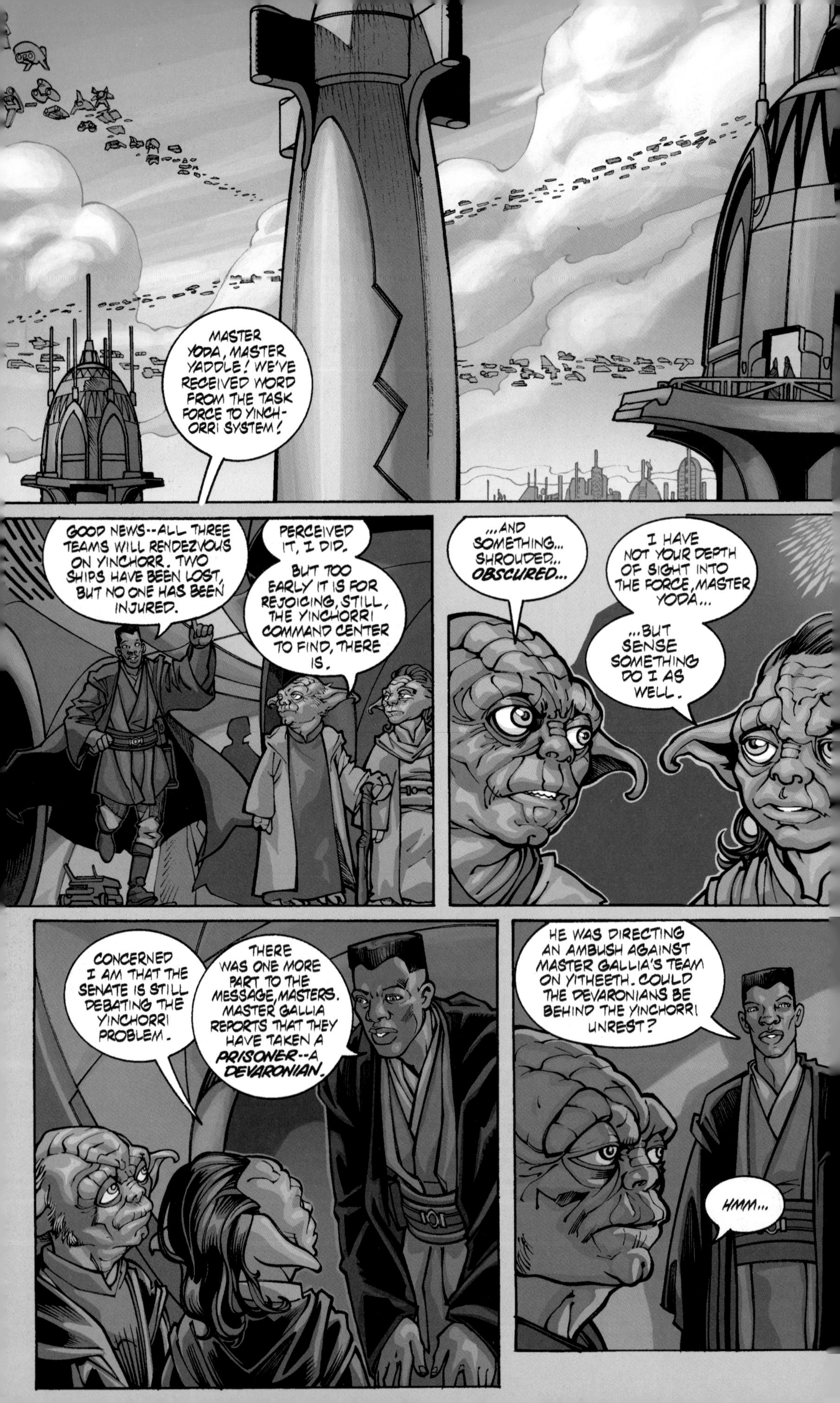
MASTER YODA, MASTER YADDLE! WE'VE RECEIVED WORD FROM THE TASK FORCE TO YINCHORRI SYSTEM!
GOOD NEWS--ALL THREE TEAMS WILL RENDEZVOUS ON YINCHORR. TWO SHIPS HAVE BEEN LOST, BUT NO ONE HAS BEEN INJURED.
PERCEIVED IT, I DID.
BUT TOO EARLY IT IS FOR REJOICING, STILL. THE YINCHORRI COMMAND CENTER TO FIND, THERE IS.
...AND SOMETHING... SHROUDED... OBSCURED...
I HAVE NOT YOUR DEPTH OF SIGHT INTO THE FORCE, MASTER YODA...
...BUT SENSE SOMETHING DO I AS WELL.
CONCERNED I AM THAT THE SENATE IS STILL DEBATING THE YINCHORRI PROBLEM.
THERE WAS ONE MORE PART TO THE MESSAGE, MASTERS. MASTER GALLIA REPORTS THAT THEY HAVE TAKEN A PRISONER--A DEVARONIAN.
HE WAS DIRECTING AN AMBUSH AGAINST MASTER GALLIA'S TEAM ON YITHEETH. COULD THE DEVARONIANS BE BEHIND THE YINCHORRI UNREST?
HMM...

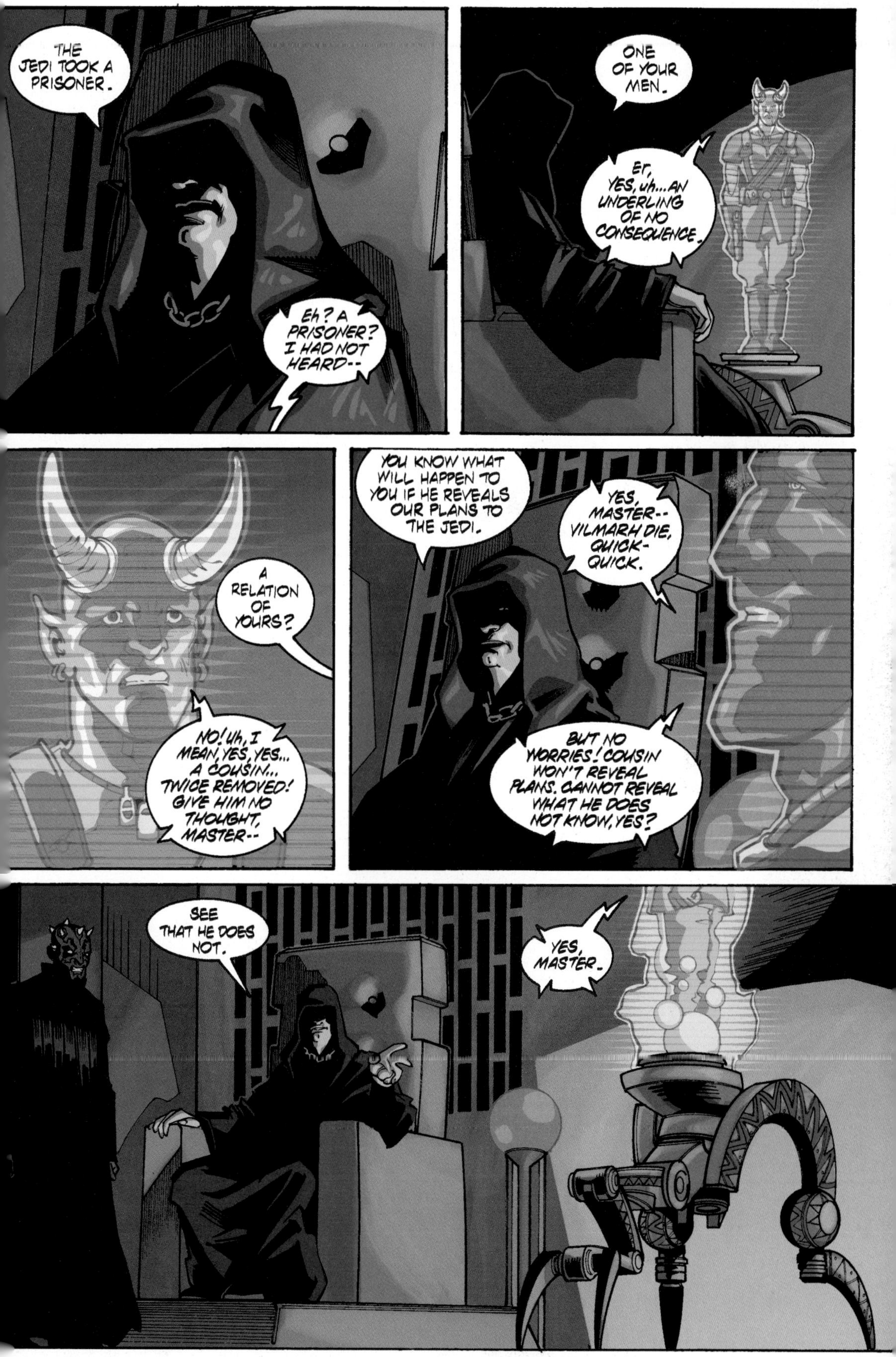
THE JEDI TOOK A PRISONER.
EH? A PRISONER? I HAD NOT HEARD--
ONE OF YOUR MEN.
Er, YES, uh...AN UNDERLING OF NO CONSEQUENCE.
A RELATION OF YOURS?
NO! uh, I MEAN, YES, YES... A COUSIN... TWICE REMOVED! GIVE HIM NO THOUGHT, MASTER--
YOU KNOW WHAT WILL HAPPEN TO YOU IF HE REVEALS OUR PLANS TO THE JEDI.
YES, MASTER-- VILMARH DIE, QUICK-QUICK.
BUT NO WORRIES! COUSIN WON'T REVEAL PLANS. CANNOT REVEAL WHAT HE DOES NOT KNOW, YES?
SEE THAT HE DOES NOT.
YES, MASTER.

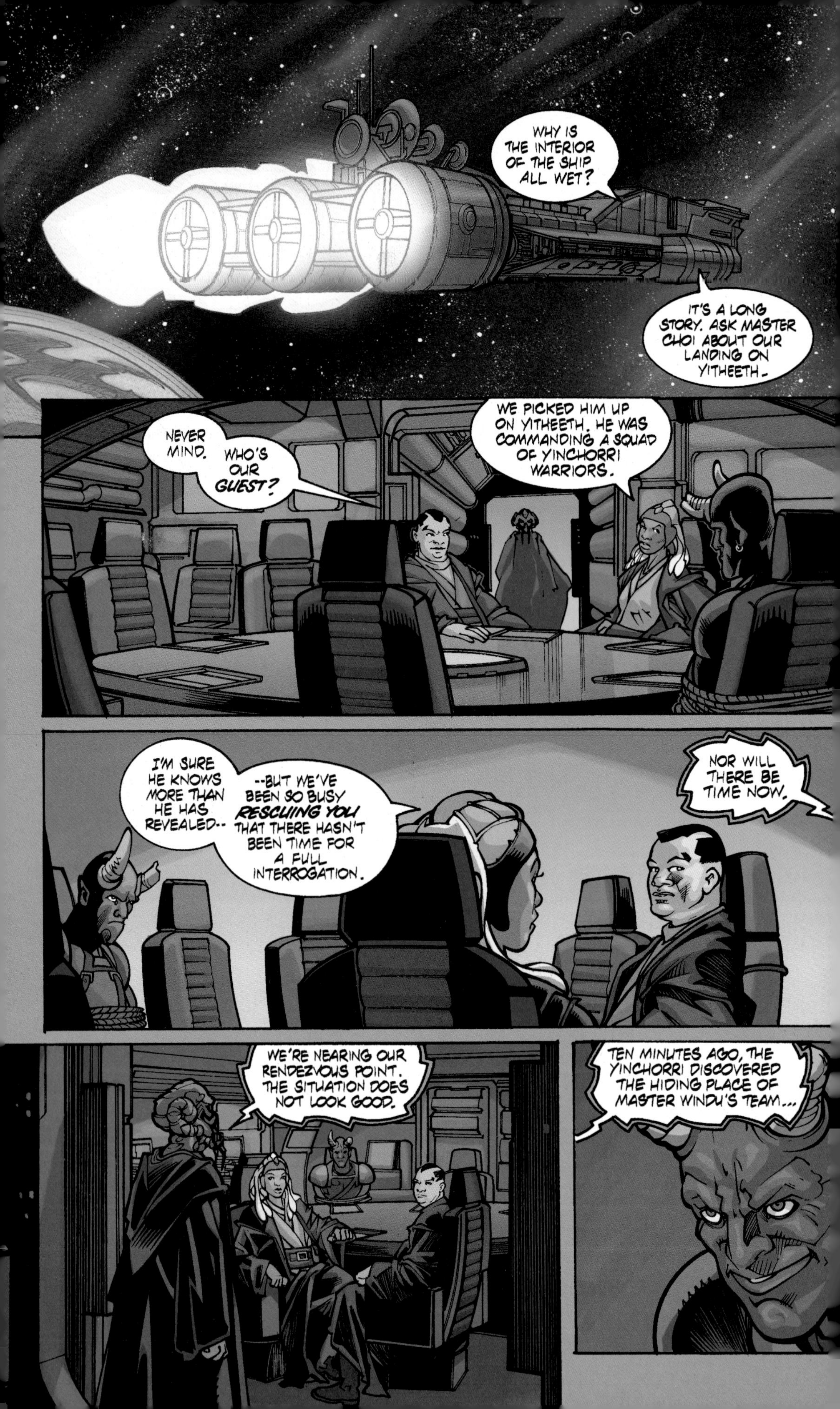
WHY IS THE INTERIOR OF THE SHIP ALL WET?
IT'S A LONG STORY. ASK MASTER CHOI ABOUT OUR LANDING ON YITHEETH.
NEVER MIND.
WHO'S OUR GUEST?
WE PICKED HIM UP ON YITHEETH. HE WAS COMMANDING A SQUAD OF YINCHORRI WARRIORS.
I'M SURE HE KNOWS MORE THAN HE HAS REVEALED--
--BUT WE'VE BEEN SO BUSY RESCUING YOU THAT THERE HASN'T BEEN TIME FOR A FULL INTERROGATION.
NOR WILL THERE BE TIME NOW.
WE'RE NEARING OUR RENDEZVOUS POINT. THE SITUATION DOES NOT LOOK GOOD.
TEN MINUTES AGO, THE YINCHORRI DISCOVERED THE HIDING PLACE OF MASTER WINDU'S TEAM...

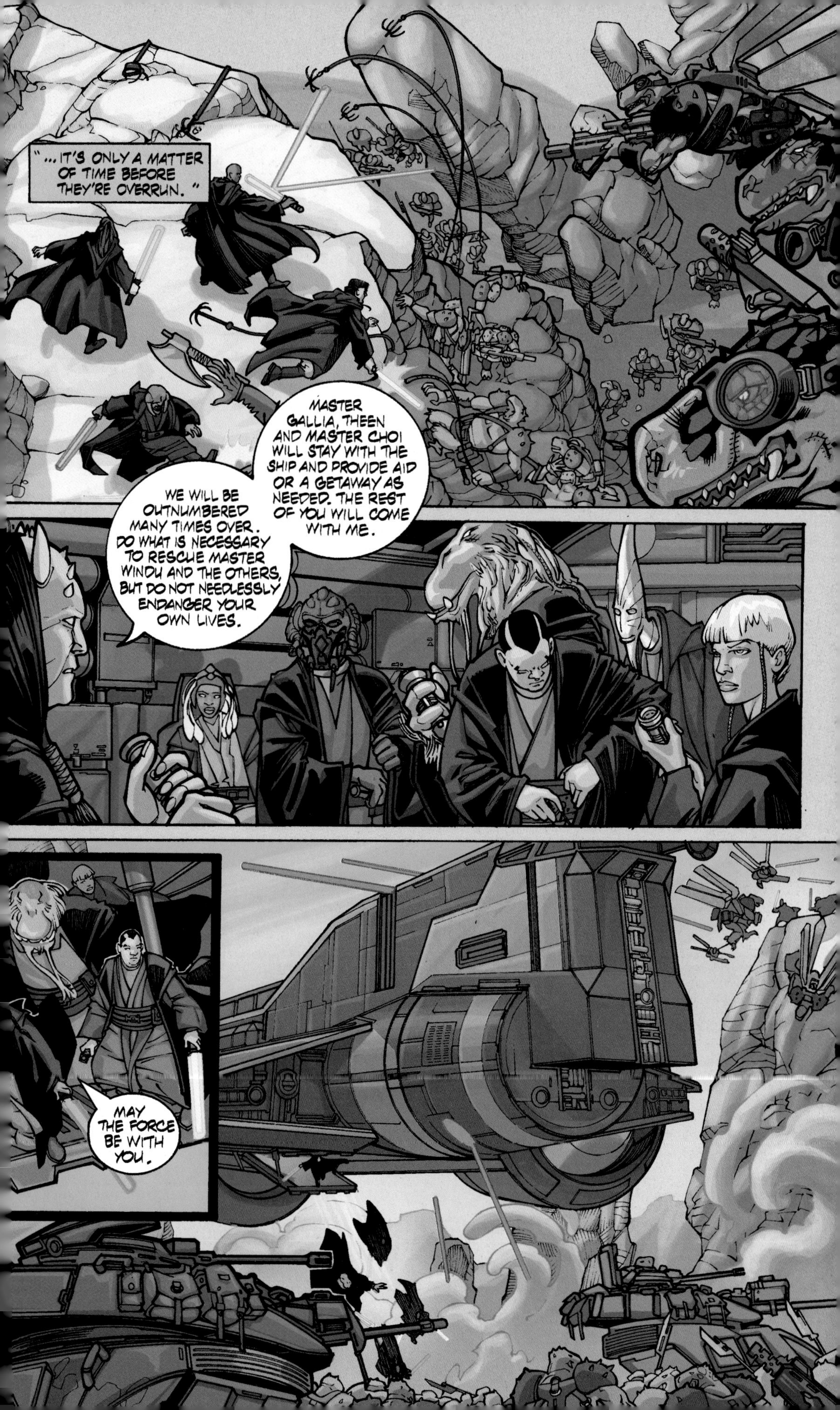
"...IT'S ONLY A MATTER OF TIME BEFORE THEY'RE OVERRUN."
MASTER GALLIA, THEEN AND MASTER CHOI WILL STAY WITH THE SHIP AND PROVIDE AID OR A GETAWAY AS NEEDED. THE REST OF YOU WILL COME WITH ME.
WE WILL BE OUTNUMBERED MANY TIMES OVER. DO WHAT IS NECESSARY TO RESCUE MASTER WINDU AND THE OTHERS, BUT DO NOT NEEDLESSLY ENDANGER YOUR OWN LIVES.
MAY THE FORCE BE WITH YOU.

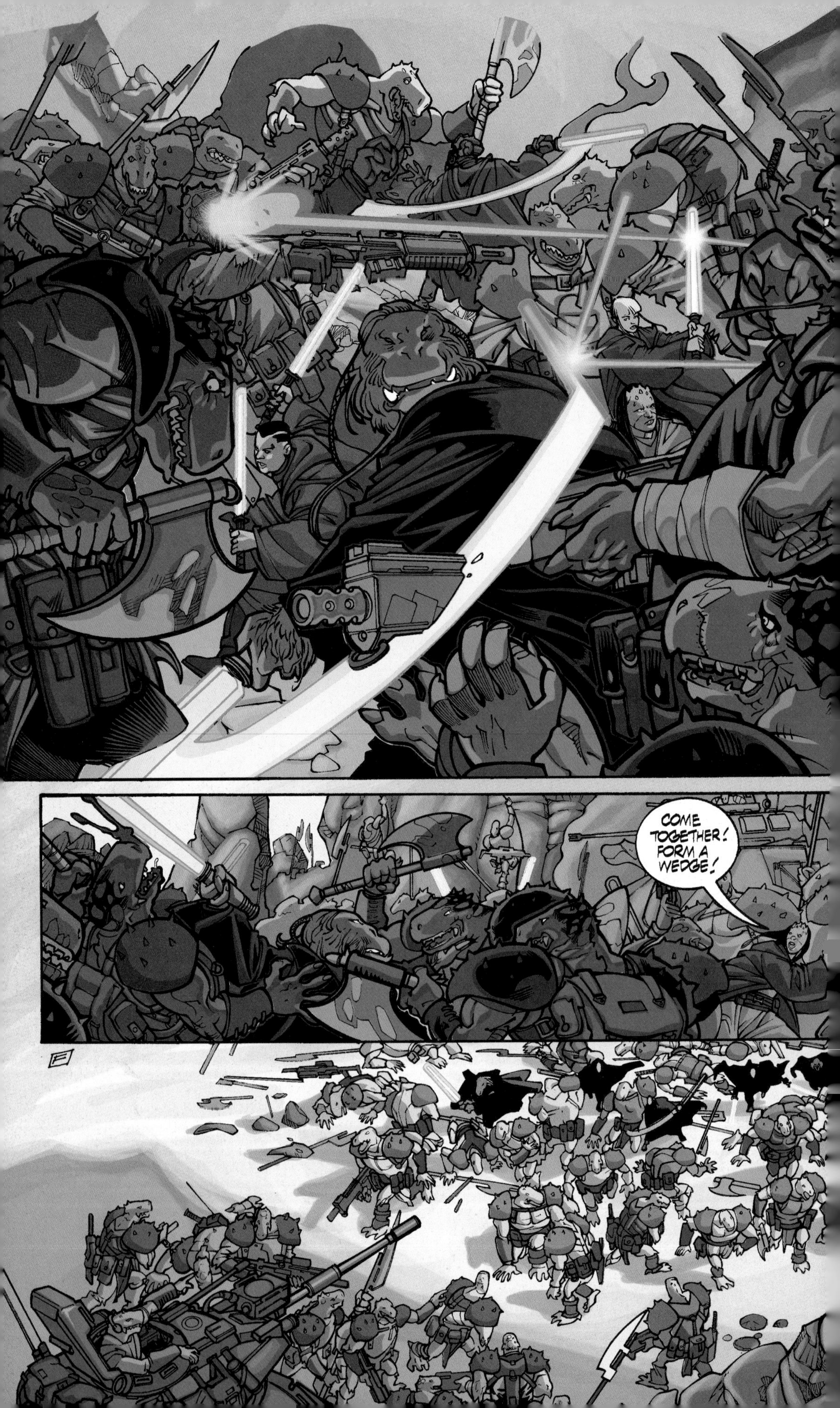
COME TOGETHER! FORM A WEDGE!

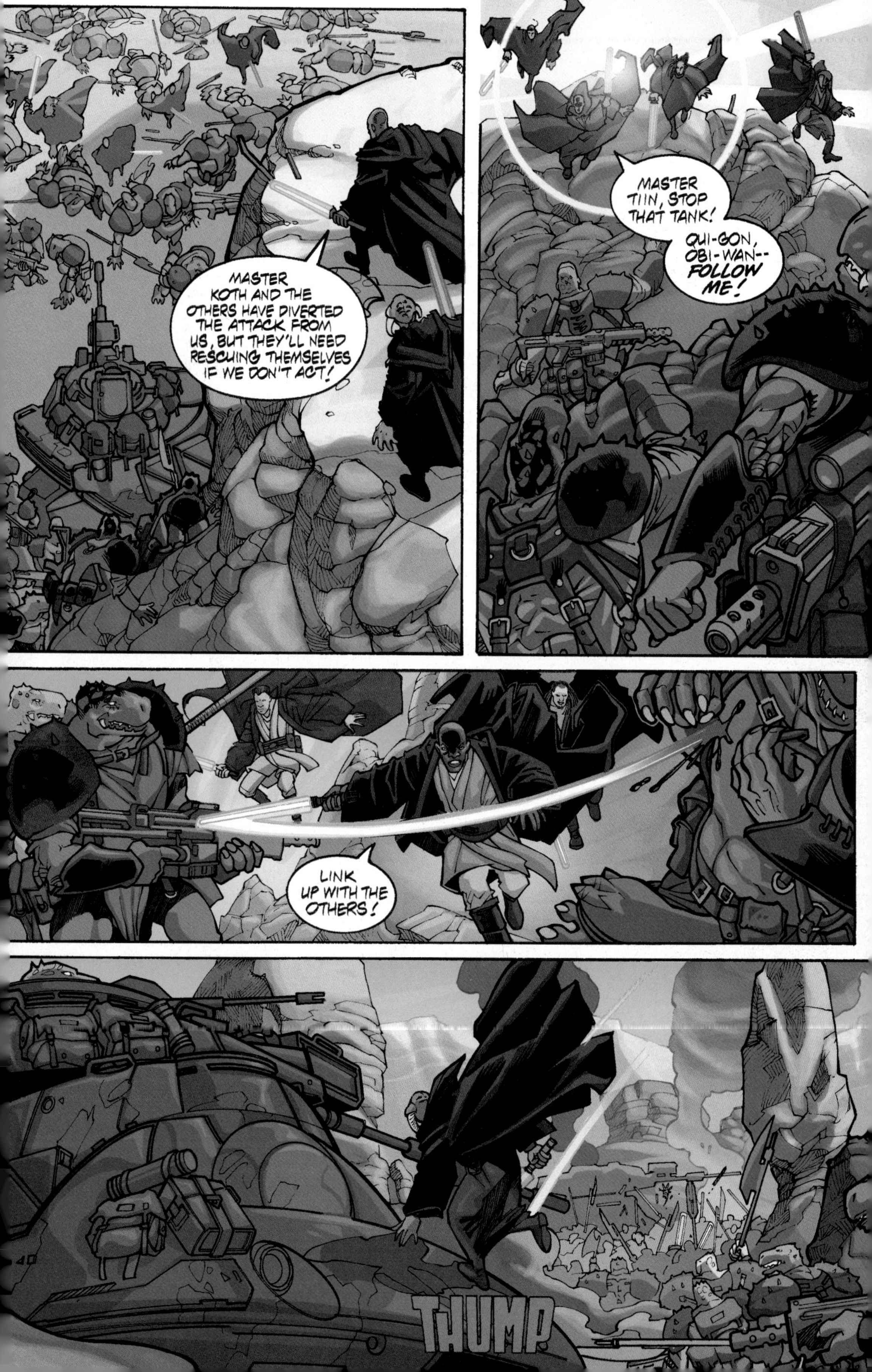
MASTER KOTH AND THE OTHERS HAVE DIVERTED THE ATTACK FROM US, BUT THEY'LL NEED RESCUING THEMSELVES IF WE DON'T ACT!
MASTER TIIN, STOP THAT TANK!
QUI-GON, OBI-WAN-- FOLLOW ME!
LINK UP WITH THE OTHERS!
THUMP

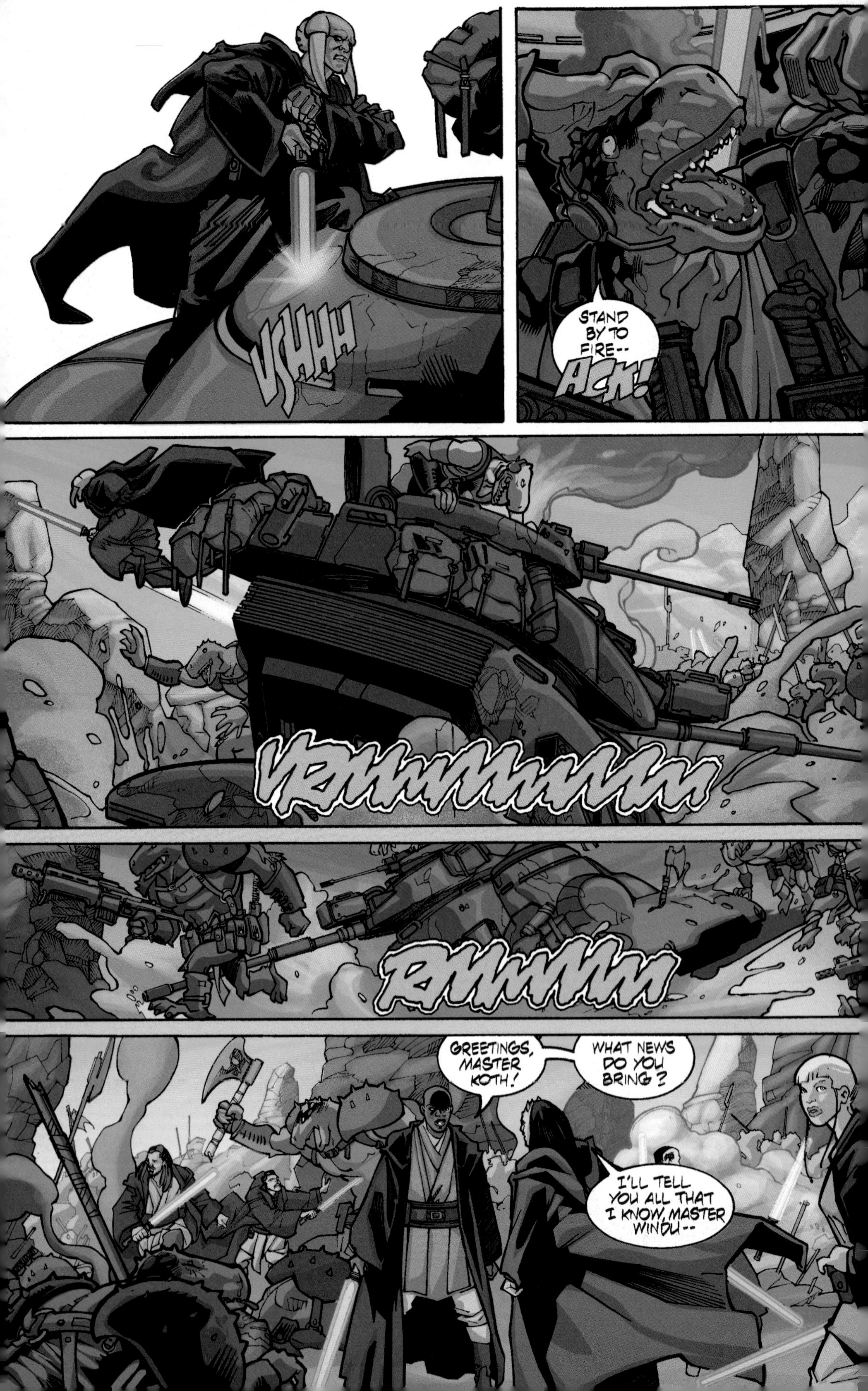
VSHHH
STAND BY TO FIRE--
ACK!
VRMMMMMMM
RMMMM
GREETINGS, MASTER KOTH!
WHAT NEWS DO YOU BRING?
I'LL TELL YOU ALL THAT I KNOW, MASTER WINDU--

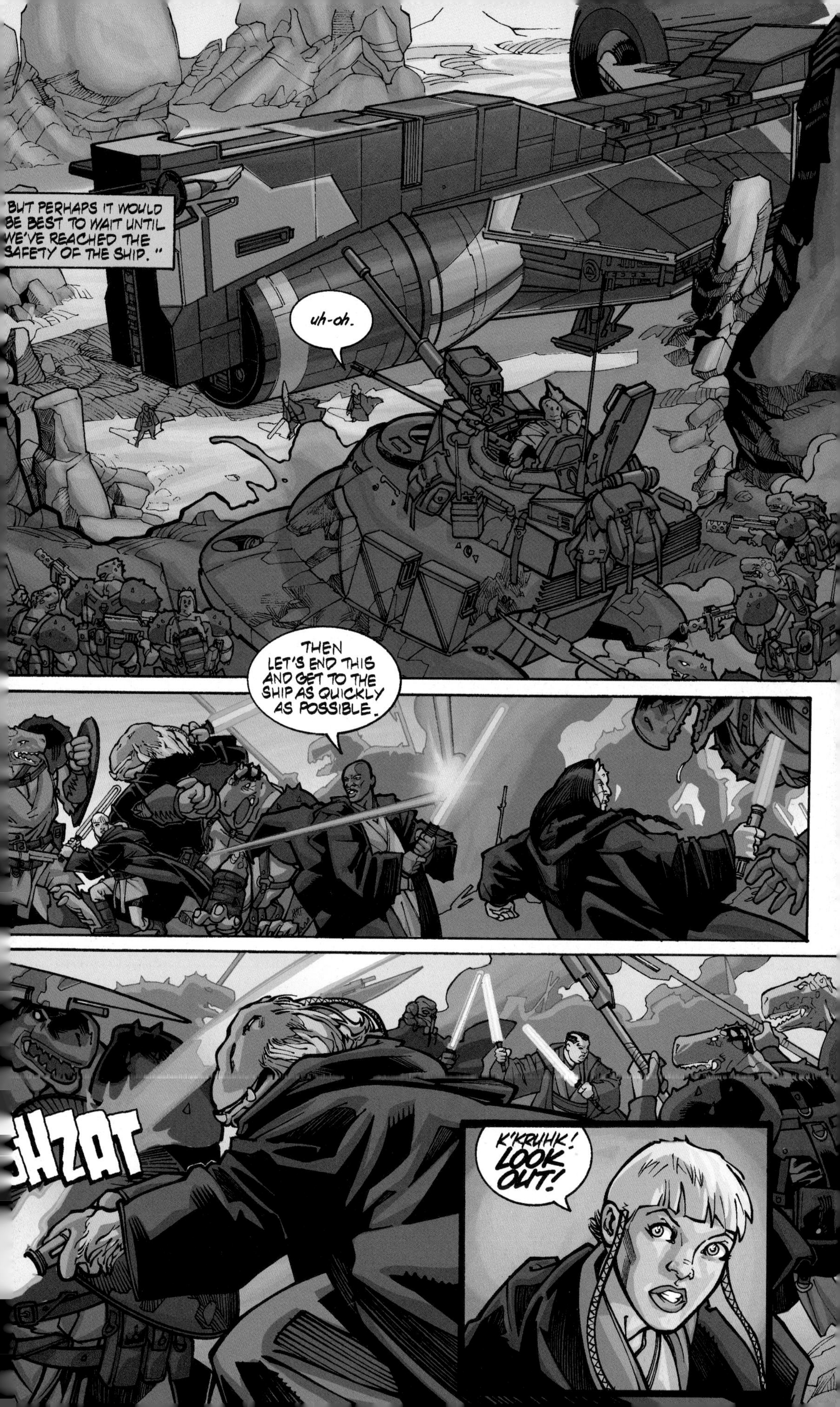
"BUT PERHAPS IT WOULD BE BEST TO WAIT UNTIL WE'VE REACHED THE SAFETY OF THE SHIP."
uh-oh.
THEN LET'S END THIS AND GET TO THE SHIP AS QUICKLY AS POSSIBLE.
HZAT
K'KRUHK! LOOK OUT!

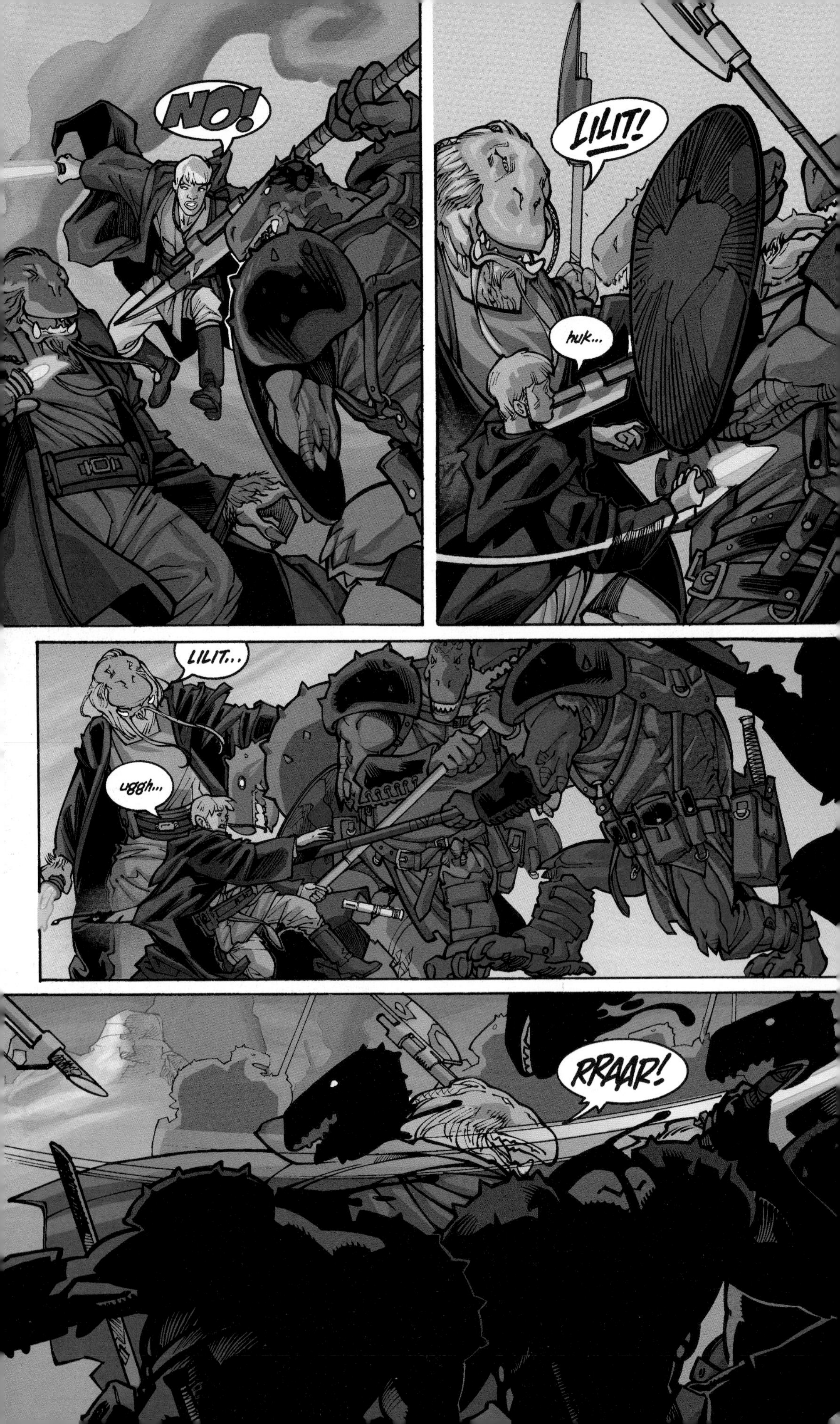
NO!
LILIT!
huk...
LILIT...
uggh...
RRAAR!

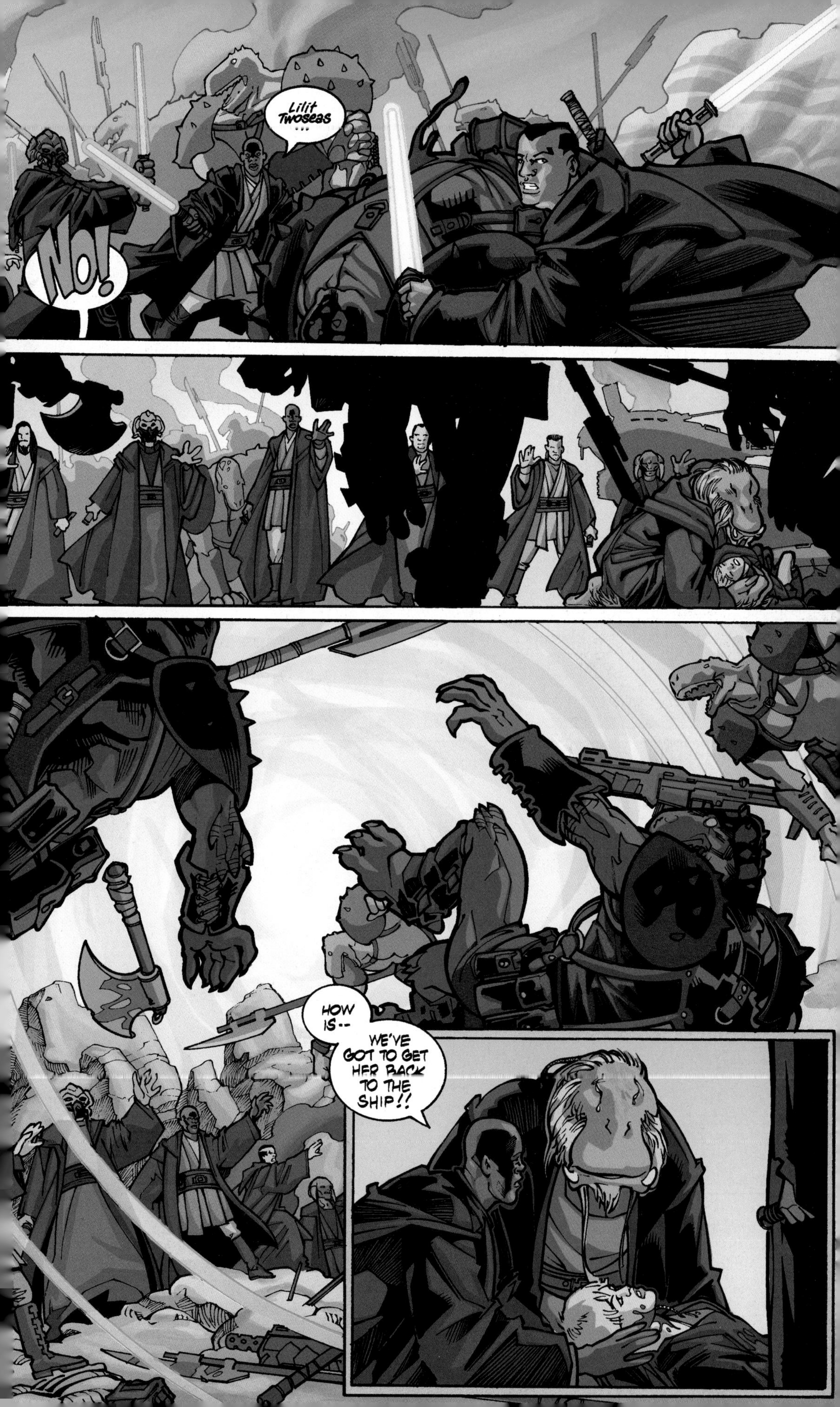
Lilit Twoseas . . .
NO!
HOW IS --
WE'VE GOT TO GET HER BACK TO THE SHIP!!

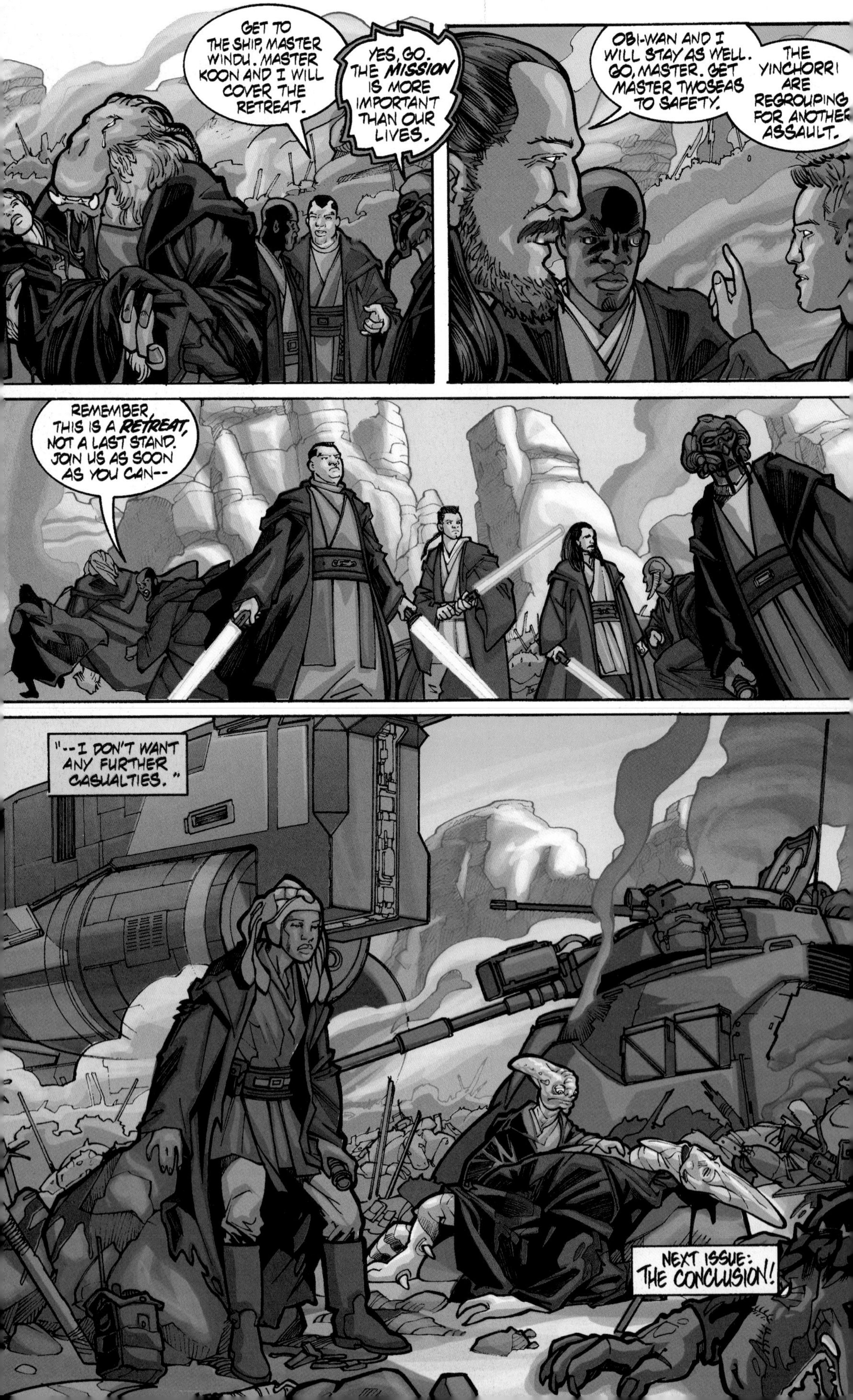
GET TO THE SHIP, MASTER WINDU. MASTER KOON AND I WILL COVER THE RETREAT.
YES, GO. THE *MISSION* IS MORE IMPORTANT THAN OUR LIVES.
OBI-WAN AND I WILL STAY AS WELL. GO, MASTER. GET MASTER TWOSEAS TO SAFETY.
THE YINCHORRI ARE REGROUPING FOR ANOTHER ASSAULT.
REMEMBER, THIS IS A *RETREAT*, NOT A LAST STAND. JOIN US AS SOON AS YOU CAN--
"--I DON'T WANT ANY FURTHER CASUALTIES."
NEXT ISSUE: THE CONCLUSION!

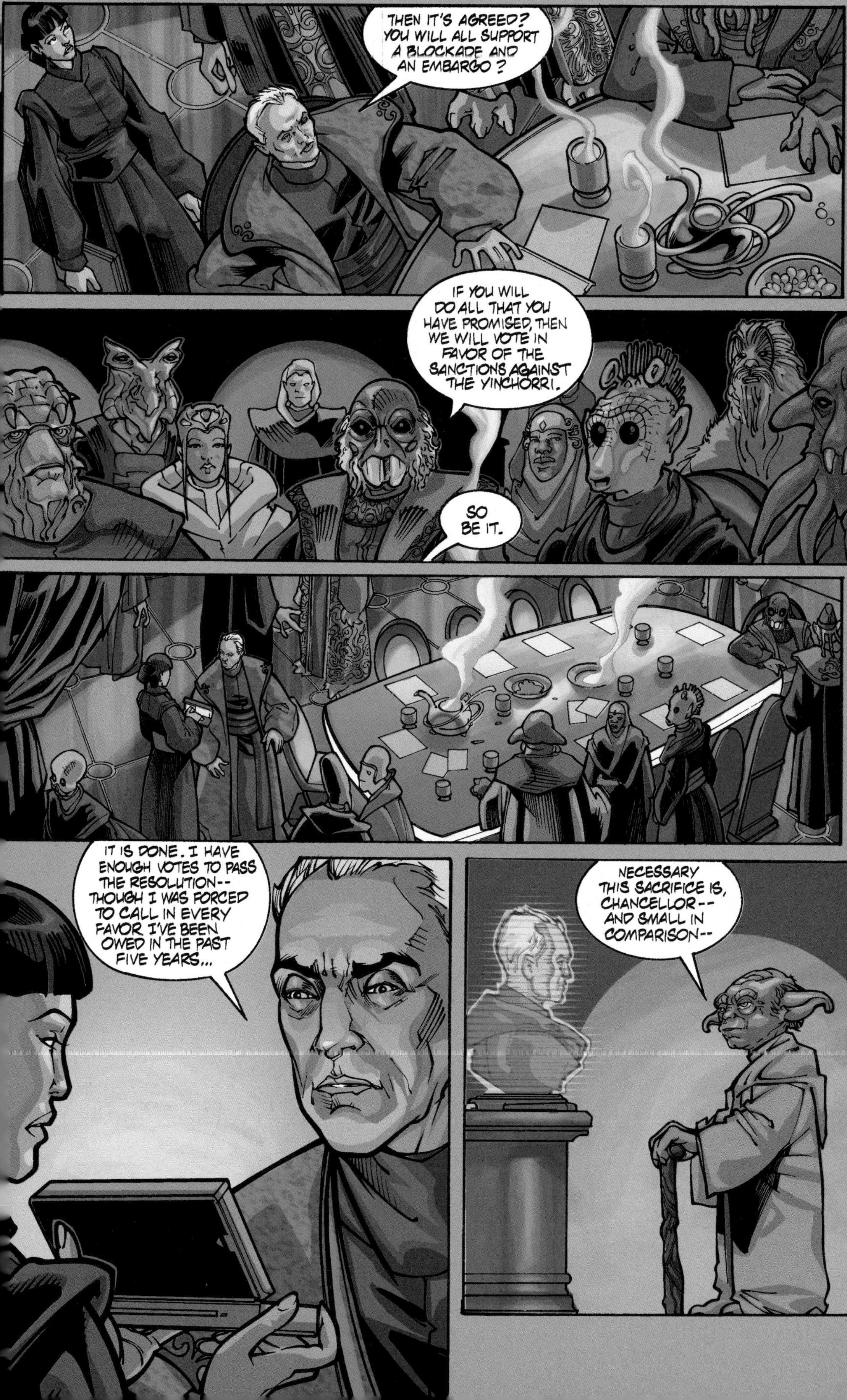
THEN IT'S AGREED? YOU WILL ALL SUPPORT A BLOCKADE AND AN EMBARGO?
IF YOU WILL DO ALL THAT YOU HAVE PROMISED, THEN WE WILL VOTE IN FAVOR OF THE SANCTIONS AGAINST THE YINCHORRI.
SO BE IT.
IT IS DONE. I HAVE ENOUGH VOTES TO PASS THE RESOLUTION-- THOUGH I WAS FORCED TO CALL IN EVERY FAVOR I'VE BEEN OWED IN THE PAST FIVE YEARS...
NECESSARY THIS SACRIFICE IS, CHANCELLOR-- AND SMALL IN COMPARISON--

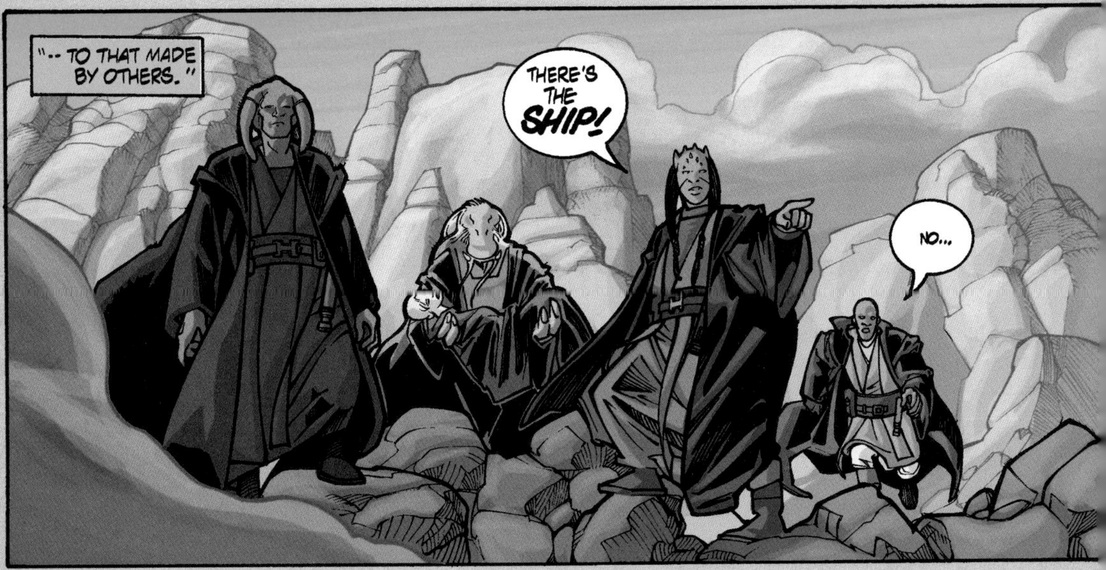
"-- TO THAT MADE BY OTHERS."
THERE'S THE SHIP!
NO...
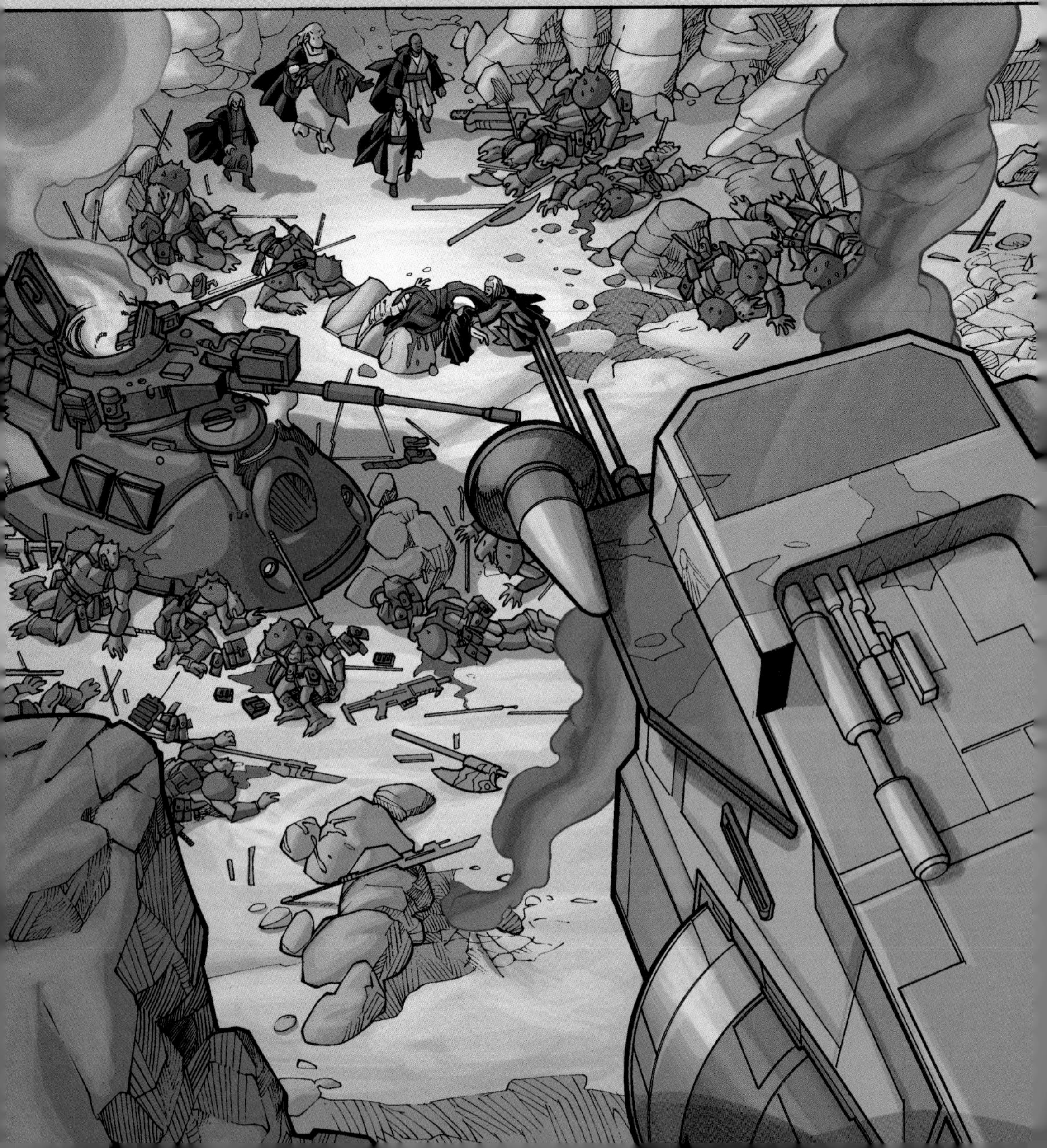

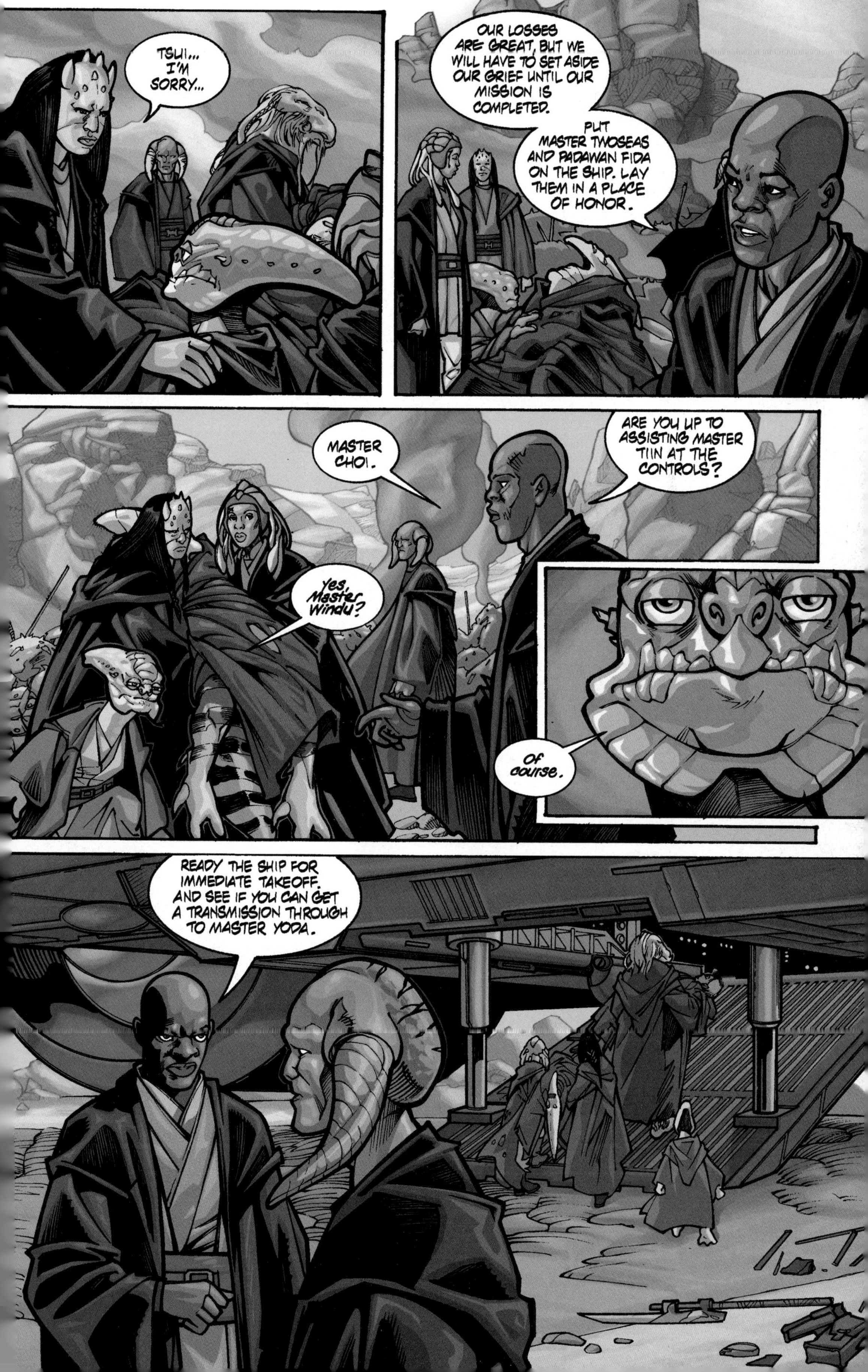
TSUI... I'M SORRY...
OUR LOSSES ARE GREAT, BUT WE WILL HAVE TO SET ASIDE OUR GRIEF UNTIL OUR MISSION IS COMPLETED.
PUT MASTER TWOSEAS AND PADAWAN FIDA ON THE SHIP. LAY THEM IN A PLACE OF HONOR.
MASTER CHOI.
ARE YOU UP TO ASSISTING MASTER TIIN AT THE CONTROLS?
Yes, Master Windu?
Of course.
READY THE SHIP FOR IMMEDIATE TAKEOFF. AND SEE IF YOU CAN GET A TRANSMISSION THROUGH TO MASTER YODA.

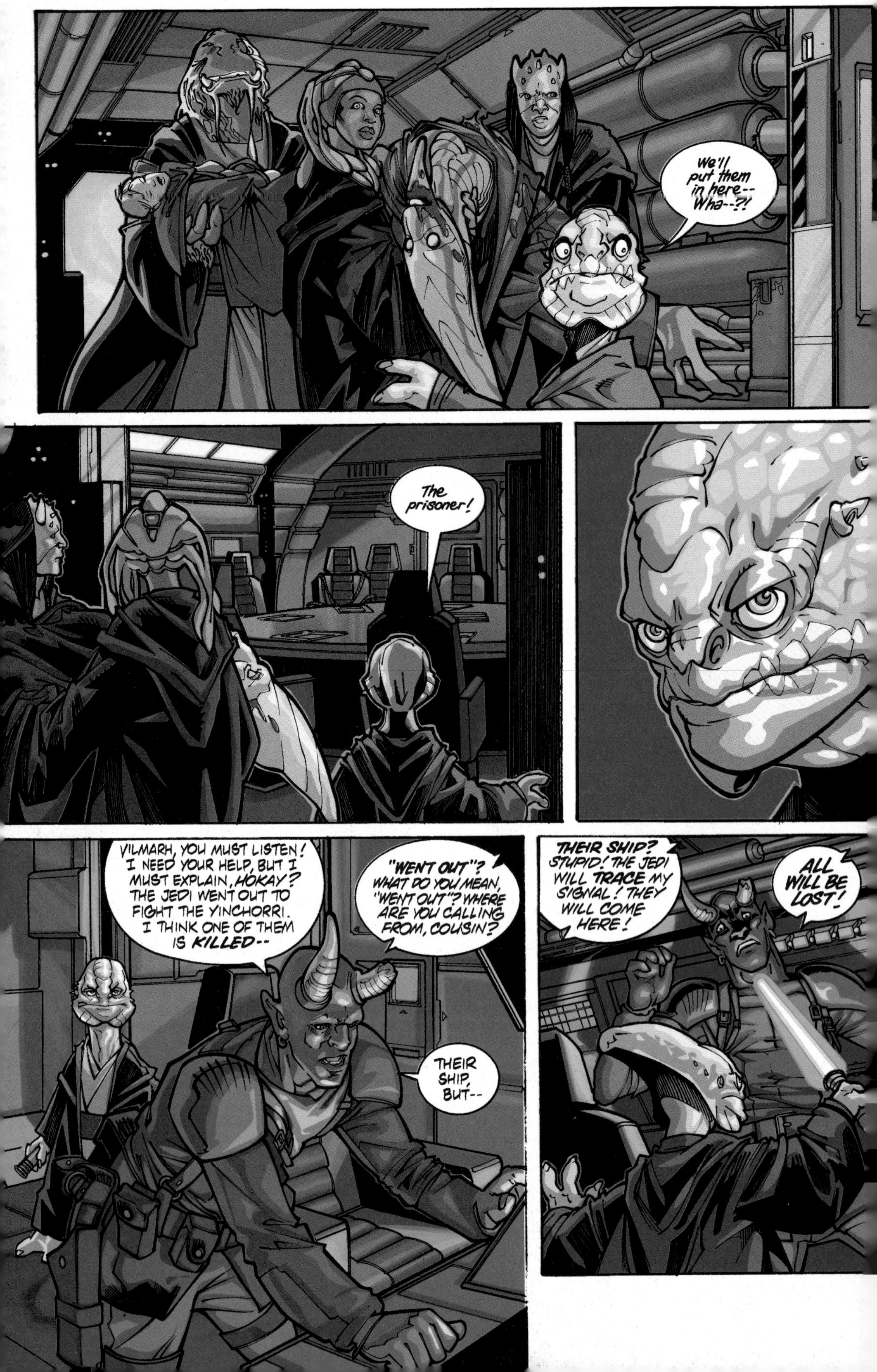
We'll put them in here-- Wha--?!
The prisoner!
VILMARH, YOU MUST LISTEN! I NEED YOUR HELP, BUT I MUST EXPLAIN, HOKAY? THE JEDI WENT OUT TO FIGHT THE YINCHORRI. I THINK ONE OF THEM IS KILLED--
"WENT OUT"? WHAT DO YOU MEAN, "WENT OUT"? WHERE ARE YOU CALLING FROM, COUSIN?
THEIR SHIP, BUT--
THEIR SHIP? STUPID! THE JEDI WILL TRACE MY SIGNAL! THEY WILL COME HERE!
ALL WILL BE LOST!

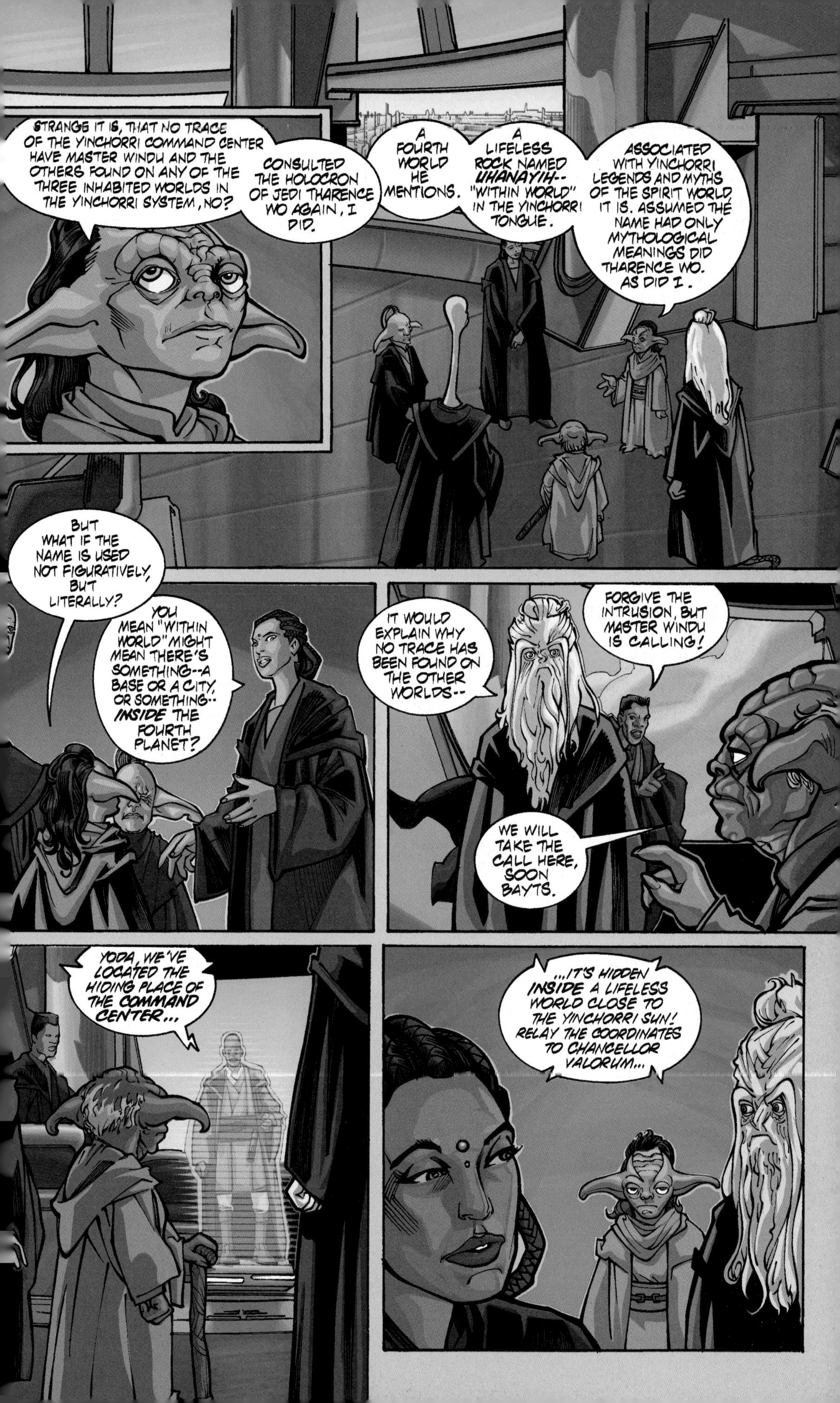
STRANGE IT IS, THAT NO TRACE OF THE YINCHORRI COMMAND CENTER HAVE MASTER WINDU AND THE OTHERS FOUND ON ANY OF THE THREE INHABITED WORLDS IN THE YINCHORRI SYSTEM, NO?
CONSULTED THE HOLOCRON OF JEDI THARENCE WO AGAIN, I DID.
A FOURTH WORLD HE MENTIONS.
A LIFELESS ROCK NAMED UHANAYIH-- "WITHIN WORLD" IN THE YINCHORRI TONGUE.
ASSOCIATED WITH YINCHORRI LEGENDS AND MYTHS OF THE SPIRIT WORLD IT IS. ASSUMED THE NAME HAD ONLY MYTHOLOGICAL MEANINGS DID THARENCE WO. AS DID I.
BUT WHAT IF THE NAME IS USED NOT FIGURATIVELY, BUT LITERALLY?
YOU MEAN "WITHIN WORLD" MIGHT MEAN THERE'S SOMETHING--A BASE OR A CITY, OR SOMETHING--INSIDE THE FOURTH PLANET?
IT WOULD EXPLAIN WHY NO TRACE HAS BEEN FOUND ON THE OTHER WORLDS--
FORGIVE THE INTRUSION, BUT MASTER WINDU IS CALLING!
WE WILL TAKE THE CALL HERE, SOON BAYTS.
YODA, WE'VE LOCATED THE HIDING PLACE OF THE COMMAND CENTER...
...IT'S HIDDEN INSIDE A LIFELESS WORLD CLOSE TO THE YINCHORRI SUN! RELAY THE COORDINATES TO CHANCELLOR VALORUM...

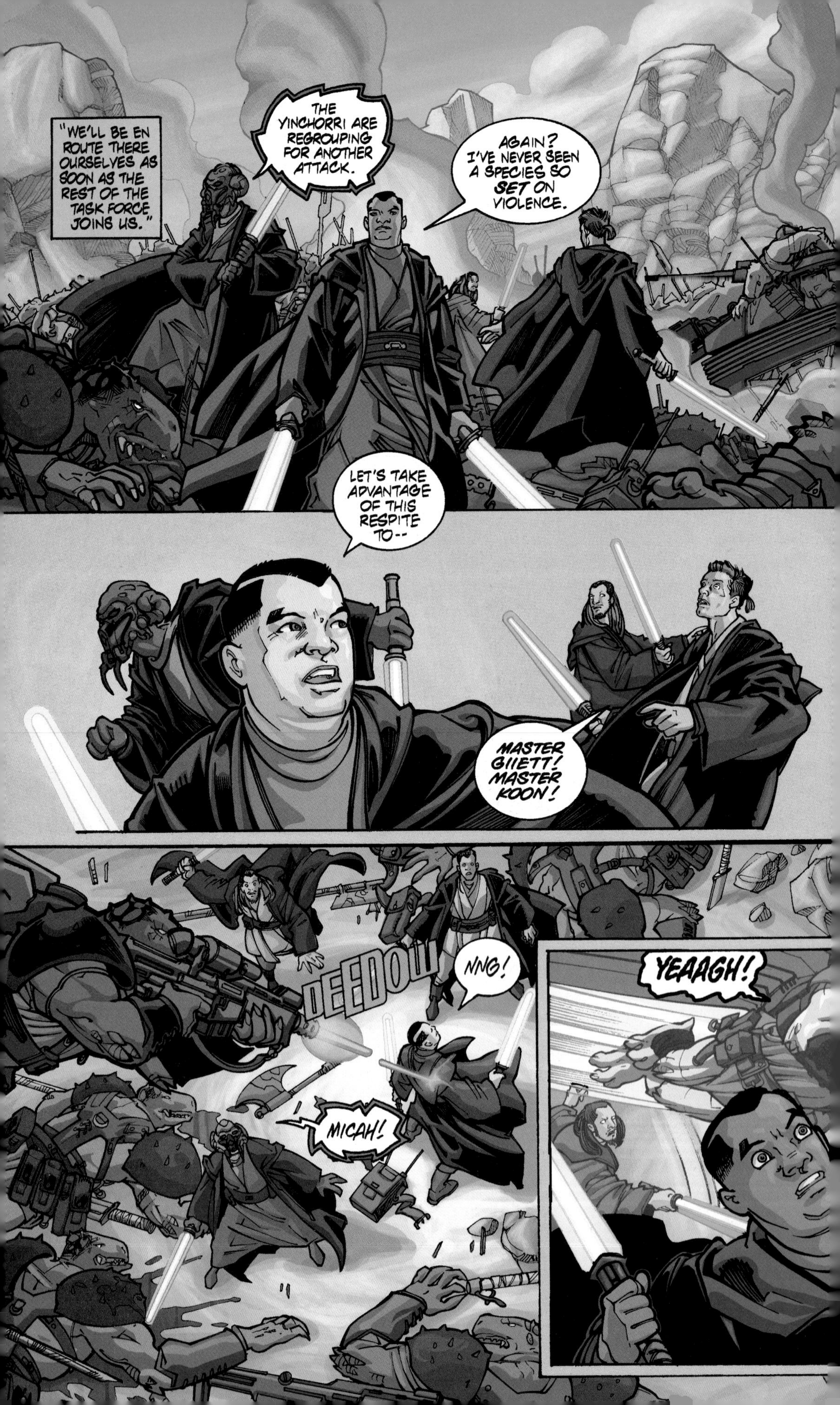

"WE'LL BE EN ROUTE THERE OURSELVES AS SOON AS THE REST OF THE TASK FORCE JOINS US."
THE YINCHORRI ARE REGROUPING FOR ANOTHER ATTACK.
AGAIN? I'VE NEVER SEEN A SPECIES SO SET ON VIOLENCE.
LET'S TAKE ADVANTAGE OF THIS RESPITE TO--
MASTER GIIETT! MASTER KOON!
DEEDOW
NNG!
MICAH!
YEAAGH!

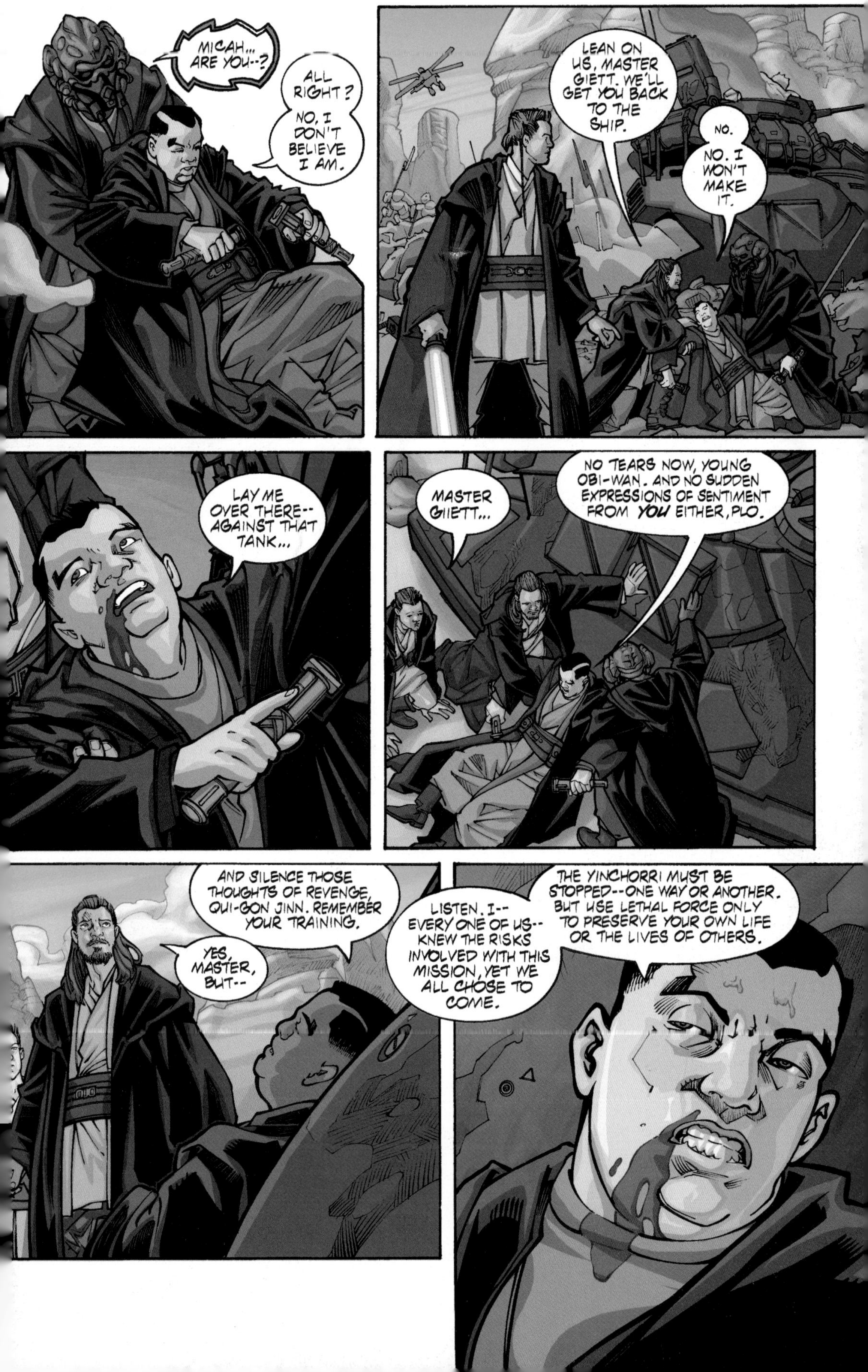
MICAH... ARE YOU--?
ALL RIGHT? NO, I DON'T BELIEVE I AM.
LEAN ON US, MASTER GIETT. WE'LL GET YOU BACK TO THE SHIP.
NO.
NO. I WON'T MAKE IT.
LAY ME OVER THERE-- AGAINST THAT TANK...
MASTER GIETT...
NO TEARS NOW, YOUNG OBI-WAN. AND NO SUDDEN EXPRESSIONS OF SENTIMENT FROM YOU EITHER, PLO.
AND SILENCE THOSE THOUGHTS OF REVENGE, QUI-GON JINN. REMEMBER YOUR TRAINING.
YES, MASTER, BUT--
LISTEN. I-- EVERY ONE OF US-- KNEW THE RISKS INVOLVED WITH THIS MISSION, YET WE ALL CHOSE TO COME.
THE YINCHORRI MUST BE STOPPED--ONE WAY OR ANOTHER. BUT USE LETHAL FORCE ONLY TO PRESERVE YOUR OWN LIFE OR THE LIVES OF OTHERS.

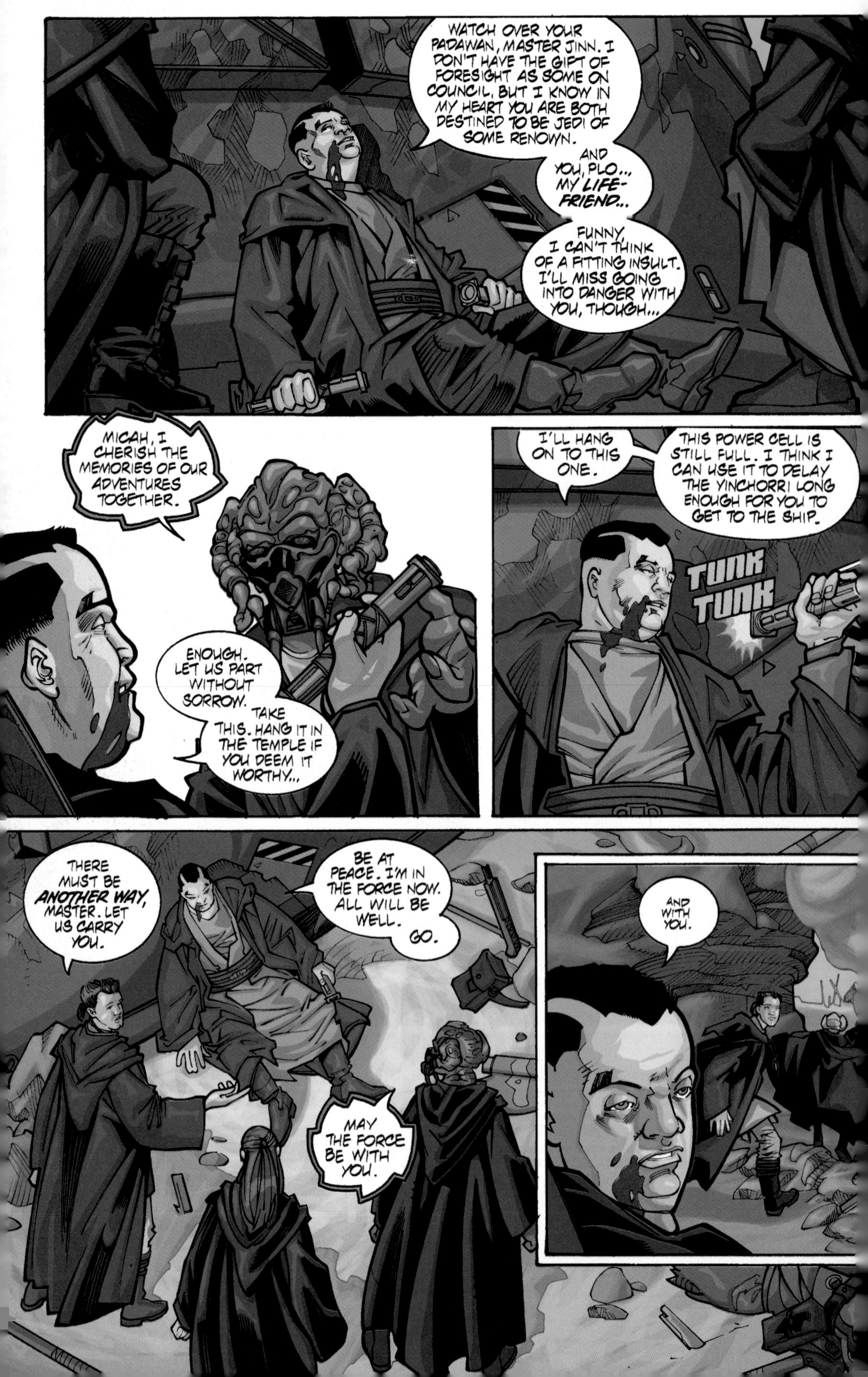

WATCH OVER YOUR PADAWAN, MASTER JINN. I DON'T HAVE THE GIFT OF FORESIGHT AS SOME ON COUNCIL, BUT I KNOW IN MY HEART YOU ARE BOTH DESTINED TO BE JEDI OF SOME RENOWN.
AND YOU, PLO... MY *LIFE-FRIEND*...
FUNNY, I CAN'T THINK OF A FITTING INSULT. I'LL MISS GOING INTO DANGER WITH YOU, THOUGH...
MICAH, I CHERISH THE MEMORIES OF OUR ADVENTURES TOGETHER.
ENOUGH. LET US PART WITHOUT SORROW.
TAKE THIS. HANG IT IN THE TEMPLE IF YOU DEEM IT WORTHY...
I'LL HANG ON TO THIS ONE.
THIS POWER CELL IS STILL FULL. I THINK I CAN USE IT TO DELAY THE YINCHORRI LONG ENOUGH FOR YOU TO GET TO THE SHIP.
TUNK TUNK
THERE MUST BE *ANOTHER WAY*, MASTER. LET US CARRY YOU.
BE AT PEACE. I'M IN THE FORCE NOW. ALL WILL BE WELL.
GO.
MAY THE FORCE BE WITH YOU.
AND WITH YOU.

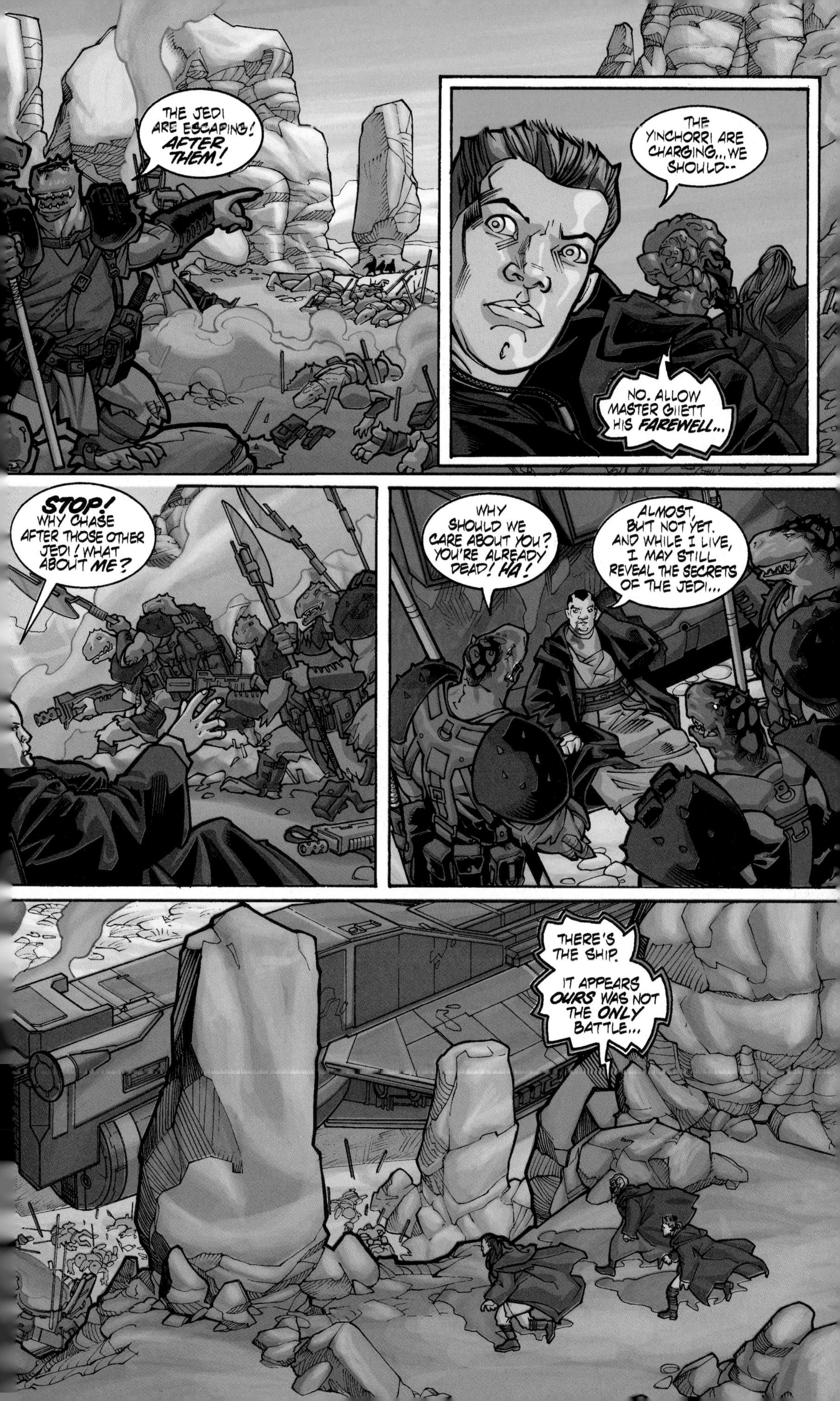
THE JEDI ARE ESCAPING! AFTER THEM!
THE YINCHORRI ARE CHARGING... WE SHOULD--
NO. ALLOW MASTER GIIETT HIS FAREWELL...
STOP! WHY CHASE AFTER THOSE OTHER JEDI! WHAT ABOUT ME?
WHY SHOULD WE CARE ABOUT YOU? YOU'RE ALREADY DEAD! HA!
ALMOST, BUT NOT YET. AND WHILE I LIVE, I MAY STILL REVEAL THE SECRETS OF THE JEDI...
THERE'S THE SHIP.
IT APPEARS OURS WAS NOT THE ONLY BATTLE...

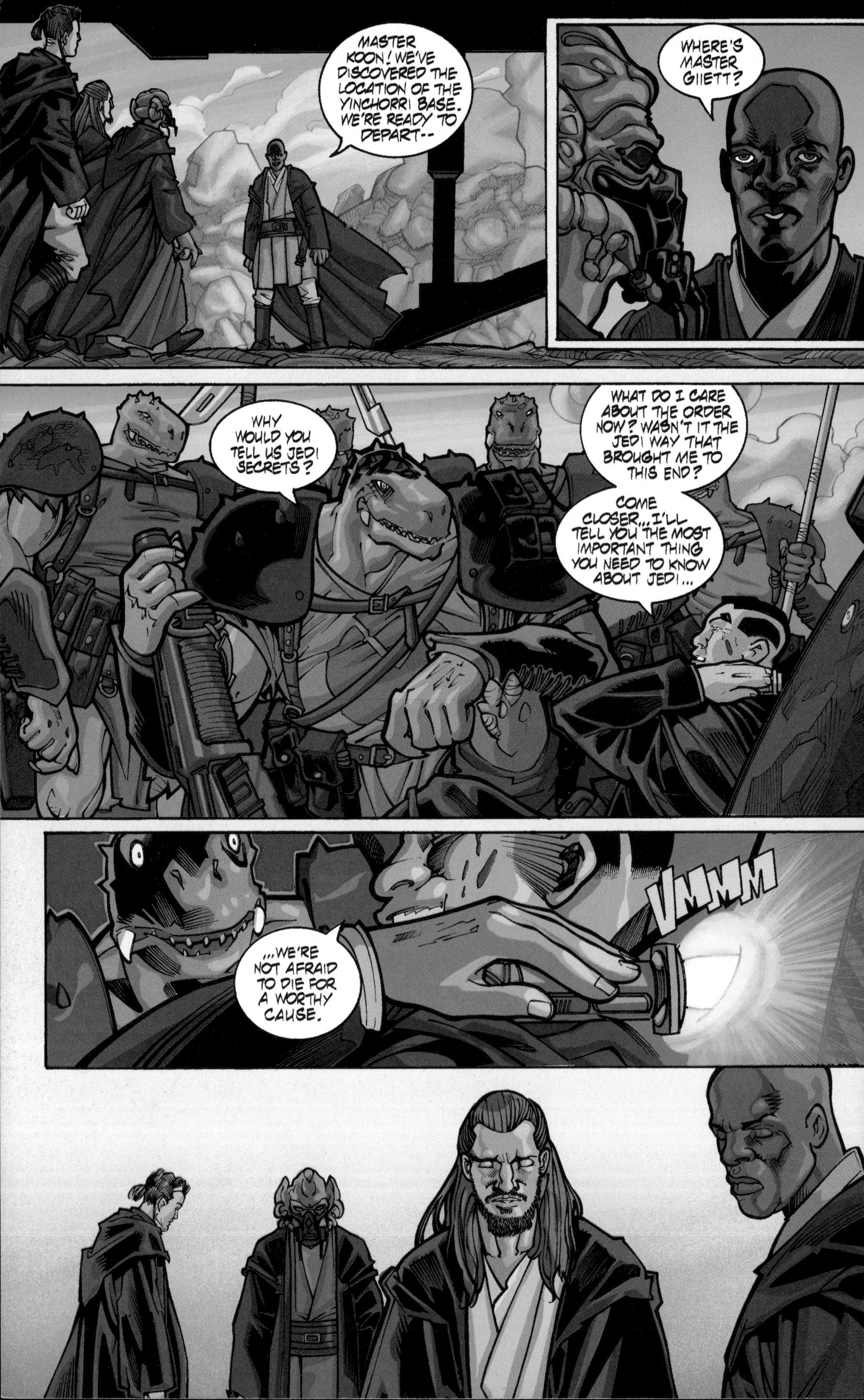
MASTER KOON! WE'VE DISCOVERED THE LOCATION OF THE YINCHORRI BASE. WE'RE READY TO DEPART--
WHERE'S MASTER GIIETT?
WHY WOULD YOU TELL US JEDI SECRETS?
WHAT DO I CARE ABOUT THE ORDER NOW? WASN'T IT THE JEDI WAY THAT BROUGHT ME TO THIS END?
COME CLOSER... I'LL TELL YOU THE MOST IMPORTANT THING YOU NEED TO KNOW ABOUT JEDI...
...WE'RE NOT AFRAID TO DIE FOR A WORTHY CAUSE.
VMMM

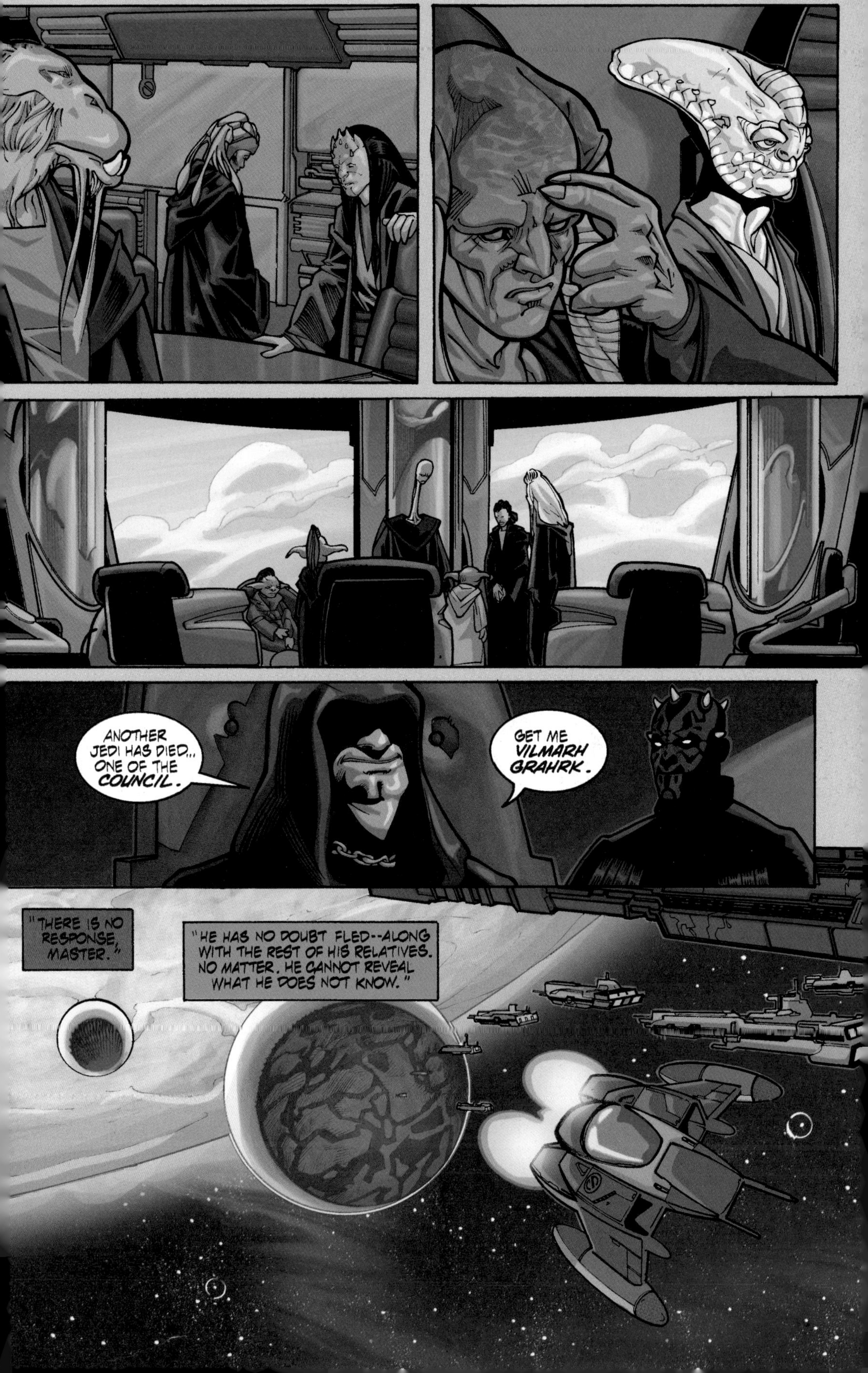
ANOTHER JEDI HAS DIED... ONE OF THE COUNCIL.
GET ME VILMARH GRAHRK.
"THERE IS NO RESPONSE, MASTER."
"HE HAS NO DOUBT FLED--ALONG WITH THE REST OF HIS RELATIVES. NO MATTER. HE CANNOT REVEAL WHAT HE DOES NOT KNOW."

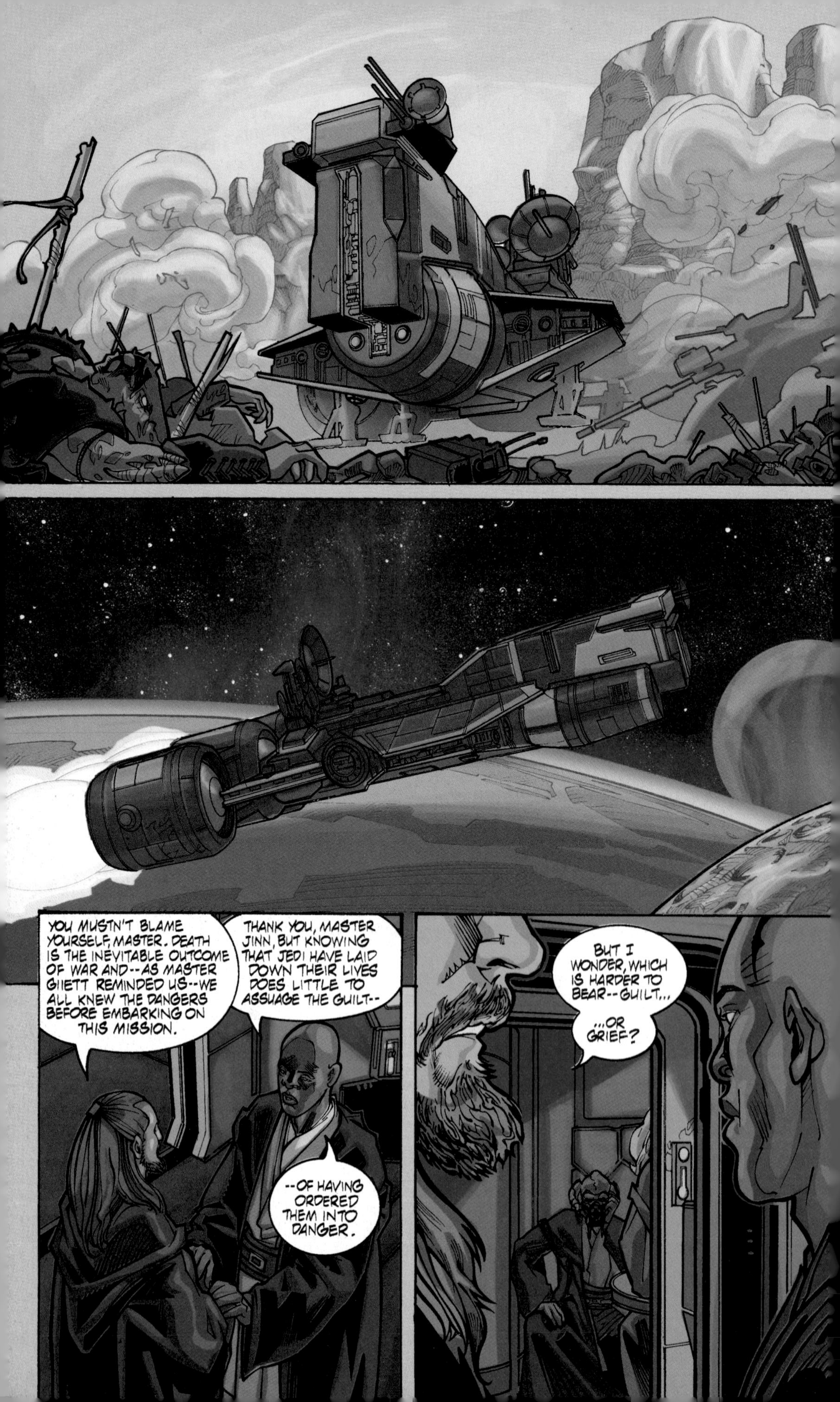
YOU MUSTN'T BLAME YOURSELF, MASTER. DEATH IS THE INEVITABLE OUTCOME OF WAR AND--AS MASTER GIIETT REMINDED US--WE ALL KNEW THE DANGERS BEFORE EMBARKING ON THIS MISSION.
THANK YOU, MASTER JINN, BUT KNOWING THAT JEDI HAVE LAID DOWN THEIR LIVES DOES LITTLE TO ASSUAGE THE GUILT--
--OF HAVING ORDERED THEM INTO DANGER.
BUT I WONDER, WHICH IS HARDER TO BEAR--GUILT...
...OR GRIEF?

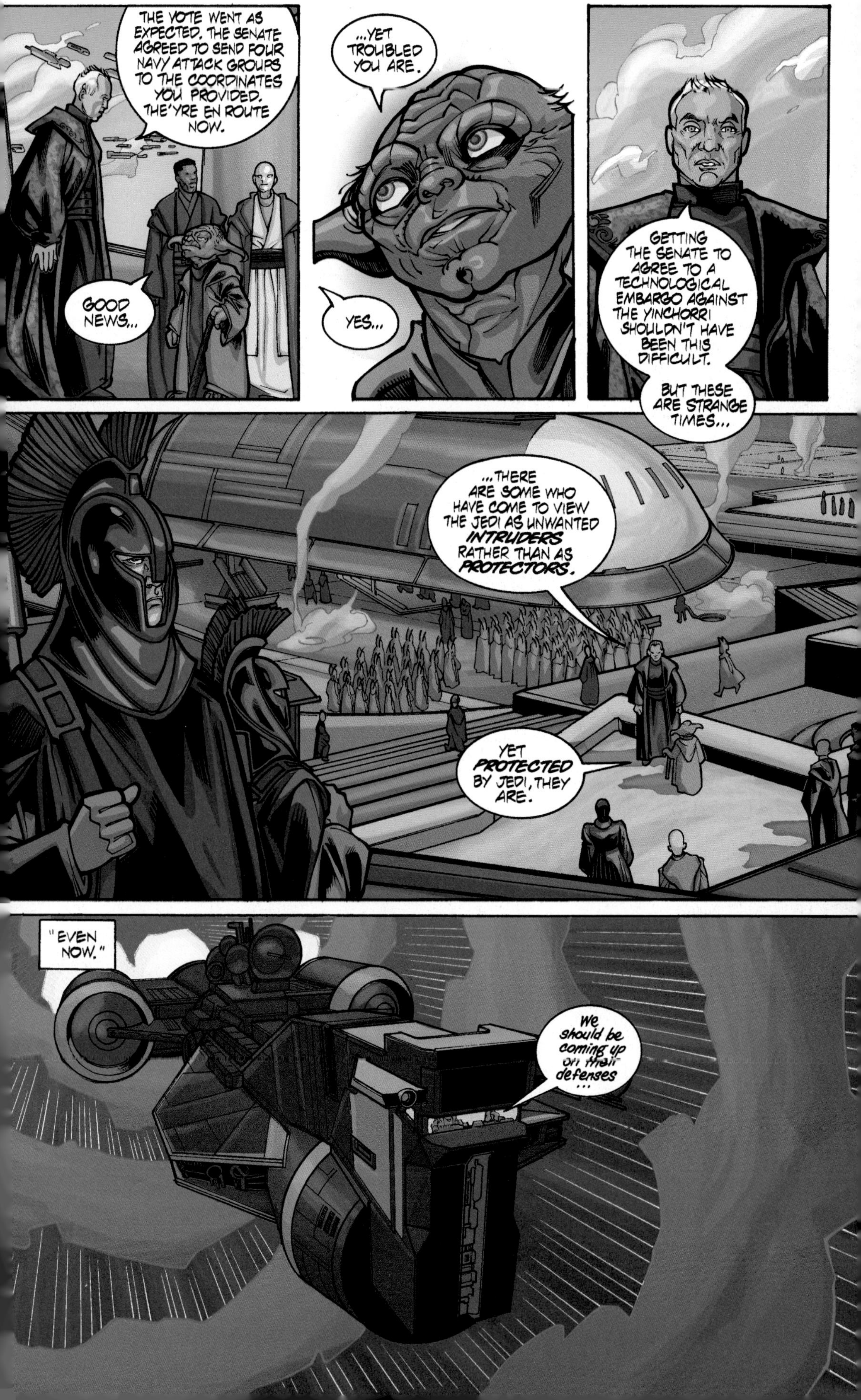
THE VOTE WENT AS EXPECTED. THE SENATE AGREED TO SEND FOUR NAVY ATTACK GROUPS TO THE COORDINATES YOU PROVIDED. THE'YRE EN ROUTE NOW.
GOOD NEWS...
...YET TROUBLED YOU ARE.
YES...
GETTING THE SENATE TO AGREE TO A TECHNOLOGICAL EMBARGO AGAINST THE YINCHORRI SHOULDN'T HAVE BEEN THIS DIFFICULT.
BUT THESE ARE STRANGE TIMES...
...THERE ARE SOME WHO HAVE COME TO VIEW THE JEDI AS UNWANTED INTRUDERS RATHER THAN AS PROTECTORS.
YET PROTECTED BY JEDI, THEY ARE.
"EVEN NOW."
We should be coming up on their defenses ...

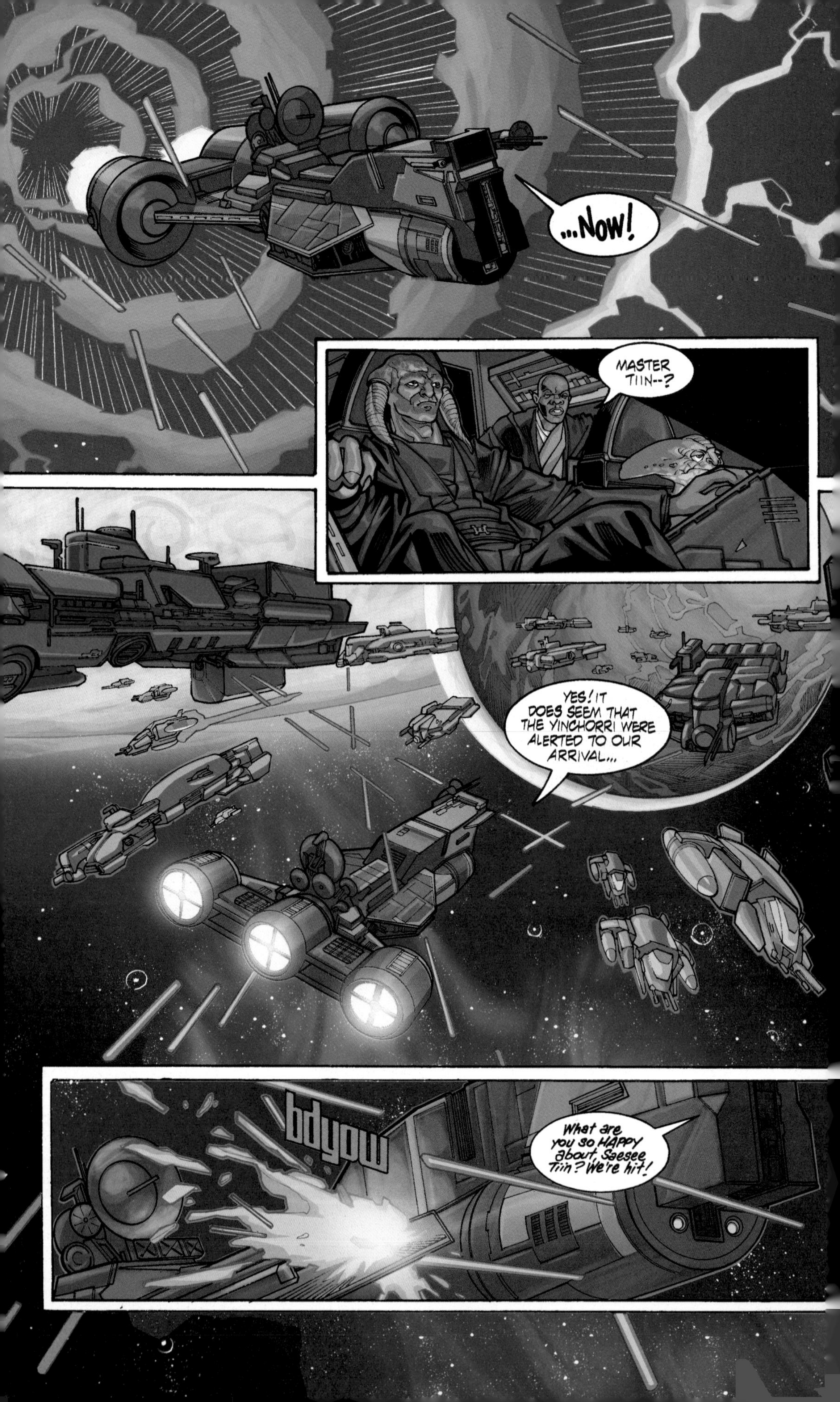
...Now!
MASTER TIIN--?
YES! IT DOES SEEM THAT THE YINCHORRI WERE ALERTED TO OUR ARRIVAL...
bdyow
What are you so HAPPY about, Saesee Tiin? We're hit!

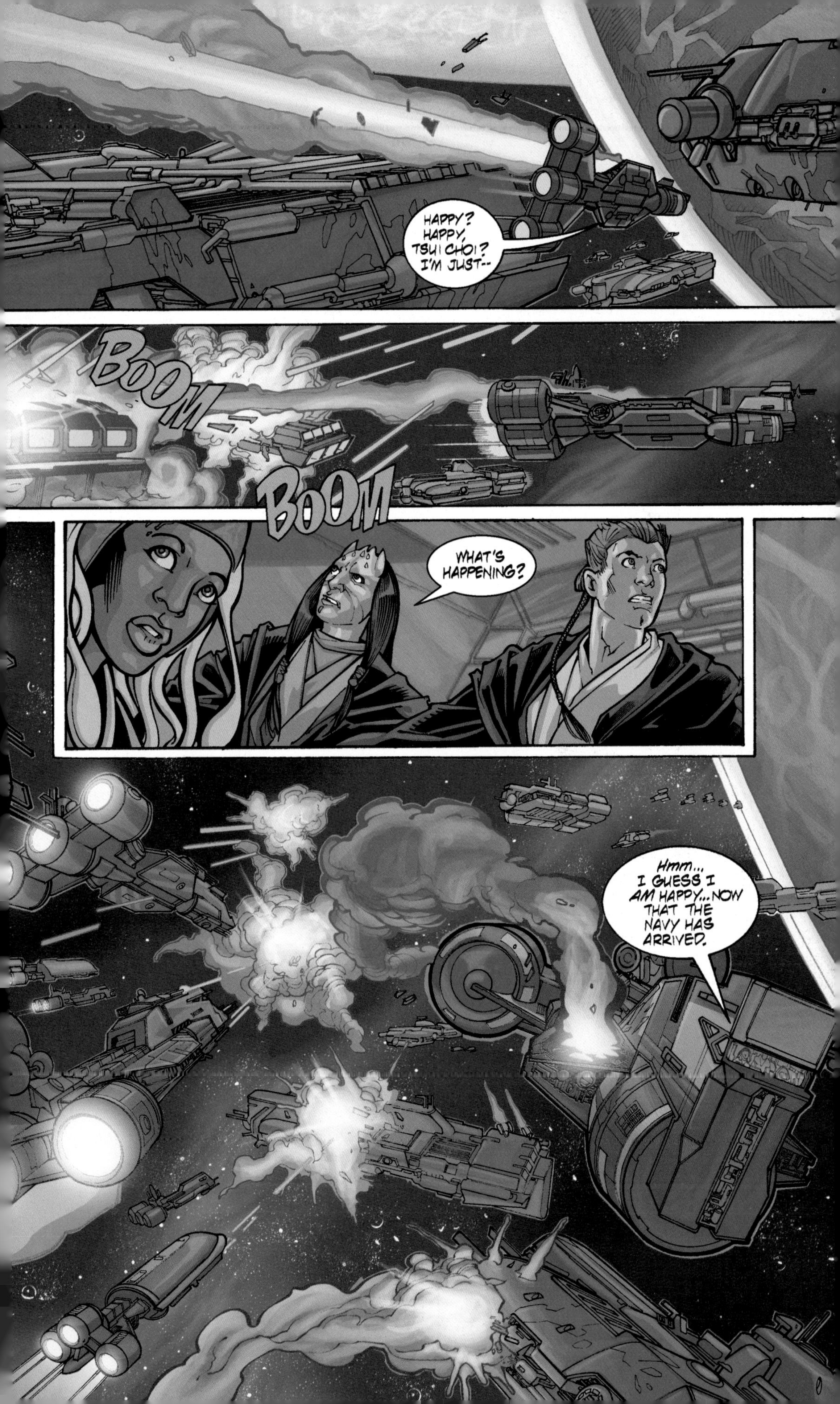
HAPPY? HAPPY, TSUI CHOI? I'M JUST--
BOOM
BOOM
WHAT'S HAPPENING?
Hmm... I GUESS I AM HAPPY...NOW THAT THE NAVY HAS ARRIVED.

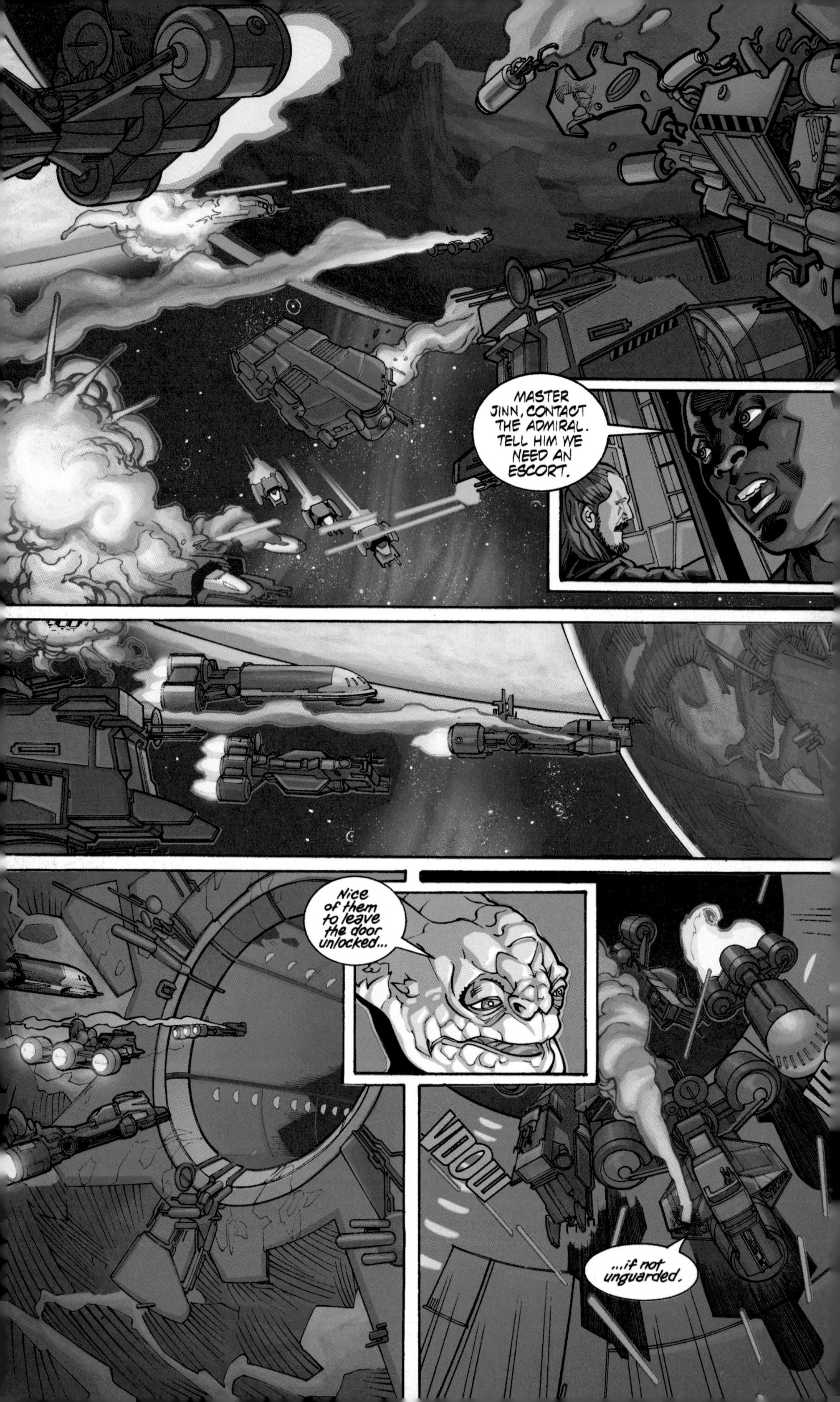
MASTER JINN, CONTACT THE ADMIRAL. TELL HIM WE NEED AN ESCORT.
Nice of them to leave the door unlocked...
...if not unguarded.

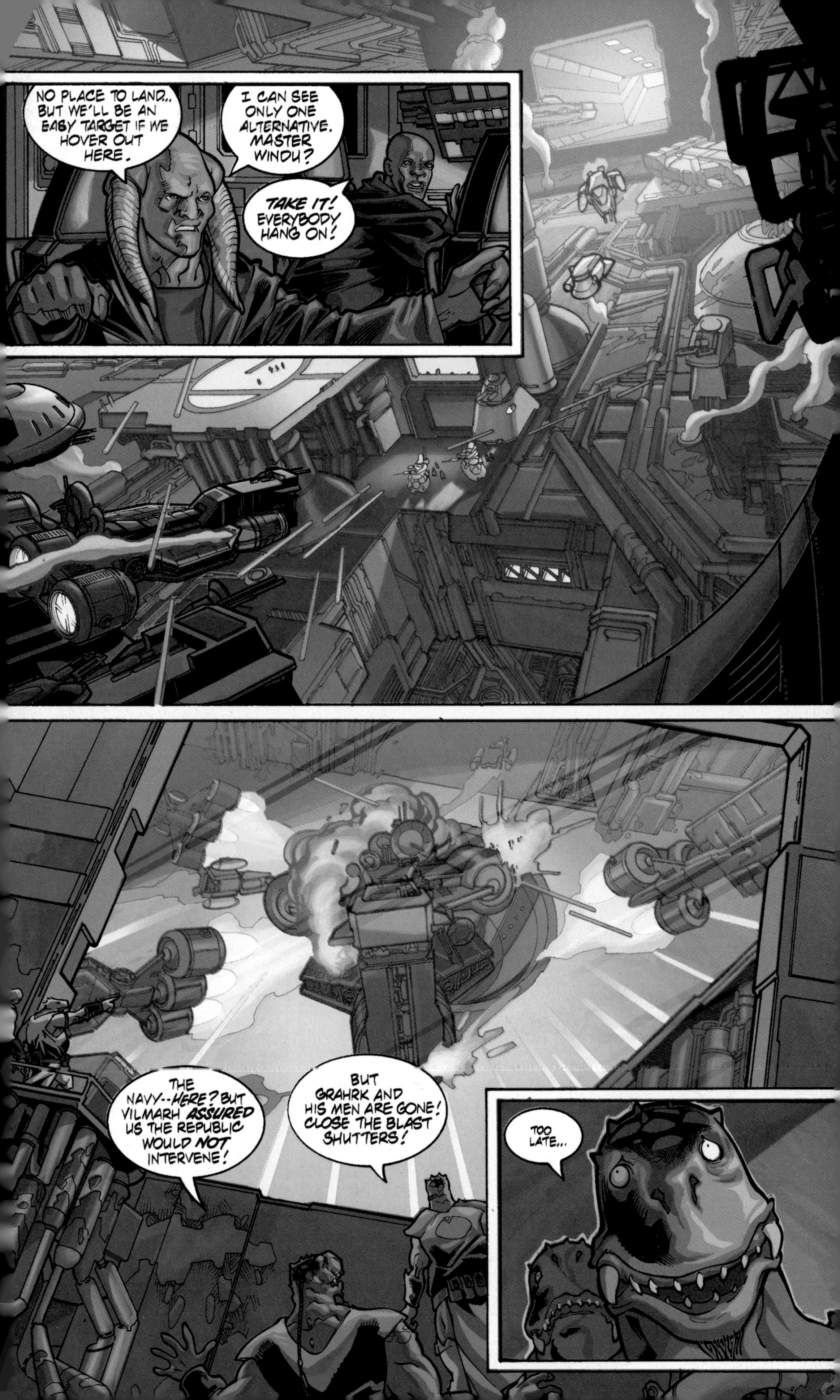
NO PLACE TO LAND.. BUT WE'LL BE AN EASY TARGET IF WE HOVER OUT HERE.
I CAN SEE ONLY ONE ALTERNATIVE. MASTER WINDU?
TAKE IT! EVERYBODY HANG ON!
THE NAVY--HERE? BUT VILMARH ASSURED US THE REPUBLIC WOULD NOT INTERVENE!
BUT GRAHRK AND HIS MEN ARE GONE! CLOSE THE BLAST SHUTTERS!
TOO LATE...

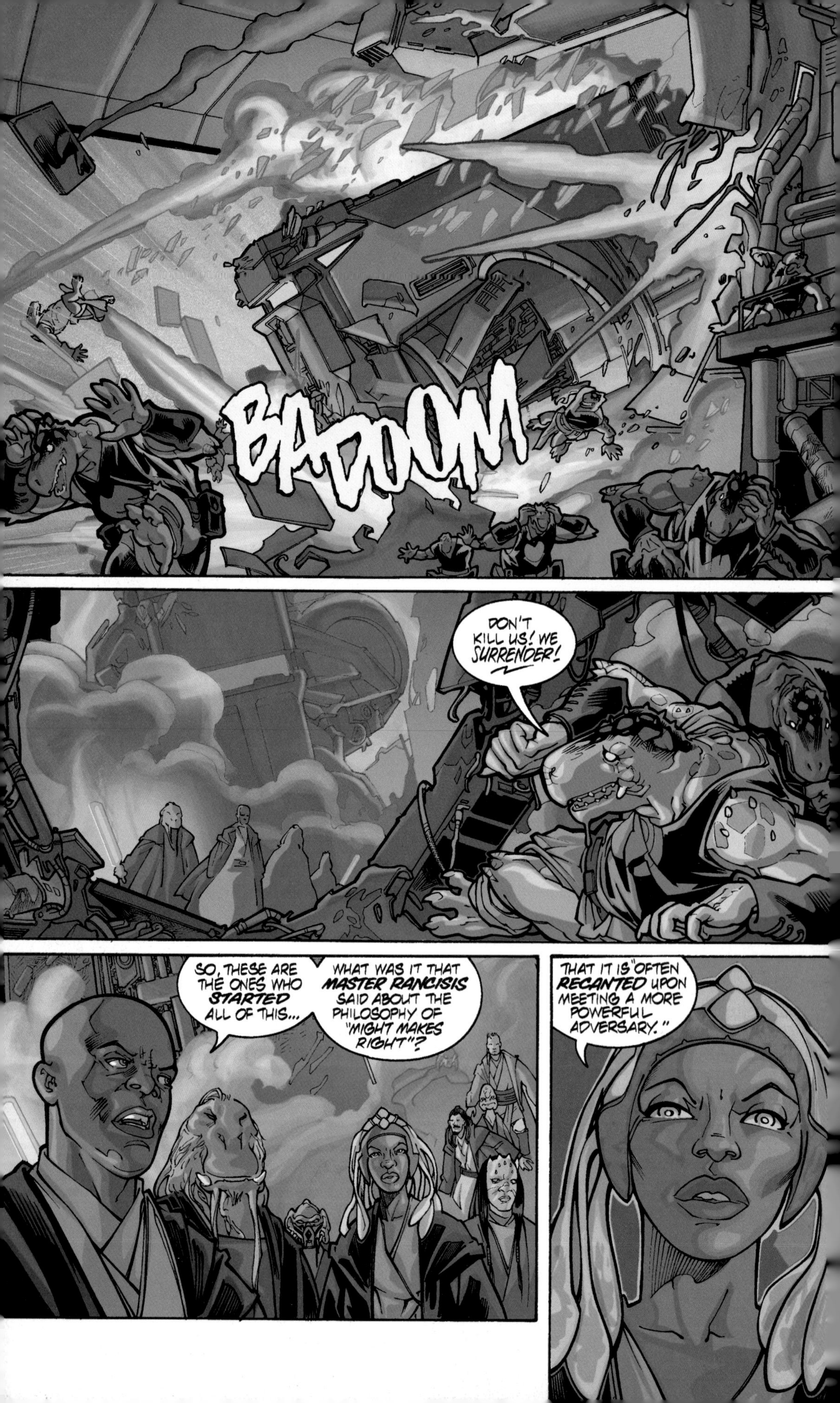
BADOOM
DON'T KILL US! WE SURRENDER!
SO, THESE ARE THE ONES WHO STARTED ALL OF THIS...
WHAT WAS IT THAT MASTER RANCISIS SAID ABOUT THE PHILOSOPHY OF "MIGHT MAKES RIGHT"?
THAT IT IS "OFTEN RECANTED UPON MEETING A MORE POWERFUL ADVERSARY."

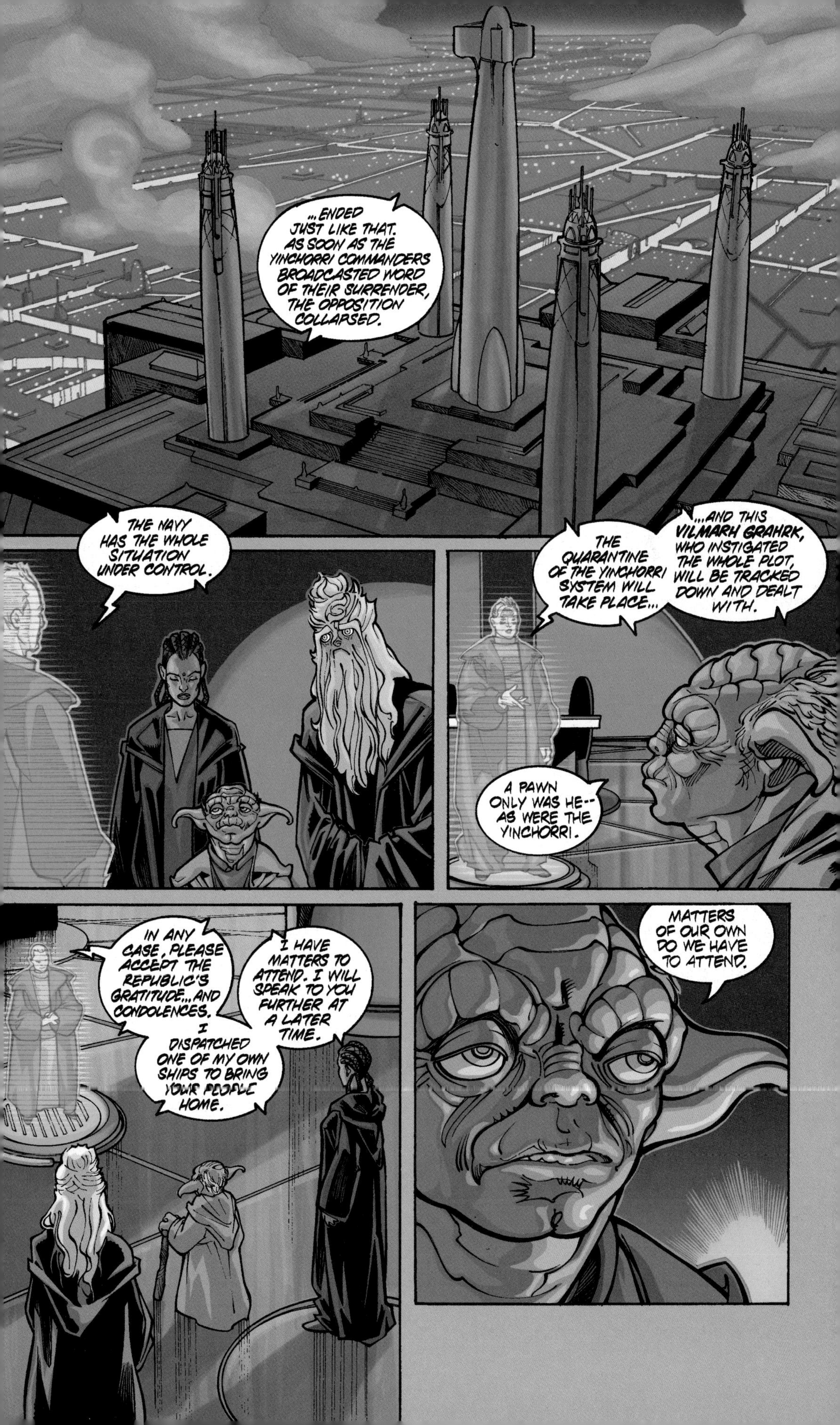
...ENDED JUST LIKE THAT. AS SOON AS THE YINCHORRI COMMANDERS BROADCASTED WORD OF THEIR SURRENDER, THE OPPOSITION COLLAPSED.
THE NAVY HAS THE WHOLE SITUATION UNDER CONTROL.
THE QUARANTINE OF THE YINCHORRI SYSTEM WILL TAKE PLACE...
...AND THIS VILMARH GRAHRK, WHO INSTIGATED THE WHOLE PLOT, WILL BE TRACKED DOWN AND DEALT WITH.
A PAWN ONLY WAS HE-- AS WERE THE YINCHORRI.
IN ANY CASE, PLEASE ACCEPT THE REPUBLIC'S GRATITUDE...AND CONDOLENCES.
I DISPATCHED ONE OF MY OWN SHIPS TO BRING YOUR PEOPLE HOME.
I HAVE MATTERS TO ATTEND. I WILL SPEAK TO YOU FURTHER AT A LATER TIME.
MATTERS OF OUR OWN DO WE HAVE TO ATTEND.

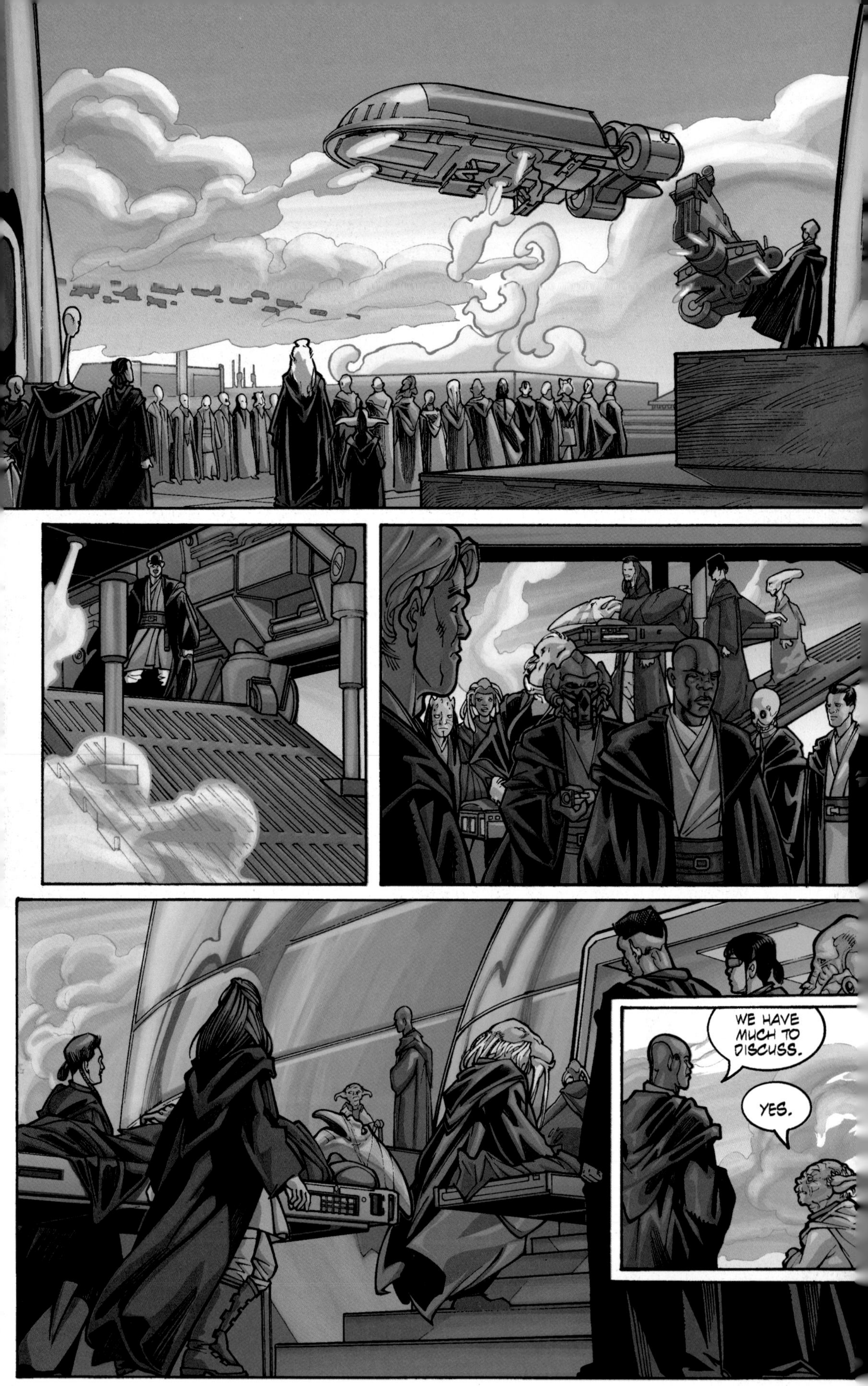
WE HAVE MUCH TO DISCUSS.
YES.

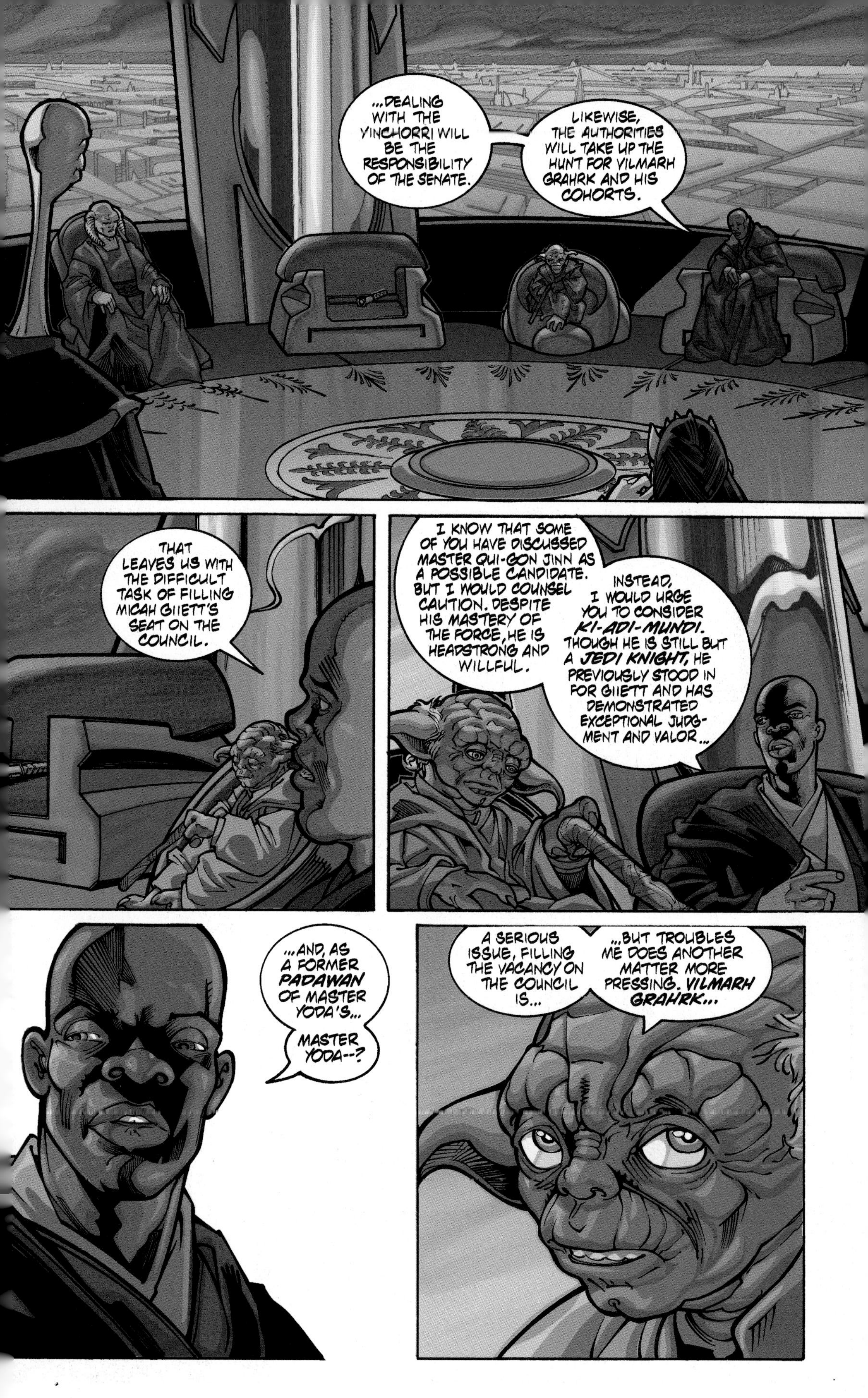
...DEALING WITH THE YINCHORRI WILL BE THE RESPONSIBILITY OF THE SENATE.
LIKEWISE, THE AUTHORITIES WILL TAKE UP THE HUNT FOR VILMARH GRAHRK AND HIS COHORTS.
THAT LEAVES US WITH THE DIFFICULT TASK OF FILLING MICAH GIIETT'S SEAT ON THE COUNCIL.
I KNOW THAT SOME OF YOU HAVE DISCUSSED MASTER QUI-GON JINN AS A POSSIBLE CANDIDATE. BUT I WOULD COUNSEL CAUTION. DESPITE HIS MASTERY OF THE FORCE, HE IS HEADSTRONG AND WILLFUL.
INSTEAD, I WOULD URGE YOU TO CONSIDER KI-ADI-MUNDI. THOUGH HE IS STILL BUT A JEDI KNIGHT, HE PREVIOUSLY STOOD IN FOR GIIETT AND HAS DEMONSTRATED EXCEPTIONAL JUDGMENT AND VALOR...
...AND, AS A FORMER PADAWAN OF MASTER YODA'S...
MASTER YODA--?
A SERIOUS ISSUE, FILLING THE VACANCY ON THE COUNCIL IS...
...BUT TROUBLES ME DOES ANOTHER MATTER MORE PRESSING. VILMARH GRAHRK...

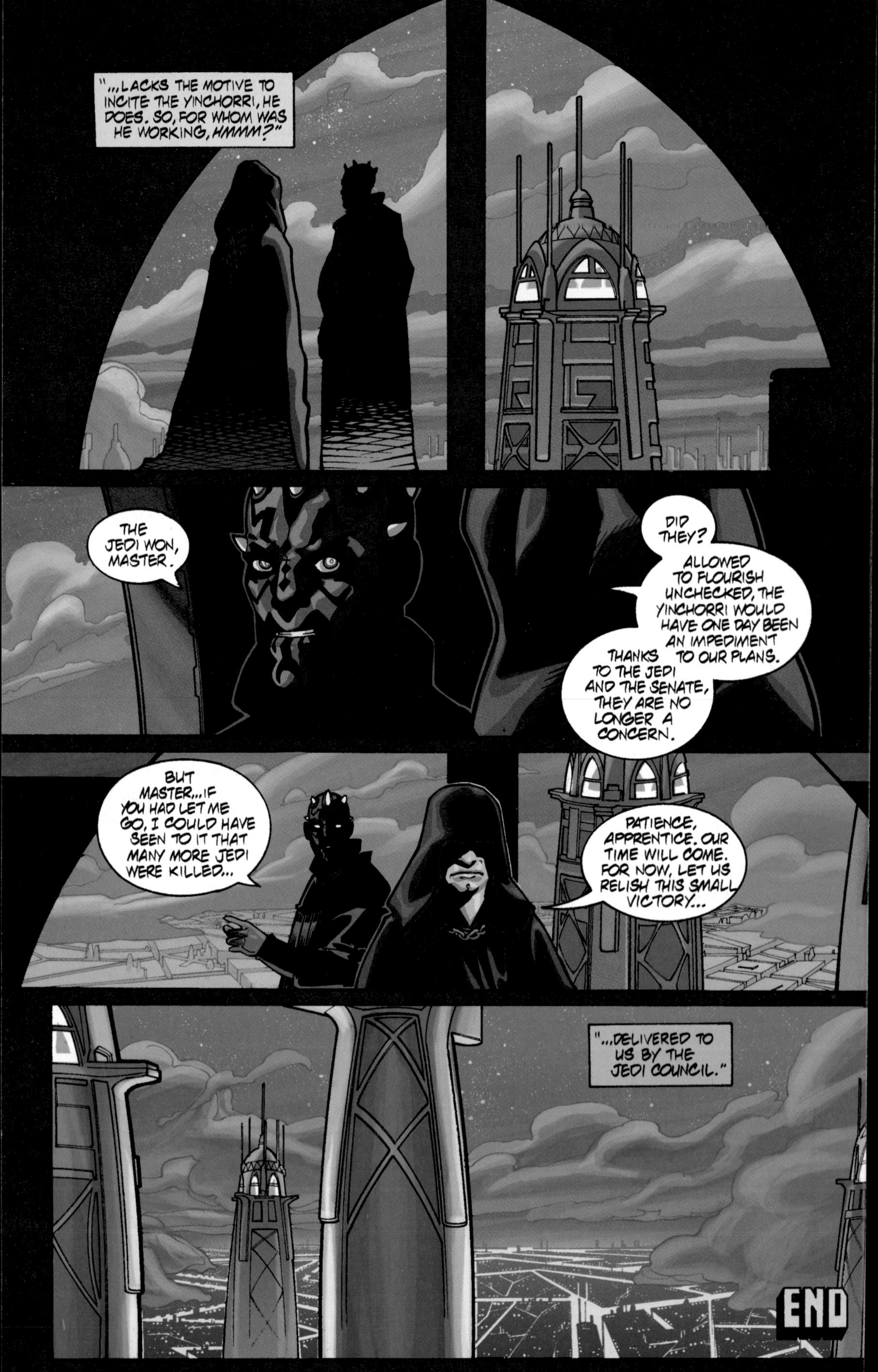
"...LACKS THE MOTIVE TO INCITE THE YINCHORRI, HE DOES. SO, FOR WHOM WAS HE WORKING, HMMM?"
THE JEDI WON, MASTER.
DID THEY?
ALLOWED TO FLOURISH UNCHECKED, THE YINCHORRI WOULD HAVE ONE DAY BEEN AN IMPEDIMENT TO OUR PLANS.
THANKS TO THE JEDI AND THE SENATE, THEY ARE NO LONGER A CONCERN.
BUT MASTER...IF YOU HAD LET ME GO, I COULD HAVE SEEN TO IT THAT MANY MORE JEDI WERE KILLED...
PATIENCE, APPRENTICE. OUR TIME WILL COME. FOR NOW, LET US RELISH THIS SMALL VICTORY...
"...DELIVERED TO US BY THE JEDI COUNCIL."
END

Creator Files

Name: Randy Stradley

Place of Birth: Thirty-some miles west of Boston, Massachusetts

Occupation: Editor, writer, luckiest boy alive

Past Comics Credits: *Aliens vs. Predator, Godzilla, Star Wars: Crimson Empire*

Favorite Artists: Francisco Ruiz Velasco, Arthur Adams, and Davidé Fabbri

Star Wars Character You Most Resemble: Qui-Gon Jinn gone to fat (or the bartender in the Cantina scene)

Name: Davidé Fabbri

Place of Birth: Forli, Italy

Occupation: Artist

Past Comics Credits: *Maelstrom (Heavy Metal)*, Starship Troopers: Insect Touch, Starship Troopers: Dominant Species, Xena: Warrior Princess, Star Wars: Jedi Council — Acts of War, and Star Wars: The Hunt for Aurra Sing*

Favorite Artists: Moebius, Adam Hughes, Mike Mignola, Magnus, Syd Mead, J. Gimenez, Masamune Shirow, Geof Darrow

Star Wars Character You Most Resemble: Chewbacca

Name: Christian Dalla Vecchia

Place of Birth: Bologna, Italy

Occupation: Inker

Past Comics Credit: *Examen* (Italian superhero), *Gabriel* (Italian comics)

Favorite Artists: Adam Hughes, Mike Mignola, Frank Cho, Kentaro Miura, and Nirasawa Yasushi

Star Wars Character You Most Resemble: *Star Wars* is full of dynamic heroes, and I'm tired and sedentary. So, I'd have to say Jabba, although I'm not as fat.

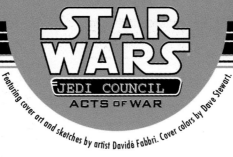

STAR WARS
JEDI COUNCIL
ACTS OF WAR

Featuring cover art and sketches by artist Davidé Fabbri. Cover colors by Dave Stewart.

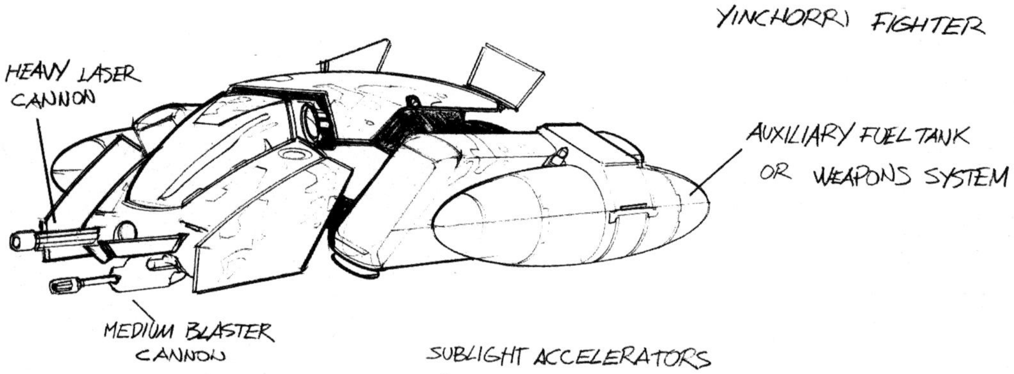
YINCHORRI FIGHTER
HEAVY LASER CANNON
AUXILIARY FUEL TANK OR WEAPONS SYSTEM
MEDIUM BLASTER CANNON

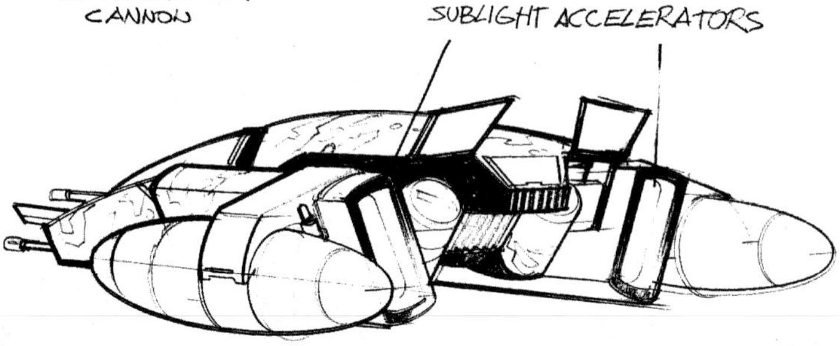
SUBLIGHT ACCELERATORS

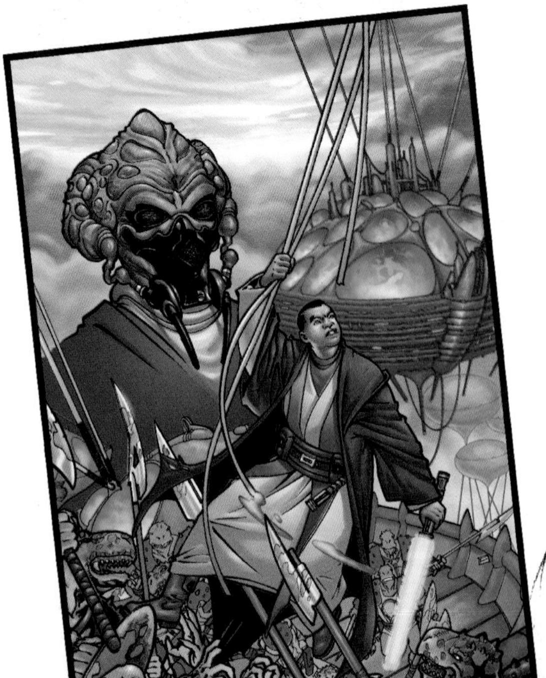

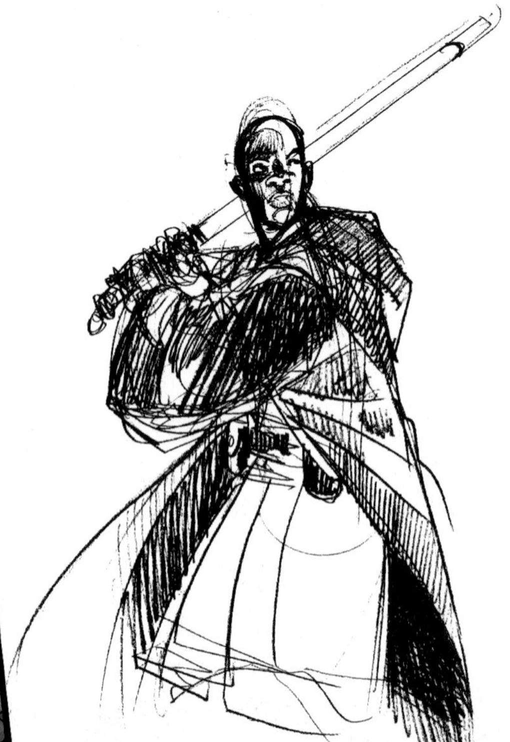

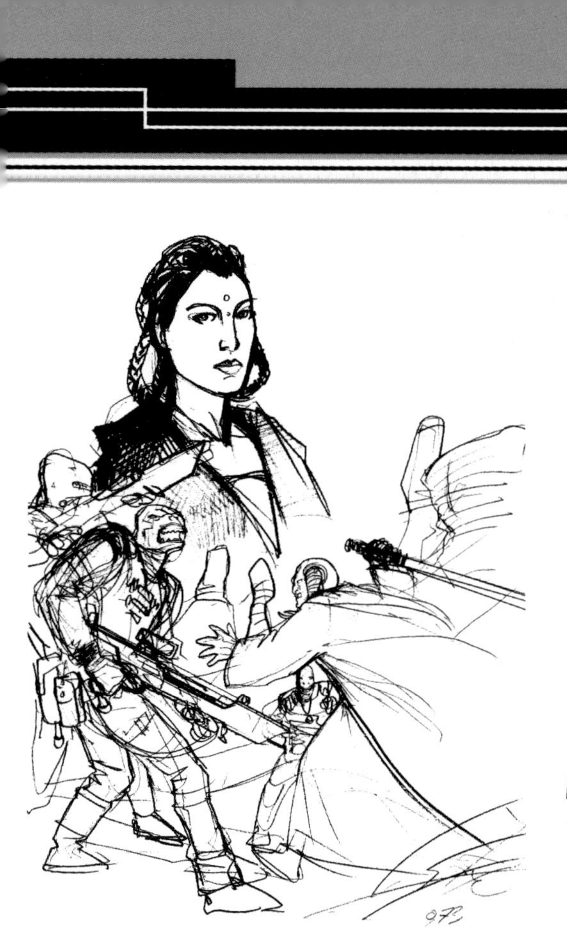
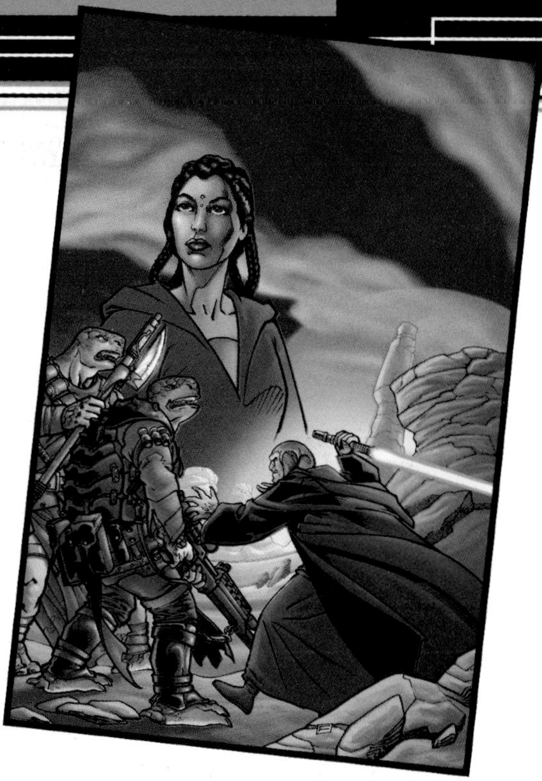
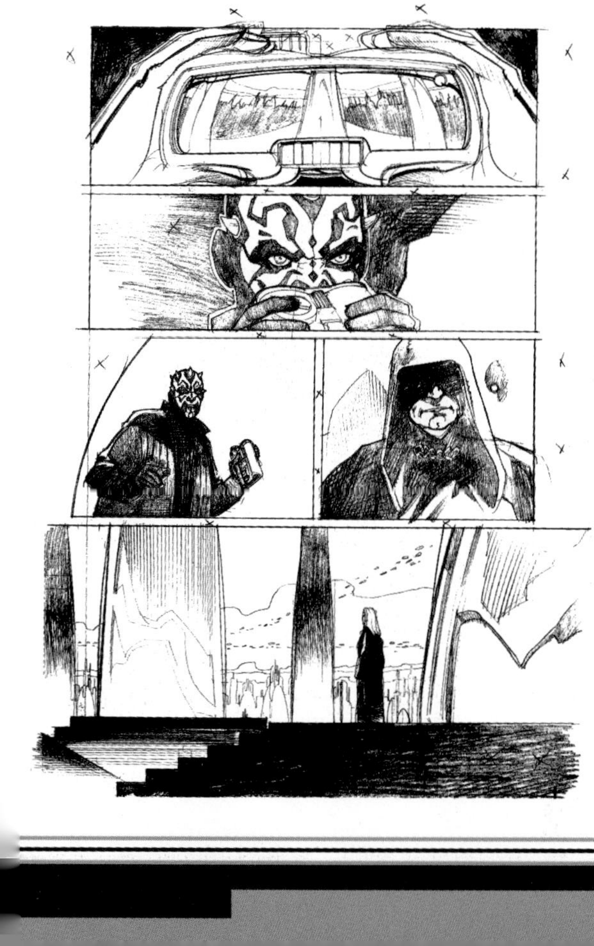
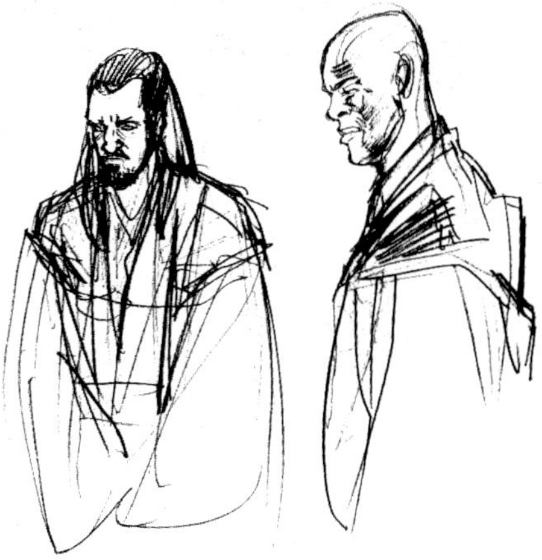
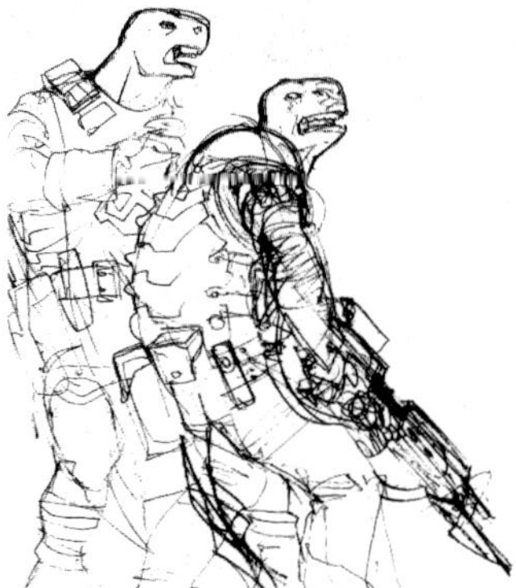

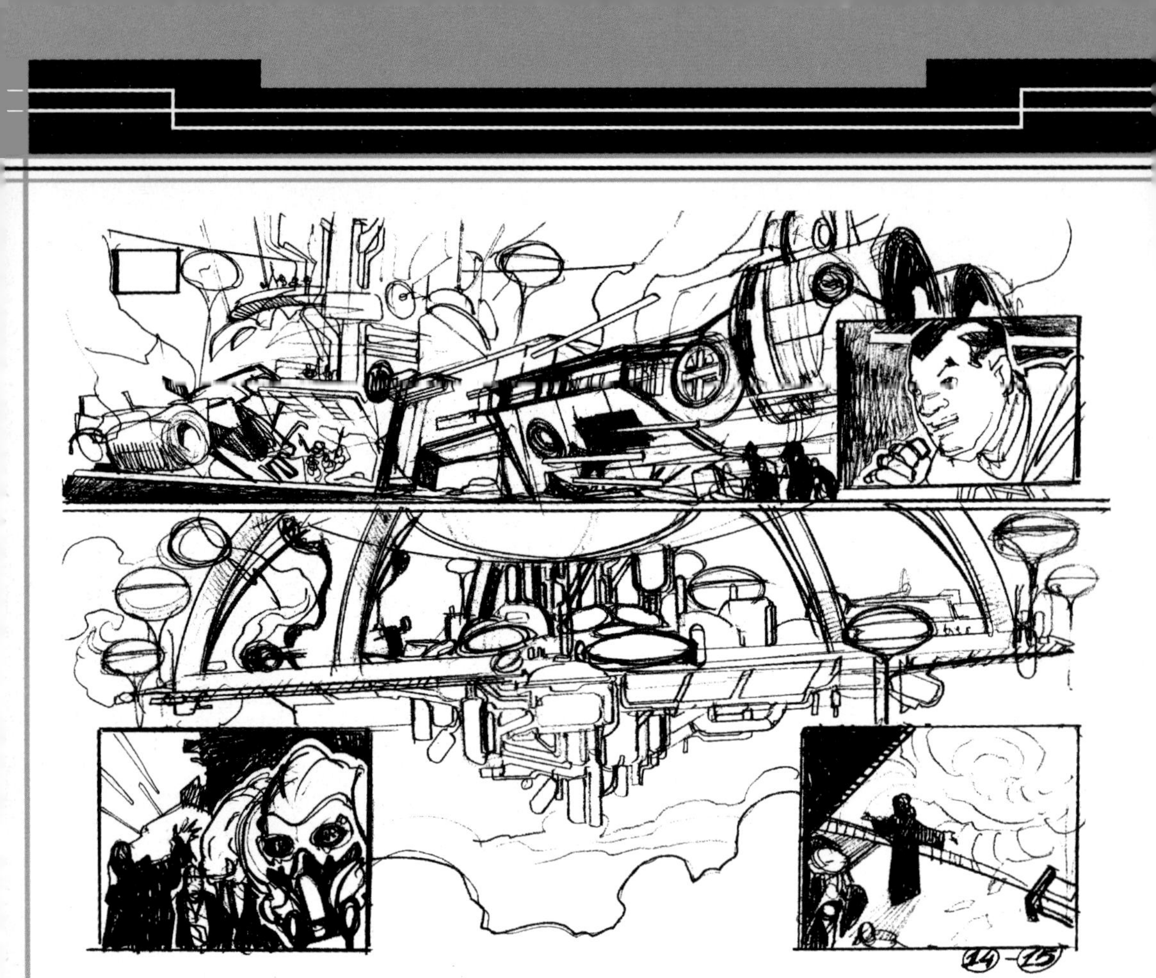
14-15

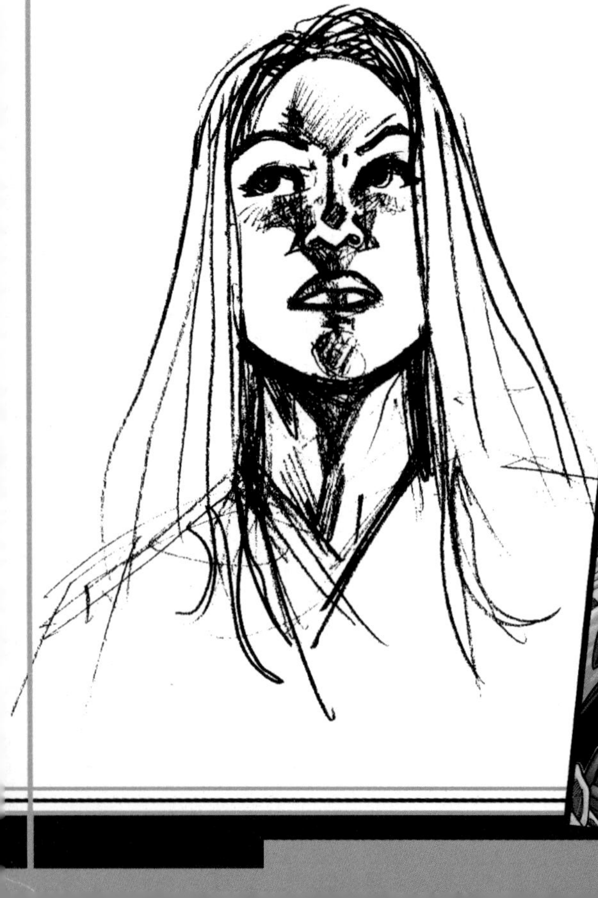

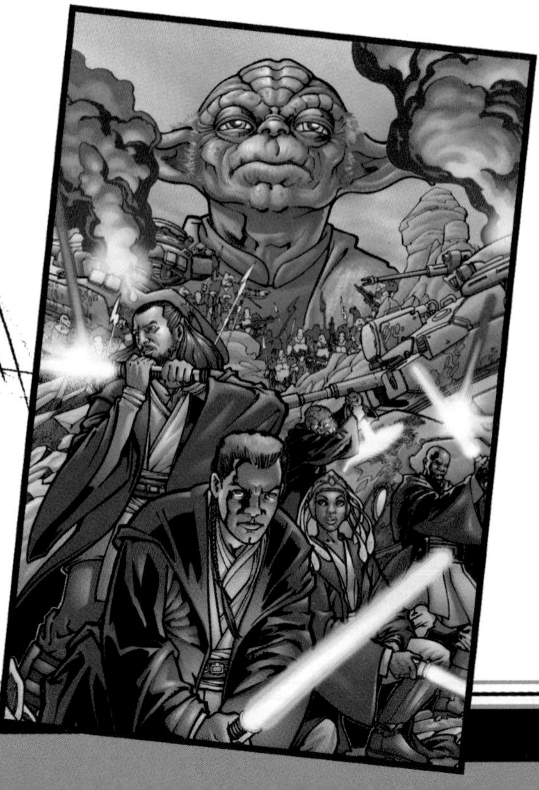